BIG SHIELD

MIKE FLORIO

ALSO BY MIKE FLORIO

Playmakers
(2022)

Father of Mine
(2023)

On Our Way Home
(2023)

Son of Mine
(2024)

This is a work of fiction. Any similarities to actual persons, living or dead, are completely coincidental. The professional football league featured in the book is also fictional. If you choose to associate any of the teams (from Las Vegas to Minnesota to Baltimore to Cincinnati to Kansas City) with actual pro football teams that play in those markets as you're reading the book, I can't stop you.

Paperback: 979-8-9879440-7-3

Ebook: 979-8-9879440-6-6

TO ALL THE MEN
WHO HAVE PLAYED
PRO FOOTBALL,
THE GREATEST
SPORT ON THE
PLANET.

1

CARSON JEFFREY

If there was an easier way to make extra money, I couldn't think of it.

Not that I spent much time trying.

I did two things. The two things almost anybody who ever lived and breathed and ate and crapped can do.

One, I kept my eyes and ears open. Two, I kept my mouth shut.

I told myself it really was easy money. Easier than easy. What was that old song?

That ain't workin'. That's the way you do it.

Case in point. We were leading Philadelphia by thirty-four and the starters were out of the game. But I was still focused. It wasn't like I needed to worry about playing. I was still the third-string quarterback on the Vegas roster. You know, the guy who wears the only uniform that never gets dirty.

Still, I had plenty to do. Not for my main job. For the other.

For that one, all I did was pay attention. To everything that was going on. There was always a chance the backup would twist his knee or something, and then I'd be playing. But that's not why I was paying attention.

I was paying attention for the easy money.

My football story fits with plenty of others who came before me, and a lot more who'll follow in my footsteps. If I even left any. That's how it goes for slappies like me.

In high school, we mopped the floor with everybody. They begged us, and paid us, to play at a college somewhere. Once we got there, we raised eyebrows all over again. It made people think we'd be playing on Sundays.

Then came the Sundays, and we found out we'd be better off spending our time in church.

The pro game moved just fast enough to be too fast for me. The window to get the ball to an open man was just small enough to go away for good right before I could slip it through that tiny slice of daylight.

There was still a place for me. With thirty-six teams in this league, there aren't enough good quarterbacks to go around. Or there aren't enough bad quarterbacks to go around, which is how my agent liked to say it.

I'd been banging my head against a ceiling I'd never shatter. No matter how hard I worked or how much I studied or how many vitamins I took or how bad I wanted it, it wasn't going to happen.

Would steroids or some other drug have made me better? A long time ago, I promised myself I'd never do that. I know that sounds strange, since I was doing the other thing instead.

It wasn't cheating. I was never quite sure what to call it. But if it didn't affect the game, how could it be cheating?

Should I have felt guilty about it? The game chews us up and spits us out, and they don't pay the players close to what they should. What was wrong with making the game I worked for work for me?

I told myself it was all harmless. *Victimless*. That was the word. A way to get a little more without hurting anybody. It worked.

I was all I'd ever be in pro football. My career was basically over, even though it hadn't ended. Or started. More than three years after landing in Las Vegas, I hadn't played in a game. I assumed I never would. There was still a place for me. But that place wasn't as a pro football player on a pro football field during a pro football game.

I'd stick around, as long as I could. At some point, I'd probably jump from team to team to team. The money would be more than what most guys my age and with my limited brainpower could make anywhere else. I knew I'd need to find another job, at some point. Until then, I decided to milk all I could from a game that didn't really want me around anymore. If it ever even did.

Was I bitter? No. I was realistic. Opportunistic. That's about as big as the words get when you go to school at North Texas. Which made it easy for me to become an Academic All-American. If they only knew the whole truth and nothing but the truth about my academics.

I loved football since I was four. I played since I was eight. I was a star everywhere I went until I got to the highest level and met my match. Pretty much every other guy on the field who tried to keep me from doing what I was trying to do was good enough to keep me from doing it the way I needed to.

It sucked, but that's the way it goes for plenty of football players who just aren't good enough to make it at the highest level of the game.

I never planned for the other thing to happen. Tooty McElwain had his bachelor party in town. I was too drunk to be playing blackjack. The guy next to me was trying to help out, giving me the side eye when I wanted to do stupid shit like hit on eighteen. We got to talking. I can't remember much of the details. I can't forget where it ended up.

At first, I started sharing some of the stuff I saw and heard in the locker room. I didn't realize it had value. Then he started saying he'd pay me for more.

I was good at it, if that even counts as something to be good at. I just had to remember things. Who was injured. Who wasn't.

What was the game plan this week? Heavy on the run? Focused on the pass? Which running back would get the bulk of the carries? Which receivers would get the most passes thrown their way? What was the defense planning to do? Load up against the run? Take away the pass? Every last bit of information had value to people.

After a while, it didn't end when the games started. They offered me more money to tip them off to the plays while they were happening. I could hear every call through the speaker inside the padding of my helmet, next to my ear. I knew whether the next play would be a run or a pass. All I had to do after that was make a signal.

It was simple. When the words and letters and numbers called for a run, I tugged on my face mask for a second and pulled my hand away. When a pass was coming, I wrapped my fingers around the bars and left them there until the snap. If the quarterback checked from pass to run or run to pass (which didn't happen very often), I pulled on the bottom of my chin strap. When the people who knew the code saw the signal, they made bets on their phones. Play after play after play.

Was it wrong? Everything about this sport is wrong. All those billions come from grown men crashing their heads into each other. We're all pieces in a machine that will be changed out for new ones.

Most players know that's how it works. And they don't care. Five years feel like fifty. Fifty years seem like five hundred. We give up our futures. What's the harm in finding a way to make a little more in the present?

They call it in-game betting. The streaming services give the people watching the games enough time to lock in the action. It's turned every game into a casino. Nowadays, there are so many different ways to drop a few bucks here and there, before every play. And there's a real advantage in knowing what the plays will be before they happen. Giving the right people that edge made me a lot of money. Sort of.

It really was easy. I'd get behind the head coach, in a place where I'd be in the shot. And I knew where all the cameras were. Whatever the score, the only thing that mattered was when the coach called something like *West Right Slot 72 Bingo U Split Can It With 58 Lexus Apple 96 Seattle* into his little microphone, I'd put my hand on those bars and leave it there until the snap. Then, the right people would know the next play would be a pass.

The cash showed up the day after the game. They gave me twenties. It was all stuck in a bag and stuffed in a planter next to the garage. Nothing about my place stood out. That made it the perfect spot for the money to be delivered.

My neighbors knew I played for the local team. They also knew I didn't really play. I had a build that made me look more like a basketball player. Otherwise, I blended.

Blending made it easier to do both of my jobs. The first one only mattered at practice, if then. The second one mattered all the way up until the end of each and every game.

I never cared about the final score. I wanted the team to make the playoffs because it would keep the gravy train going. I wanted to win the Super Bowl because I could sell the ring for a nice chunk of change. Why shouldn't I cash in? It'd be something I didn't earn, something I don't want.

Right place at the right time. They shouldn't give out jewelry for that.

None of the trophies or trinkets meant shit to me. Everybody was in it for the money. Pretty much everybody connected to the game was making a lot more money than me, officially. Unofficially, I was doing OK, thank you very much. I decided to keep doing it as long as I could justify it. Which was easy, as long as I never gave much thought to not justifying it.

Why should I have? The sportsbooks make a lot more money than my tiny little project ever cost them. If I was careful—and I was—I knew that thing would keep going, for as long as I could hold my spot as a third-string scrub at the bottom of the Las Vegas roster.

I just didn't know I wouldn't be holding it much longer.

2

JOHNNY MOTTS

I fucking hate sending messages.

It don't bug me to get rough with somebody. I just don't see the point. If people can't do whatever they're supposed to do, why give out warnings? Just get rid of them. For everybody in this world of ours, there's a hundred more who would give a left nut to be in it.

Most people who do this job don't know how bad they wanna do it until they get a taste. You know how people complain about having to sit at a desk all day and type emails and talk on the phone? Not many people complain about this life.

I guess I'm sort of complaining now. I ain't complaining about the work. I'm just complaining about this one piece of it. Most of the messages I ever sent ended up being a preview of coming attractions, so to speak. If a guy's a fuckup, he's gonna keep fucking up. We break his arm. He gets the message. He straightens up and flies right. Then his arm heals. He forgets how bad his arm hurt. He don't forget he's still a fuckup.

I can't wait until I climb high enough that I don't have to be the one sending messages. When I do, maybe I'll get rid of messages altogether. If a guy can't handle this shit, there ain't no message to send. He knew the risk when he signed up.

Do we print it on a card? Nope. There's been enough

movies and TV shows about how it works. What's them words? *Occupational hazard*? It ain't no different than a lumberjack who has a tree fall on him. If you screw up with how you put your saw in the bark, you pay for it. If you screw up here, same ending. Personally, I'd rather get shot than have a trunk squash my skull.

The guy I visited tonight took a bullet to the knee. He'll live, unfortunately. At some point, they're gonna tell me to do what I should've done when I shot his leg.

What if I had? Maybe one of these times when they tell me to send a message, I'll take it too far. I'll call it an accident. I probably can't get away with that more than once or twice. At some point, they'll figure out they wasn't accidents. Then I'll be the one who gets sent a message.

We're pretty much like the army. Some of the people give orders. Other people follow them. I wish I was only giving orders. Sure, I get to give some now. I've got guys who work for me. I still have to follow all the orders I get. I don't like that part, especially when I don't agree with them.

Will I ever be the one giving all the orders? Even Carmine answers to somebody. I don't know how high it goes. I heard some stuff that makes me wonder who's really in charge. At the very top, I mean. It's not like the old days, when the crews ran their own thing and they found a way to work together, until they didn't. Now, I feel like everything rolls up higher. I wonder if it rolls past the point where the people calling the shots are even in this life.

It's just a feeling I get sometimes. If I'm right, I'll never really be the one calling all the shots. To be that guy, maybe I should have started off as one of them schnooks sitting with a thumb up my ass in a cubicle.

I could have. I took classes on some computer bullshit for two years after high school. I didn't learn much other than how to hack into a network. That shit comes in handy when it's time to blackmail somebody. It's usually a lot cleaner to break his thumbs or even better blow his head off.

It's too late for me to get a real job. I've been at this six years now. I think I'm doing OK, mainly because if I wasn't I already would have had a cast on one of my own arms or a bullet in one of my own kneecaps. I just need to make sure I keep doing OK with whatever they give me.

They trust me. They even put me in charge of cozying up to ball players. Most of them like coming to Vegas. They wanna be big shots, which means they ain't hard to spot. They've got the clothes and the jewelry and that cloud of cologne at a few grand for a bottle the size of your last toenail.

I'm good at spotting them. I'm good at getting close to them. I'm good at talking to them. I give off just enough of a whiff of danger. They get drawn to it. Moth to a flame. Most of them don't realize the flame is real before it's too late to fly away.

I'm up to eighteen guys. Got some in every sport. Most are in football. That's where the real money's at. There's so much action on football now that the sportsbooks barely even notice when we use the information we buy.

It wasn't too hard to get the players on board. For most, it's a lot easier to keep them on board. The money does the trick. Plus, they know what they got themselves into. Yeah, them movies and TV shows help plenty.

I need to keep looking for more guys. The more I get, the better I do. The boss knows I'm doing a good job for him and whoever he answers to. He knows I'm getting information that tips the odds our way. We've made good money from this. I don't know how much. I know it's a lot.

I usually hang out at the Wynn. Sometimes, I'll get started at the bar on the twenty-third floor of the Waldorf-Astoria. Even though that place don't have a casino, it attracts money. Which attracts me.

That's how I found Jimmy King. He was drinking expensive wine at the Waldorf and talking about all the dough he was gonna make at the tables. I told him to skip the Wynn and go to the Aria, that I know one of the craps dealers there. I said it like it would make a difference, although shit like that never does. Besides, I didn't have no friend there. I'd say my friend must be off tonight. Jimmy King was drinking enough fancy purple shit that by the time we got there he wouldn't think to give me the third degree.

I knew it was him right away. Basketball players are easier to spot than football players. They ain't got helmets on when they're working. Plus, they're fucking giants.

The wiseguy act works. I sound like I'm from Jersey, because I am. I talk with my hands all the time. I got a bunch of shiny rings. I wear a gold chain. I got the vibe. Guys not in this world can sense it. They like it. It makes them feel like hot shit, in a different way than they already are.

Yeah, Jimmy King was easy. We played craps. I took him to the blackjack table, where it's always easier to talk. I told him to hit a few times when he was thinking about staying. I told him to stay a few times when he was thinking about hitting. I got lucky. He got lucky. Bing bang boom, I got me a friend.

The key with guys like that is don't ask them no questions about what they do. They don't wanna talk about it. They wanna forget. I act like I ain't impressed by none of that. I act like what I do is more important. They end up asking me all the questions. Maybe I should be the one whose mugshot is on a bubblegum card.

After we won some and I told him it's the right time to walk away, he listened. We went back to the Waldorf, away from all them cameras and microphones at the casinos.

When we settled in, I mentioned that gambling only feels like easy money when you win, that there's easier ways to make easy money. And away we went.

That's how I did it with Jimmy King. It's different with every guy. For some of them, you have to take it slow. For others, I can tell the door's already open a little. Or a lot.

Once I get them, alls I gotta do is keep them in line. Make sure they do what they're told, when they're told. Most of them are happy to do it. I've been focusing on the right ones. Guys who don't stand out. Guys who are in a position to get what we need. Guys who are making good money but not great money from their teams. Guys who realize how easy it is to make more of it.

I've been doing that part for about three years, give or take. I need to be looking for a way to step up. I need to start thinking about finding somebody who can take over doing what I've been doing. That's the biggest problem with being good at something. They want you to keep doing it. I wanna go higher. I won't have a chance to do it if I keep doing what I'm doing as good as I've been doing it.

Not many of my guys ever give me any trouble. Maybe it's because they know the stakes. Maybe it's because I'm lucky. Maybe it won't last.

I got one now that's starting to be an issue. I don't wanna tell Carmine about it. I'm at the point where maybe I have to. Whatever he tells me to do, I'll be ready to deal with it. Even if it means sending a message before doing whatever comes next. Because whatever comes next usually does.

Like I said, I fucking hate sending messages.

3

ALICE SMITHSON

I kept the door to the conference room closed. I'd twisted the interior blinds on the windows along the length of the table. It had been a good day, so far. I savored the rare seclusion from a life that ordinarily required me to engage in non-stop interactions from the moment I climbed out of my car until the instant I eased my sore hips back into the driver's seat.

I brought a granola bar, a pack of crackers, and two bottles of water. The conference room had its own private washroom. That allowed me to hunker down for more than five hours. I'd taken a few calls, ignored more than a few others, and otherwise kept grinding through the busy work I rarely had the luxury to do in the hours between sunup and sundown.

I'd gotten so much accomplished that I didn't experience the familiar cringe of irritation when someone knocked on the door. It opened before I could say anything.

"Is Sally accepting visitors to her own personal slammer?"

I smiled at Will. We'd been hired the same day. We stood shoulder to shoulder as we repeated the magic words that made us lawyers, after I'd gotten a nearly perfect score on the bar exam (I'm still pissed about the two I missed) and Will had barely passed. He became my closest ally right away, mainly because he wasn't threatened or intimidated by anything about me, brains or work ethic or looks.

Not that I was a beauty queen, but it was enough to stand out in the office. That might sound boastful. It's also accurate. It matters to be self-aware about certain things.

Here's another. If I ever cared enough to compile a scorecard, I would have realized Will was my only true friend in the entire building.

"Why are you in here?" he said.

"My office smells like a morgue with a broken refrigerator. Again."

"My office smells like farts. But they're mine. As far as I know."

"I hope you emptied the tank in there," I said as he moved inside and closed the door.

"I've always got one in the cylinder. You never know when it's going to come in handy."

"That's what you get for eating all those bananas."

"You assume it's a condition I don't welcome."

"You look tired," I said.

"You realize that's an insult?"

"It's an observation."

"Plenty of observations are also insults."

"Fine, you look extremely well rested and not under the slightest bit of stress."

"That's not an insult. It's also a lie. I definitely am tired, and without question I'm stressed."

"How's the trial going?"

"We ended early today because the defense expert's flight got canceled. I have some extra time to get ready for tomorrow."

"How does it look?"

"Do we ever know?" he said. "We just keep going until it's over."

"When do you think that'll be?"

"The jury gets it Thursday afternoon, I think. Hopefully, we'll have a verdict the next day. Either way, I'm going out Friday night. And I plan to drink every last banana out of my system."

"We don't need another trip to the emergency room."

"That happened once. Will I ever live it down?"

"You almost didn't live it down that night."

"Thanks to you, I did."

"You're welcome," I said.

"What are you doing Friday night?" He raised his eyebrows in the innocent plea of a child hoping to score an extra spoonful of chocolate pudding after dinner.

"Is this your way of asking me to join you?"

"Isn't it always?"

"I plan to relax at home."

"How are you ever going to find a husband?"

"You assume I want one."

"Well, then, how am I ever going to find one? I need you to help me break the ice if I spot an eligible bachelor."

"I didn't know you were looking."

"I'm always looking. I just don't do much finding."

"I'll be sending you positive vibes from my couch."

"You'd have as many drinks with me as you'll have alone."

I rolled my eyes. I knew he'd be persistent. I knew at some point before Friday night I'd give in. I might as well get it over with.

"This is the last time. I'm too old to go bar hopping."

"I'm older than you."

"You're too old for it, too."

"I'm too old for a lot of things. It doesn't stop me from doing them."

"You can do them without me."

"It's more fun when you're there. And we'll have fun on Friday night. I guarantee it."

"I guarantee you'll have fun."

"You will, too. You work too hard."

"We all work too hard."

"Pretty soon, thirty-four becomes forty-four becomes fifty-four."

"If I'm happy, why do I need to change a thing?"

"You surely don't plan to be single your whole life."

"There will be time for that."

"You plan every minute of every day of your life. Some things can't be planned. They just have to happen."

I didn't want to argue. He was right, but I had no interest in complicating my life. I decided indulging him for one more night of too much booze and a wasted Saturday morning with a hangover wouldn't make things much more complicated.

Was it a bad decision? No, and yes.

4

CARSON JEFFREY

I always sat in the last row of the meeting room. Not to hide. To watch. While I listened to whatever the coach said, I kept my eyes on everyone else. Who was paying attention, who wasn't. I looked for anything that could add something to what I'd share when the time came to make that Saturday night call.

I took pride in doing my second job well. Maybe the satisfaction that came from handing over the best possible information made it feel less wrong.

I always assumed it was illegal, even if I couldn't rattle off any of the laws I was breaking. When it comes to gambling, the sportsbooks always know more than the people making the bets. The way I saw it, all's fair in love, war, and covering the spread.

Yes, the sportsbooks have their ways of getting inside information. How else could they set the lines so perfectly? They always know what's going to happen. It's a question of who's getting better data. Thinking about it that way made it easier for me to not feel bad about it.

And it wasn't hurting the team, at all. If I'd been giving information to opponents, that would've been different. This wasn't sabotage. I was helping folks get an edge of their own.

Well, one specific group of folks.

I didn't know much about everything Johnny Motts was doing.

I knew he wasn't working as a florist when he wasn't grabbing information for whoever was making the bets. The gold chain and the collection of rings gave that much away.

The meeting was getting started. The head coach stood at the front of the room. Rik Trellis. Short for Henrik, not some asshole move to drop the "c" because it looks cool. It's probably the only thing about Rik Trellis that doesn't put him smack dab in the middle of the asshole category.

It's not his fault. The job attracts assholes. Or it makes guys who weren't assholes into assholes. They're all competitive. Too competitive. If they weren't, they'd never get the job. They also wouldn't keep it for long.

Then again, most don't. Almost every head coach will get fired. Until they're told to pack up and scram, they'll bust their asses and worry themselves green about everything they can control, and plenty of things they can't. They'll drive themselves nuts thinking through all the angles, even though plenty of games come down to a gust of wind, a bounce of the ball, a brain fart by the wrong player at the wrong time, or a bad call by the referee.

I've been around long enough to know a really smart decision by the head coach rarely delivers a win. But one bad decision can lose a game. One loss can sink a season. Sink enough seasons, and the head coach ends up looking for a job somewhere else as an assistant coach. Then he starts waiting for another chance to do it all over again. For most guys, it doesn't happen.

Pro football coaches can age like presidents. I've seen it. During the season, they never stop. They'll sleep in their offices two, three nights a week. And they don't sleep much when they do. Cheeseburgers, Coca-Cola, and pills keep it all going.

When the season ends, they're right back at it, getting ready to do it again. They'll make decisions about who stays and who goes and who gets signed and who gets drafted and how the playbook will change. They'll try to get ahead of the things other teams are doing well. They'll start putting new players and fresh ideas to work in May. Then, after they get about four weeks off and spend the whole time losing sleep about their players possibly getting in trouble, training camp opens.

"We got a few guys banged up yesterday," Trellis said. That caught my ear. "Carter fucked up his leg. He'll miss a few weeks."

Willie Carter was the starting running back. He'd been gaining more than one hundred and twenty yards per game. I didn't even know he'd gotten hurt. Apparently, nobody else did—Willie included—until he tried to walk to his toilet the morning after the Philadelphia game and his foot felt like it had a steak knife stuck in it.

"We'll bring in a few guys tomorrow for tryouts, and we'll sign one of them," the coach said. "I don't want to see that on my phone. Do not tell your agents."

He ripped through other injuries, bruises and scratches in comparison to Carter's. I wondered who'd get the starting job while he was on the mend. Would it be one guy carrying the load, or two? I'd have to figure it all out before Saturday night's call to Johnny Motts.

The meeting kept going. No-C Rik played the film from the game. Like all coaches, he loves to rip guys in front of the team. There wasn't much ripping to do after another blowout. Trellis still found just enough to bitch about. He thinks it keeps us from getting soft, from thinking we're as good as everyone on the outside says. Even if everyone on the inside knew it.

I tried to pick up whatever I could. The plan for the next game wasn't ready yet. I tried to guess whether anything he complained about would mean any real changes, or whether he was blowing off steam. By Saturday night, I'd know which mistakes would be forgiven, and which ones wouldn't. Sometimes, that part would be clear even before practice ended on Wednesday.

Anything I see or hear or feel could matter when it was time to make the call to Johnny Motts. That became my own game. Absorb all I could, every minute of every hour of every day I was in the building, on the practice field, or anywhere else I could see or hear anything that might help me understand whatever could happen in the next game.

Ten weeks of the season had flown by. We'd played nine games. There were eleven more to go. I'd have a good pile of cash by the time it was all over. I'd keep it with the rest, even if I was running out of room to stash it. I should have asked for something bigger than twenties.

The meeting was about to end. Plenty of teams get Mondays off after a Sunday win. Not the team in Las Vegas, not under Rik Trellis.

It wouldn't be a full-blown workday. I'd get a lift in, grab some lunch, go to the quarterbacks meeting. I'd sit there, taking it in and speaking only when I had to. That'd be it for the day. We'd have Tuesday off, and we'd be back on Wednesday.

When Trellis said we were done, I picked up the tablet with my playbook in it. I'd scribbled words and half sentences in an old-school spiral notebook. I knew what it all meant, and no one else could have ever figured it out. I closed the notebook and stood.

Rik Trellis came up the steps to my left, making his way to the exit at the top of the room. I nodded, expecting him to return the gesture. But his head didn't move.

"Jeffrey," he said. "Stop by my office. Ten minutes."

I had a feeling my plans for the rest of the day were going to change.

5

JOHNNY MOTTS

Didn't I say I hate sending messages? I never said it to nobody that matters. Not that I ever would. They tell me to send a message, I send a message.

Even if I wanna do more than that.

Maybe I won't need to with this one. Baseball players are smarter. Maybe it comes from knowing how to avoid getting hit by that fucking ball. Hockey players will take a puck to the face and spit out three teeth and smile. Baseball players got some regard for their health. It must be from all that time they sit around and think when not a damn thing is happening.

I wish this guy had done a little more thinking. He made a few mistakes with the shit he told me. Shit he was supposed to know. Shit he said he knew. He was wrong about the pitcher who wasn't supposed to make his next start because his elbow was swollen. The guy ended up throwing anyway, and it fucked up the action we put down ahead of time.

I could let one slide. He's had a few now. It makes me look bad. I ain't gonna take the heat. The only way to keep my own ass clean was to tell Carmine about it and then wait for whatever he told me to do.

So I did. I was hoping he'd be fine with talking to the guy.

Carmine wanted a little more than that. Which might make me think twice the next time it's time to tell something to Carmine.

When they want me to do more than talk, I'd rather just make the guy gone. Yeah, it could get a little dicey if a ball player on a big league team ends up disappearing. It's still gonna be an issue once I break his arm. He'll have to come up with a damn good story about how it happened. But guys fall down the steps all the time, don't they?

Besides, baseball season is almost over. I was hoping that'd be enough to get them to let it float. But they didn't ask what I thought. They never do.

I had to wait a few days until the team got back from the road. I told him to call me as soon as he got home. He didn't ask no questions. He knows he's in trouble. The last thing he's gonna do is make things worse by not doing what I say.

I didn't tell him I was stopping by. Who knows what he would have done if he thought something was gonna happen? I drove over to his place. He lived alone. I make sure all my guys live alone. The less family they got, the better. I don't need wives or girlfriends or God forbid kids getting in the way of whatever I need to do. Plus, it's easier to trust them to keep their mouths shut if they don't have somebody hanging around who might get wise.

I parked a couple streets over. I cussed the whole way to his door. I felt the sweat starting in my pits and up my ass. If I wanted a job like that, I'd be moving refrigerators.

I put my finger over the lens on the camera by the door and pushed the bell. I heard feet coming. They stopped.

"Who is it?"

"It's the pizza boy." I said it in a loud voice. I hoped like hell he remembered the signal.

"I didn't order a pizza," he said. I could tell by the way it came out that he remembered the signal.

"I think you did. C'mon, it's getting cold."

I kept waiting with my finger on the lens.

"What do you want?"

"I wanna give you your pizza. I just said it's getting cold."

I was starting to think he wasn't gonna let me in. That would make it easier for me to skip this step. I started looking for the best window to bust.

The door opened just as I figured out how to get inside.

"Why didn't you tell me you were coming over?"

He was holding a bat. "Working on your swing?"

He looked at the wood. "I just like to be careful."

"That's the problem. You ain't been. Now, are you gonna invite me in or is this problem we have about to get a little bigger?"

He stepped back. I reached out my hand. He was smart enough to know what I needed him to do. He gave me the bat. I took my finger off the camera and went inside.

I moved slow. I didn't want him doing nothing dumb. Maybe deep down I did.

I held up the bat. "I ain't swung one of these in years."

I pushed the door shut behind me. It closed with a slam. He jumped at the sound.

"Calm down," I said.

"I am calm. Are you?"

The place smelled like nasty food. I made a face. "It stinks in here."

"I just had dinner."

"You save some for me?"

He seemed confused by that. I smiled.

"I can make something else, if you're hungry," he said.

"I'm always hungry, but not for whatever you cooked."

"I can make something else. You want some pasta?"

He backed away from me as I went deeper into the house. "You know, us Italians eat more than spaghetti."

"I didn't mean it like that," he said. He was nervous. I glanced around to see if he had any more bats close by. I wasn't interested in getting in a sword fight with a couple of Louisville Sluggers. I pulled back my jacket with my free hand so he could see the piece in the front of my pants.

"I'm sorry about the other day. I fucked up."

"You fucked up more than once, Larry."

"It won't happen again."

"You're right about that."

He got a little more nervous. "I thought I had good information."

"If I thought you was fucking up on purpose, I wouldn't have rung the bell."

He kept walking backward. He bumped into the wall.

"How many times do I have to tell you to calm down?"

"I can give back some of the money. I have plenty upstairs."

"I don't want your money. You earned it. Well, most of it. You won't be getting paid for the next two weeks."

"That's fair." I could tell he was looking for any reason to think I wasn't gonna do what I was about to do.

"I'm glad you think it's fair. What would you do if you thought it wasn't?"

"What do you mean?"

"What would you do? Call the cops? Sue me?"

"Nothing, I guess."

He'd moved into the kitchen. It smelled even worse in there. I wondered what the fuck he'd eaten. I realized this was taking too long.

"Stand still," I said.

"I am."

"Well, keep standing still."

He looked at the gun. He looked back at me. He didn't say nothing else. I thought for a second it was the smartest thing he done all month.

Until he did the dumbest thing he ever done in his life.

6

ALICE SMITHSON

I went by my office again. The aroma was considerably worse than the day before. The guy from maintenance insisted he couldn't smell a thing. I told him something must have gotten inside the walls and died. Mouse, rat, cat, dog. Maybe a deer. It was something organic, something deceased, something decomposing. Maybe it came and went. That day, it showed up and never left.

Once I concluded I couldn't and wouldn't try to get used to it, I went back to the conference room at the end of the hall. After Debbie the receptionist told me no one had reserved it for the day, I'd written my nickname on the sheet she keeps at the right corner of her desk. I wrote it again over the grid of squares that covered the remainder of the day.

Sally Slammer. How and when they came up with it, I do not know. I'd grown to like it. I had a well-earned reputation for putting people behind bars. I convinced myself not to wonder whether whoever had coined it was referring to my reputation for unwinding with a cocktail or two. Or more.

It was a fair assessment. The job is stressful. We all need a way to blow off steam. Mine, I'll admit, was very different from the image I portrayed when it was time to work.

It was nice to have a full day without a bunch of different places to be. That happened maybe once every three or four weeks. Usually, I'd skitter around the courthouse, attending hearings, meeting with colleagues, negotiating with defense counsel, basically running myself ragged, knowing I'd spend several hours each night clearing the paperwork that had piled up during my absence from home base.

With home base reeking, the conference room was good enough. I was able to get a lot done. I reviewed and responded to letters. I revised plea agreements. I marked up a couple of sentencing reports. I replied to email messages within a few minutes instead of a few hours, or maybe a few days.

I'd been working as an assistant U.S. attorney for seven years. (Most in the profession refer to us as AUSAs. I don't.) I'd won most of my trials. Anyone who's never lost in court has never stood before a jury very often. It's too much of a crapshoot. Even though prosecutors like me have the discretion to pick and choose only the strongest cases to pursue, any combination of factors can come together to create a shade of reasonable doubt.

Reasonable doubt. I always hated those words.

The biggest challenge came from facing a good lawyer representing clients who could afford the fee, either from their own pockets or from the bank account of a rich relative. Public defenders got and held low-paying jobs for a reason. Although every once in a while I'd stumble across a court-appointed, low-rent lawyer who'd give me a run for my money, PDs with talent rarely last long in an office that doesn't pay much, to the competent and incompetent alike.

It would take more than courtroom talent to fulfill my ambitions. I planned to move back to Cumberland at the right time. I'd put together a run for Congress. I'd spend a few terms there (if I won, and I'd do whatever I had to do to make that happen). At the right time, I'd make a play for a Senate seat. After that, who knows?

I tried not to think that far ahead. How could I not? I knew

I had the passion, the tenacity, the poise under pressure to shine in an arena where so many don't know how to communicate with other people in a way that inspires confidence. I could do it.

How far could it take me?

I stopped myself every time that question popped up. It was stupid to even consider it. Still, no one who ever ended up in a spot like that stumbled their way to the top. Many have the ambition, hardly any have the ability. Without the ambition, all the ability in the world wouldn't mean a thing when the time came to pursue the biggest jobs around.

I also knew my goals needed to be kept to myself. Anyone who tells the world *I want to be the president* (officially, I've never even told myself that) comes off as delusional in the short term and a failure in the long term. My grandfather had parlayed running a small chain of popular local grocery stores into what appeared to be an accidental decade in the Maryland statehouse. He told me before I got my first period to never share my own plans with anyone. I never had. I never would.

I'd keep working relentlessly toward my secret objectives. Every hearing and every trial sharpened my ability to think on my feet, to speak extemporaneously in a persuasive way, to handle any and all unexpected curve balls, knuckleballs, and spitters. I used to watch baseball with my grandfather. The Orioles. I loved the Orioles so much because I'd loved him so much.

I also hated football, because he hated it. He'd known years before they recognized the connection between head trauma and long-term cognitive problems that football would turn many of its gladiators into gardenias.

He'd boxed a little when he was in his twenties. He stopped after he woke up flat on a table with a doctor shining a flashlight into his pupils, thinking he was still in the bed of his apartment that same morning. The whole day had been erased from his brain by an uppercut they told him he never saw coming.

Plenty of his friends who kept fighting ended up punch drunk. He'd known, long before the experts discovered medical proof, that the game of football, like boxing, poses a unique and specific hazard to the human brain.

But football kept on growing in popularity. Even after the risks became as obvious as the surgeon general's warning on a pack of Camels, boys smitten by the money and the glory would keep flocking to the sport, thinking it won't ever happen to them.

It had taken over as the top sport in the country long before I was born. And it just kept growing. The rich kept getting richer. The powerful kept getting more powerful. The families that had owned franchises for years became billionaires, several times over. The billionaires who made their money in other lines of work lined up to buy teams.

Hollywood for the ugly. That's what my grandfather called it. A way for the rich to become famous, even though he always told me the only thing better than being rich and famous is being rich.

He also told me politics wouldn't be much different. I wasn't drawn to it for the fame. I couldn't have been drawn to it for the money. The money wouldn't be there until the political part ended, if then. It sounded naive, but I wanted to make a difference. I'd managed to remain idealistic, even after I turned thirty. I was determined to keep it that way, if only to properly honor his memory and to do justice to the name he'd given to my father, and that my father had unintentionally given to me before walking away and never looking back.

Pro football. In quiet moments like that, I'd dream about finding a way to take on the biggest, baddest bully on the block. To expose the corruption I knew in my heart permeated the sport. Behind every great fortune there is a crime. My grandfather loved quoting that line to me, too. My instincts told me that, when it comes to pro football, a crime is right in front of every great fortune, too.

He was convinced pro football had real ties to the mob, and to gambling specifically—long before it was legal pretty much everywhere. I always sensed he was right. I hoped I'd come across a chance to prove it.

The powers of my office, under the right circumstances, could give me a chance to expose it. It would take a lot of work. It would take even more luck. Still, a conviction or two of pro football's bigwigs who had broken the law could be the perfect foundation for launching the political aspirations of which I'd never breathe a word until it was time for action.

My brain was overacting. That's the only downside to having an abnormally normal day. Without something always happening, I had too much time to churn through my thoughts. It would be better to just keep going as hard as I could and wait for things to take care of themselves.

They always seemed to do just that. So often that I never dreamed things might change.

7

CARSON JEFFREY

The coach said ten minutes. I didn't want to be early. I didn't want to be late. I refused to make assumptions. I told myself it could be nothing. I told myself it could be anything. I only knew it was something.

I checked the time on my phone while I stood on the other side of his closed door. It was broad and tall and thick and solid. Exactly ten minutes had passed since I'd gotten the unexpected invitation. I took a breath, held it in. I banged the knuckles of my left hand against the wood, three times.

I could hear him on the other side, talking on the phone. I couldn't make out the words. I could tell my knocking hadn't disrupted the conversation. I listened until it sounded like the call ended. I knocked again.

As the door swung open, my neck stiffened.

"Right," he said. "It's you. Sorry. My wife is having an issue with the kids. The young one is finally big enough to fight back against his brother, and his brother isn't handling it well."

"Older kids in the neighborhood ran over me until the day they realized I could kick all their asses at the same time."

"That day has arrived in my household. I wish I was there to see it, but I'm sort of glad I wasn't."

He walked back to his desk. Even though I was dead set against making assumptions, I assumed he wanted me to go in.

"Get the door," he said. I felt something deep in my gut twisting around, looking for a way out—up or down or maybe both. I pushed the large panel that probably cost more than a Chevy. It closed with a thud. An elephant in heat probably couldn't break that thing down.

I walked toward a seat on the other side of his desk. There was a large computer in one corner. Two others were on the table behind it. I glanced up at a huge monitor on the wall above a fancy leather chair that smelled even more expensive than the door.

The screen was paused in the middle of a play. He was studying our next opponent. I recognized right away what the defense was doing. I also knew how it ended; I'd seen the highlights from the game.

"Seattle got caught on that one," I said.

He seemed confused until he realized what I was talking about. "They love that delayed safety blitz. They used it one time too many yesterday. We'll be ready."

I nodded. I tried to read his face. He was wearing that same black visor with the team logo in the middle. He reached up and tugged the bill.

"No matter how many times I do this, it never gets easier," he said.

I sunk into the seat. I kept waiting for what I knew was coming.

"We'll be signing a running back to the roster, and we'll add one to the practice squad. We need your spot."

I nodded again, because it was all I could do.

"It might be temporary," he said. "Johnson is raw. We'll have to call him up and make him the number three on game days. You know how this goes. If the third-string quarterback ever has to play in a game, we're already fucked."

"I get it." There was no point arguing. I'd been cut when the roster trimmed from ninety-five to sixty every year since I first signed with Las Vegas, after being drafted by no one. Nobody ever claimed me on waivers before Vegas brought me back to the practice squad, each and every year. This time around, I'd have to sit at home and wait.

"It's a numbers game," he said. "You've been a good soldier. We've pulled you up for game day almost every week since you got here. That's been a nice little bump."

He was right. It paid a lot better to be in uniform. For four years, that had been me. Now, it'd be Freddie Johnson, the undrafted rookie I'd once been.

I didn't need an explanation. I'd seen enough guys come and go in four years to know those who don't play in the games are always at risk of getting a *Thank you!* on social media while essentially being told, *Get the fuck out!*

"I'll stay ready," I said. "I appreciate all the opportunities you've given me."

"I can't tell you not to take another spot. Money's money. A job's a job. Don't feel like you have to say no."

I didn't like the sound of that. He was hinting this might not be very temporary.

"Thank you," I said.

He told me to keep in touch. I wondered if he meant it. It was also his way of telling me to leave. I tried not to fumble with the tablet when I put it on the desk. I didn't want to seem rattled, even though I was. I thanked the coach again and walked out. I closed that huge door behind me.

I went back to the locker room and tried to act like everything was normal. Music was playing. It wasn't anything I'd put on my playlist. I'd heard enough to start liking some of it. The guys hanging out near their regular spots noticed me as much as they ever did, which for most of them was hardly at all.

I looked at the scattered shit I kept in my locker. My red

practice jersey was hanging there. My practice pants were nice and folded in one of the drawers. I wasn't one to keep photographs on the shelves, mainly because I didn't have any. There wasn't anything I couldn't replace.

I didn't want it to be obvious I was going home and not coming back, so I grabbed my keys and kept going. I didn't say a word to anybody. Nobody said a word to me.

The players' parking lot was full of expensive cars of every size, shape, and model. The Jeep I'd bought with my NIL money at North Texas stood out like a weed in a bouquet. I got inside and checked my phone. I knew I needed to call my agent.

I also knew that, before I called my agent, I needed to call Johnny Motts.

8

JOHNNY MOTTS

I told the fucking guy to stand still. Alls he had to do was stand still.

I know it's hard to stand still when a thick wooden bat is coming straight for the arm you throw with.

But why the hell did he have to bend over? What the fuck was that? Did he think I'd stop swinging if I saw I was about to hit him in the head? Or was he willing to sacrifice his brains for his moneymaker? Why didn't he just turn his back and take it there?

It don't matter. He did it. He took his own bat square to the skull. It made a loud crack. I knew right then I couldn't stop. I hit him again in the head. And again. Maybe again. I don't fucking know. Once the mission changed, the only thing left to do was hit him until he was dead.

I called Nicky No-Nose for help. He owed me. Now, I guess I owe him.

We had to chop the body up in the tub and stuff the pieces in a couple different garbage bags. It wasn't the first time I done it. I figure it won't be the last.

I had to tell Carmine. He brung me in for a sit down. I had to explain it all. He believed me. Why shouldn't he? It was the truth.

I know what I said about not wanting to send messages. But this one wasn't my fault. The fucking guy bent over. I wasn't trying to hit him in the head. His head got in the way.

Do I wonder sometimes whether that's how it went? I can't completely control myself in spots like that. Maybe I swung a little higher than I had to. Maybe I wanted the accident to happen on purpose.

It made the news fast. That didn't surprise me. Starting shortstop for the Las Vegas baseball team don't show up for work. Nobody hears from him. Nobody knows where he is. His condo is empty. There's no sign of him nowhere.

But here's the weird thing. Them stories fizzle out when there ain't no family involved. Pro athlete disappears. That's a big deal. Then what? No body. No sign of him. No news. They say no news is good news. Nowadays, no news is no news. With no news, one story goes away and another one takes its place.

I didn't expect that part. It made me think if any of my other guys start fucking up, I'll tell the bosses it makes a lot more sense for the guy to disappear.

I thought about making the case to Carmine that, with these athletes, we should just get rid of them. As long as they ain't got nobody, no news is no news. I almost told him that. I didn't, right as my mouth was about to say it.

I decided to wait for the next time somebody fucks up. Maybe nobody would. My life would be a hell of a lot easier if it goes that way.

If the rest of them find out about Larry Ballentine, maybe that'll happen. They won't. Carmine told me to say nothing to nobody about anybody who's working for us. I get that. Still, I wonder whether mentioning Larry Ballentine at the right time to the right guy might send the right message, without me having to send a message.

I didn't wanna think about none of that. Life'll be easier for me and everybody else if everything goes smooth. It was going smooth until Larry Ballentine started fucking up. I can't sit around worrying about my other guys fucking up, too.

The more guys I have doing this, the bigger the chance one of them is gonna fuck up. One of them did. And now there's one less guy for me to worry about.

I'm feel like I'm waiting for the next one to fuck up. I try not to. If I spend too much time thinking somebody else will make a mess, it'll happen. I still think about it too much.

It's stupid to think that way. But that's how us Italians are. We've got all kinds of dumb superstitions. We think everything is cursed or jinxed. That makes me not wanna think somebody else is gonna fuck up. It also makes it impossible for me to not think it.

All of that made me feel like I knew what was coming when that prick Carson Jeffrey called my burner out of the blue on a Monday morning, five days before I was supposed to hear from him and a month or so after Larry Ballentine went away. I called back, and I swear I already knew what that mutherfucker was gonna say.

9

ALICE SMITHSON

I overslept the next morning. I developed long ago the unfortunate skill of waking up just long enough to turn off the alarm on my phone and going back to sleep without realizing what I'd done. I started setting a slew of reminders two minutes apart, backed up by an old-school clock radio on the other side of the room.

I'd fallen asleep before remembering to slide my finger across the various times on my phone. Then, I managed to keep sleeping while the sound of pop music and deejays yukking it up infiltrated the final phases of my dreams.

A half-hour later, I snapped out of it. It took me a few seconds to remember what was going on that day. When I did, I shot out of bed and rushed through my routine. I skipped any step I could. The hair was easy; I pulled up the pieces that would have slipped over my collar and clamped them together at the back of my head. I forced myself to take the time to apply makeup, not that I used much. The end result couldn't look haphazard, because haphazard would look cheap. This was not the day to look cheap.

I skipped a normal breakfast (no big deal) and coffee (slightly bigger deal), grabbing a protein bar to gobble while driving my car to the office. It wouldn't have been the same as being late for court. Still, we'd managed to get him to agree to come in for a meeting. I didn't want him storming out because I was fifteen minutes late.

I wasn't fifteen minutes late. Only ten. Debbie the receptionist widened her eyes when she saw me. I hustled my bag to the office, grabbed the file and a legal pad, and swung back to the conference room where I'd spent most of the prior day.

As I stood by the door to gather myself, I tried not to think about who was on the other side. The CEO of Traxxion Industries was just another man. Another citizen to whom the various requirements of federal law applied. Sure, Henderson Robertson had a net worth of more than ninety billion dollars. I kept telling myself the money didn't give him a license to do whatever he wanted to do.

It helped that a Democrat still occupied the White House. Most of the many American corporate fat cats lean hard to the right, primarily because most of them vote only with their tax breaks and brackets. I've tried to keep political ideologies out of my work. Regardless, if the current president were a Republican, the investigation would not have been happening.

At a minimum, it wouldn't have been happening with Henderson Robertson choosing not-so-voluntarily to sit for a voluntary interview with the Assistant United States Attorney who was running the probe into whether key Traxxion executives had amassed through hidden (but not completely untraceable) blockchain transactions thousands of units of a new cryptocurrency that was going to be added to one of the most popular exchanges.

Using coded communications our highly skilled and specialized FBI agents had managed to uncover and crack on the dark web, I'd learned that the chief executive of the crypto exchange, a fraternity brother of Henderson Robertson's at Dartmouth, had funneled information to Robertson about the new offering early enough to act on it. Robertson, smart enough not to buy any of it himself and cheap enough to not properly compensate his top-level Vice Presidents, had shared the information with one of them. Who shared it with another. Who shared it with another. And so on. Five decided to buy large amounts of the new crypto product.

Its value spiked when the exchange finally announced it would be added to the platform. They all dumped it within a week. The total profit, as best our people could calculate it, was $135.45 million.

It would be a complex and tedious effort to prove the digital connections in court. I knew I could pull it off. I also believed Henderson Robertson was arrogant enough to think no one would be able to show he was the link between Rory Nicholas and the executives who had cheated their way to a nine-figure windfall. I pushed for the interview in order to give Henderson Robertson a chance to lie to my face. It would be yet another charge for the eventual indictment.

It wasn't entrapment. It would land squarely within his nature to lie about anything and everything. I merely wanted to let nature take its course.

I inhaled and exhaled one last time before turning the knob and slipping into Sally Slammer mode. When I entered, I saw the lead investigator and his top assistant on one side of the table. On the other, Henderson Robertson sat among a phalanx of men in dark suits with white shirts held together by ties in various shades of red.

Sitting to Henderson Robertson's right was Joyce Fuller-Watson. She used to be a federal prosecutor. She left two years before I arrived. She now charged her time at two thousand dollars per hour, maybe more. She worked for clients who paid her monthly invoices without blinking.

Henderson Robertson didn't look up at me. "I see we're keeping banker's hours around here," he said. I ignored him and went to my seat.

"We agreed to make Mr. Roberston available for thirty minutes," Joyce Fuller-Watson said. "We're leaving in nineteen."

I dropped the legal pad on the table and opened a pen. "You can leave now, if you'd like." I looked at the row of men, one by one. Each was glaring at me, except for their boss. Henderson Robertson kept his head down, staring at his phone with a foul look on his face. It was the same expression I'd seen in nearly every photo ever taken of him.

I waited a little longer to see if any of them would get up. I remembered I had less than nineteen minutes to get my business concluded.

"Thank you for coming in," I said. "I know your time is valuable."

Henderson Robertson kept his eyes on the screen. "You have no idea how valuable it is, young lady."

"When did you last communicate with Rory Nicholas?" I said.

"Mr. Robertson hasn't seen Rory Nicholas in more than ten years," Joyce Fuller-Watson said.

"I'm sorry, ma'am, we're not interviewing you today. Mr. Robertson?"

"I haven't seen Rory Nicholas in more than ten years."

"My question isn't when you last saw him. I asked when you last communicated with him."

"I communicate with many people."

"I assume you do. When did you last communicate with Rory Nicholas?"

"I can't recall."

"Your class had a reunion last year. Mr. Nicholas chaired the committee. Did you communicate with him then?"

"I didn't go. I was out of the country."

"Again, that's not my question."

"Do you think those emails come to my personal account?

Do you think I sit around and chat with college classmates I haven't seen in more than a decade about a reunion I'm not able to attend?"

"I'm just asking if you communicated with him then."

"I'm telling you I don't recall."

"Do we have to subpoena all of your digital communications from the past decade?"

"You'll need a court order. I know a thing or two about what it takes to get one. Do you think you're the first prosecutor who has tried to make a name for himself by taking me on?"

"As you may have noticed, I'm not a him."

"Here we go. I apologize for offending your sensibilities with my selection of pronouns."

I stared at him. Silence is powerful in these situations. Humans don't like awkward pauses. Most people will keep talking. I waited to see whether Henderson Roberston would stumble into the lowest of low-tech traps. I waited a little longer.

"The clock is ticking," Joyce Fuller-Watson said.

I kept staring at Henderson Robertson. He'd been well coached. Unlike most men of his wealth and power, he'd taken the coaching to heart.

He wasn't going to say anything. His expression hadn't changed. Plenty of jurors would be inclined to dislike him, right away. That face would be a valuable asset for me at trial.

"Did Rory Nicholas provide you information, in any way and in any format, about the plans to include the RabbitRun cryptocurrency in the Vesuvio exchange?"

"He did not."

"If you don't recall your communications with him, how can you remember he didn't?"

He threw his phone down in front of him. It banged against the table. "I think I would recall something like that. Are you being serious right now?"

"I want to be sure I understand your version of the events."

"Here's my version of the events. Rory Nicholas and I attended Dartmouth together. We were members of the same fraternity. You obviously know that. I haven't seen him in years. We don't regularly communicate. I would recall if he decided out of the blue to share that kind of inside information with me, because I know the consequences of acting on it."

"How can you explain the fact that five of your senior executives purchased, between them, seven hundred and fifty thousand units of RunRabbit currency?"

"I have no involvement in or knowledge of the manner in which my senior executives make investment decisions. I've told them to steer clear of crypto. It's too volatile. It's backed up by nothing. I'm confident you'd find, if you ever had access to my full range of holdings, very limited activity with cryptocurrencies."

"So you don't know why they bought it?"

"I have no idea."

"You don't know why they sold it?"

"Maybe they're the ones you should be talking to."

I went with silence again. I knew he wouldn't keep talking. I just wanted to be sure I had what I needed.

"To be clear, would it be accurate to say you had no communications, directly or indirectly, with anyone regarding the RunRabbit cryptocurrency?"

"That's awfully broad," Joyce Fuller-Watson said.

"Again, you're not the person we're interviewing today. Mr. Robertson?"

Something approaching the beginning of a smile crept along the thin lips of his resting just-smelled-a-fart face.

"That's awfully broad," he said, reciting the words with the exact same inflections his lawyer had used.

"I'll narrow it down. Would it be accurate to say you had no communications, directly or indirectly, with anyone regarding the fact that the Vesuvio cryptocurrency exchange planned to add the RunRabbit cryptocurrency to its listing?"

"That would be accurate."

I turned to Joyce Fuller-Watson. "If we issue a subpoena for Mr. Robertson's communications, I trust you'll accept it. I assume Mr. Robertson would prefer not to be served in person."

"Send it to my attention. I trust I should send any documents arising from our efforts to oppose the subpoena to your attention?"

"I'm easy to find," I said.

Henderson Robertson picked up his phone and began to stand. "So I can go?"

"I said you can leave whenever you'd like."

The other lawyers aligned to each side of him scrambled to their feet, and the procession out of the conference room commenced. Joyce Fuller-Watson stayed close to Henderson Robertson, practically nudging him out of the room. Before he walked through the door, he stopped and turned back to me. I noticed the hint of a cringe beginning in the dark circles under Joyce Fuller-Watson's eyes, before she blinked it away.

"I'll tell you something a wise man told me a long time ago," Henderson Robertson said. "No amount of power is abused more than hardly any at all."

I kept calm. I stayed firm. I said nothing. Henderson Robertson was looking a little disappointed I didn't take the bait. He flipped his chin at the collection of lawyers who had started then stopped then started again to leave.

After they were gone and the door was pulled shut just hard enough to send the intended message, I leaned back in my chair. I smiled. Without turning to the two men who had stayed silent on either side of me during the meeting, I said the same words twice.

"We've got the bastard."

10

CARSON JEFFREY

Johnny Motts didn't answer the call I made from the newest burner. I wondered if he was still asleep, like one of those gangsters from the movies who works all night and sleeps all day. Like vampires. I guess that makes sense.

I was still sitting in the front seat of my Jeep. I hadn't left the parking lot, but I didn't want to stay for long.

There was no point in hearing how sorry anyone was about what happened. Shit, it's amazing I lasted as long as I did. The only thing that made me any different from the other slappies who constantly come and go is that, one, I never caused trouble and, two, I played a position that's got to be fully staffed to get a team through a season. Plenty of guys catch passes at every practice. Every team keeps at least three or four quarterbacks around to throw them.

I dialed my agent's number as I drove away. I pressed the button for the speaker. After all these years of using the same car, I never figured out how to run my phone through the system in the dashboard.

"I heard," Paul Templeton said immediately after he answered.

"Good news travels faster than I realized."

"I was talking to them about one of my other guys. They're bringing in running backs. They mentioned they were letting you go."

"Thanks so much for letting me know."

"It was literally three minutes ago."

"Why didn't you call me?"

"I figured you found out."

I still would have liked a call from my agent, as soon as he got the news. Of course, that level of care isn't usually given to clients clinging to the bottom rung of the ladder.

"So what's next?" I said as the Wrangler started taking me home. The only good news was my side project with Johnny Motts would make rent there not an issue, for a long time.

"I'll make some calls," Paul said. "I'll check the rosters and see if anyone is down a quarterback. Maybe I can call in favor."

"I won't be a charity case. I only want to play for a team that wants me."

"You'd say no to a spot?"

"I can afford to be a little bit picky."

"There aren't enough openings to be picky."

"All I'm saying is we don't have to rush it."

"Well, it's my nature to rush it, I'll start—"

I cut him off when I noticed the burner ringing.

"I need to call you back." I could hear Paul starting to ask what could be more important than not being unemployed.

I pressed the button and reached for the burner. I jerked the steering wheel when I noticed the Jeep crossing the yellow line in the middle of the road. A guy in a pickup truck blared his horn at me. I waved an embarrassed apology and answered the call.

"Ain't it a little early in the week for a report?"

"I got cut this morning."

"What the fuck did you do?"

"They needed the spot. Willie Carter got hurt yesterday and they're bringing in more running backs."

"What the fuck are they gonna do for a third quarterback?"

"They're keeping the new guy. There's nothing I can do about it."

"This ain't good news for me."

"I'm not exactly getting ready to throw a party."

"You need to be on a new team. This thing is working too good. It don't work at all if your ass is on your couch."

"It's not as easy as you think."

"Get your agent on it."

"He is."

"He don't know about your other thing, right?"

I always hated when people thought I was stupid. It would have been worse than stupid to tell Paul what I'd been doing. Besides, Paul probably would have wanted a piece of the action after he found out how much extra money I'd been making.

"Nobody knows about my other thing."

"Well, he needs to get you on a team, fast."

"There's only so much that can be done."

"Can't you stay on as like an assistant coach?"

"They have a full staff. I just need to find a new team."

"Make it happen."

"I have no control over that."

"I got a lot of people counting on this project. After we're done, I'm gonna have to make some calls I'd rather not make."

I cursed myself for not thinking this through any better. I figured Johnny Motts and whoever he works for understood I could be let go at any time. I shouldn't have to spell it out. But there I was, caught between one employer who didn't want me on the payroll and another who wasn't willing to let me leave it.

"Don't do anything yet," I said. "Maybe he'll find something else for me today."

"You might think you don't need to pack up and move to a new town because you got enough cash to ride things out for a while. This ain't about the money you already made. This is about the money you need to keep making."

"I'll keep you posted."

"You don't need to. I'll be calling every hour until you get yourself on a new team."

Johnny Motts hung up. I held the burner. I thought about rolling down the window and throwing it into the street. I knew that would be the wrong move.

I had a feeling I'd keep getting that urge.

11

JOHNNY MOTTS

This is all I fucking need.

Just when everything was going smooth. First, the shortstop gets himself killed. Now, that overgrown bull rider gets himself fired.

Am I playing a little dumb with him? Yeah. I get how it works. Guys get cut. Especially the guys who are barely hanging on. I'm surprised it didn't happen to the kid sooner.

I still can't let him get soft. I know how much money we give him. He might think he can coast for the rest of the season. Maybe he thinks he's got enough that he don't need to play no more at all. I can't let that happen.

Alls I can do is push him. Bust his balls. Call him non-stop. Make him keep looking and looking if only to get me off his ass.

Should I let Carmine know? He's still pissed about Larry Ballentine, even though that was a while ago. I'll give it a day or two. It's only Monday. Maybe I'll get lucky and the kid'll end up on another team.

They all need quarterbacks. That's probably why he lasted in Vegas as long as he did.

Shit, he could end up with one of the teams we already got covered. We ain't got that many, but all it takes is one. If we get two guys on the same team, then what?

Will two of them give us even more information? Or will we be paying twice for the same shit? And why the hell didn't I think of that before? The more guys we get, the better the chances two of them end up together. What if one tells us one thing, and the other tells us something different?

Maybe it means Larry Ballentine will get some company in that landfill.

The more I think about it, the more I think I should tell Carmine. I know he answers to somebody else. I wish I knew who. I still can't shake the feeling that what we do crosses over into something legit, somewhere.

Of course, how can it really be legit, if that's what's going on? It'd just be a front. Not a front like a phony candy store with the real business in the back. There could be a real business connected to this. Something that makes plenty of money without breaking no laws. Something that makes extra money through us.

Who would do that? Who would risk something that don't break the law by messing with something that did?

Then I remembered the guys I've been recruiting. Already making great money legally from sports. Ready to risk it to make even more by working for us on the side.

It's greed. That's what would get someone to do it. Spin the wheel with your life, your money, your freedom. For more.

I wonder how many of those guys even do it for the money. They got enough. There's something about getting more. I never thought about it, but that's the perfect word for what it is.

More.

They want more. I want more. We all want more. And I can't get no more if this fucking kid who got cut today don't find another gig soon.

I keep thinking I should let Carmine know what's happening. Part of me says I should. Part of me says to wait. You know how in the movies sometimes a guy gets a devil on one shoulder telling him to do one thing and an angel on the other telling him to do the opposite? That's how I'm feeling. I just didn't know which one is the devil and which one is the angel.

Maybe I should ask one of the other guys for advice. But can I trust them? Either they'd be stupid enough to say something to the wrong person, or they'd be smart enough to make it look like they was stupid enough to do it. I know that game. I've played it myself.

We're in this thing that has ranks and layers and levels, but it's still every man for himself. You can't count on nobody. You tell somebody your secrets, they'll find a way to use them against you. Even if they don't mean to, they will.

That's what we are. It's who we are. We fuck over everybody on the outside. When the chance comes along, we fuck over everybody on the inside, too.

If I'm gonna say anything to anybody, I'm gonna say it to Carmine. Yeah, I'll give it some time. Maybe the kid will get another spot. I'm gonna wear that fucker out until he does.

Does he deserve that? I don't give a shit. He's the one who lost his job. He can call it a numbers game or whatever. If he was worth a shit they wouldn't have got rid of him.

Hopefully, he's worth enough of a shit that somebody else wants him. I don't wanna make another one of these guys disappear. If I have to, I got a decent idea how it will go.

No news is no news.

That's how it went with the guy who was in the starting nine for a pro baseball team. Nobody's gonna think twice about a failed football player that washed out of the league and then fell off the face of the earth.

12

ALICE SMITHSON

The meeting with Henderson Robertson was short, but it left me feeling drained for the rest of the day. Not having coffee within thirty minutes of waking up didn't help. By the time I filled a cup from the stale pot in the break room, it was too late for the caffeine to make a difference. The engine would sputter until I had a chance to pull the ripcord the right way the next morning.

I powered through it. I ignored that dull ache behind my eyes, stronger on the left side than the right. More meetings, two hearings, three conference calls. I missed my day of solitude. I tried not to think about the catching up I'd have to do later.

Why did I agree to join Will for his Friday night manhunt? I needed an evening of doing nothing, a morning with no alarms. I couldn't get out of it. Will wouldn't let me. I wouldn't let myself. I always keep my word, always follow through on everything I say I'll do. It's nothing my grandfather ever told me to do. It was part of the example he set.

The clock crept toward six. I didn't feel compelled to supplement my growing list of good results by making a show of staying late when I could finish my work at home. In comfortable clothes. In a comfortable chair. With the expensive tequila I'd sip. Neat. Usually two glasses. Sometimes a third. It gave me a glow as I trudged through emails and documents and whatever else came from the pile that would keep filling up, each and every day. It also made it easier to fall asleep without fretting over whatever was waiting for me the next morning.

I packed up a few files for the trip home. The door swung open. Just as I was starting to make a joke about coming into my office without knocking (the joke would have carried a very real message about coming into my office without knocking), I realized it was the boss.

The big boss.

I'd crossed paths with Roger McClelland when he was in private practice, before his efforts to raise money for the current president and associated PACs delivered an appointment as the U.S. Attorney for the District of Maryland. He had worked at one of the big firms, representing white-collar defendants who had the money and urgency to pay whatever he wanted. Before that, he'd been an assistant in this office, same as me.

He managed to have it both ways, making great money while remaining sufficiently connected to secure the job he now held. He'd stay there at least until a Republican president took the oath, and then he'd go back to his old firm or maybe start one of his own. He'd be able to charge even more to help those who were factually guilty finagle a verdict of legally innocent.

"Am I interrupting anything?" he said.

"Not at all." I hoped my face hadn't revealed my initial reaction.

"Really, we can do this another time."

"Now is fine." I stood up with my briefcase and dropped it. It landed on the floor and flew open. "I was just getting my things together."

"You can sit down then," he said. "I'll take a seat as well, if that's OK."

I fell back into my chair. He lifted a box of files from the seat across from my desk and lowered it to the carpet. It still had that sickening new smell, even after almost a year. Better than the funk that drove me out of there the day before. I hoped it was gone, that I hadn't simply gotten used to it that day.

Possibilities ricocheted in my brain. I didn't like not knowing what was happening. I wouldn't have to wait long to find out.

"How has everything been going?" he said.

I didn't know whether he was looking for something perfunctory, or whether he truly wanted to know. When in doubt, keep it simple.

"Just staying busy in the business of doing justice."

"You're doing us proud."

I smiled at that. There's no way he knew much about what I'd been doing. I still liked hearing him say it out loud.

"Sally Slammer. That's a great nickname. It keeps the people you deal with on their toes. Makes them nervous. You made Bobby Brunfeld nervous. When I told him that's what they call you, it made it a lot easier for me to sell the plea."

"It was a fair deal. It would have been a tough case."

"I left a lot of money in that file."

"Billable hours," I said. "I try to never divide my annual salary by the total time I put in."

"If you ever did, you'd be taking more than a briefcase out of here. And you'd never come back."

"One of these days, I guess."

"You'll be hell on the folks around here once you're on the other side."

I didn't know what to say to that, so I just thanked him.

"There's no need to thank me for stating the obvious."

"I guess not," I said, mainly because I couldn't think of anything else to say.

"Life becomes a lot easier when you don't have to state the obvious to the people who work with you."

"That's for sure," I said. (So much for being witty and articulate during an unprecedented audience with the man in charge.)

"Good, because I'd rather not state the obvious about your meeting from this morning."

There it was. I should have realized that's what this was about.

I gathered myself for whatever was coming next.

13

CARSON JEFFREY

When the wing of the jet dipped toward the runway, everything went white. I couldn't remember the last time I'd seen snow.

Paul Templeton hadn't found me another job, yet. For now, he'd lined up a workout on Tuesday morning. In Minnesota.

On the red eye, I slept for maybe ten or fifteen minutes at a time. I'd drift off for a bit and wake up and try all over again. I aimed to get maybe two or three hours of actual sack time at the hotel room, before they put me through the paces. Basically, I'd be throwing footballs to a bunch of strangers in front of a bunch of strangers who'd figure out whether I'm good enough.

I didn't want to do it. I couldn't tell Johnny Motts I said *no thanks* to a chance to get another job. Still, I didn't know shit about this team. Didn't know the coaches, the players, the city. I did know that the sooner I landed on a roster, the sooner I'd stop hearing from Johnny Motts.

Teams give tryouts all season long. Most of them happen on Tuesdays, when the current players are off. It makes things less awkward, since they don't have to see the guys who might end up taking their jobs.

That's how it goes, throughout the league. Each team is one big machine, always looking for better or cheaper parts. When they find one, the old one gets ripped out and the new one gets jammed in.

I didn't know how many other quarterbacks were trying out. Paul said it would be better if there were more than just me. Sometimes, a team brings in a quarterback only because it needs someone to throw the ball to the ones they're thinking about signing.

Someone was waiting for me close to baggage claim, not that I had a bag to claim. The kid was standing there, holding a sign with my name on it. It wasn't like he'd recognize me. I haven't done enough in pro football to be recognized, by anybody.

"Howdy," he said. I didn't know if that was a Minnesota thing. Maybe he just wanted me to feel comfortable, since he probably knew I went to school in Texas.

"Howdy," I replied, pulling at the brim of an invisible cowboy hat. He offered to carry the backpack I brought on the plane. I thanked him and told him I'll do it.

I knew the game. I had to act like this scrawny, little intern in a polo shirt two sizes too big for his body and fresh acne on both cheeks and half of his forehead has real juice. Anything I said while he drove me to the hotel would get back to the people in charge. Most guys who get rides like this don't realize it, or they just don't care.

He led me to the car. It was an SUV painted in the same shade as the team's purple helmet. He started to open the door to the back seat. I waved him off and climbed in the front, across from him. I knew I should treat this guy like he was the head coach. Hell, I treated him like he was the owner.

"Sorry about what happened in Vegas," he said.

He was the first person to say that to me. My agent hadn't. There's no way Johnny Motts ever would. They both wanted me to get to my next job, but for very different reasons.

"Thanks," I said. "I get how things work."

"We'd love to have you here. I hope it works out."

"So do I," I said, even though I didn't.

It hit me that I could get an easy ticket out of Minnesota by being a dick to the kid. But that wasn't my way. No, I'd never been naturally disposed to being an asshole. Four seasons of being on the bench in Vegas tipped any horns I might've had.

Of course, this would've been the right time to get a little pissy. I had the rug yanked out from under me, without warning. I'd spent the last day being harassed non-stop by Johnny Motts. I had barely enough sleep to think straight. Next, I'd be going through the motions in a place I didn't want to be.

Knowing I'd keep getting calls from Johnny Motts helped me stay focused. I'd be back in Vegas soon enough. I promised myself that, once I was home, I'd shut off both phones and sleep until I woke up.

The kid dropped me off a few minutes after eight o'clock. He said he'd be back at eleven. I thought about asking for a little more time, but they had a schedule to keep. Also, I wasn't in a position to negotiate—with anyone about anything.

The mattress wasn't very comfortable. It didn't matter. I was tired enough to conk out in the last row of a rollercoaster. So I turned off the burner, put my main phone on silent, and set an alarm for ten minutes to eleven. Thanks to the buzz cut, all I'd have to do was step out of the shower, get dressed, and go.

I waited inside the main doors to the hotel for the kid to pull up in that purple SUV. I wondered if I'd ever get used to wearing a helmet that color, with whatever that thing is on the sides. I hoped like hell I wouldn't have to try.

The practice facility was close to the hotel. I saw it from my room, on the other side of a lake. One out of fifty thousand. Or is it ten thousand? I didn't plan to be there long enough to take inventory.

The SUV rolled to the front door. Another intern waited to take me wherever I needed to go. The second one was even more talkative. Peppy, with that Minnesota accent. I acted grateful. I followed him through the hallways to a small locker room away from where the real players spend their time. I saw other bags and clothes, which told me I wouldn't be alone for the tryout.

The intern took me to a stall with some of the newest gear for me to wear, even though I would have been fine with a hoodie and sweatpants. He asked for my general measurements and came back in less than a minute with a new pair of size fourteen cleats. I got changed while the intern waited on the other side of the door to take me to the practice field.

Once we got there, I saw four men in team gear standing off to themselves. Assistant coaches, apparently. The head coach wasn't around. Neither was the one who runs the offense. A few of the faces looked familiar.

I did a quick count of players. Eight in all. Some were getting loose. Some were standing around, talking. Half seemed nervous. Two came off as disinterested. One acted like he didn't know why he was even there.

I perked up when I spotted Walker Parker. He was the guy in Vegas I used to be, before I got there. Third-stringer who never played. They let him go once they decided they could trust me as the emergency option, even if that would be like trying to put out a five-alarm fire with a trickle of chihuahua piss.

He hollered at me and jogged over. "Welcome to Club Slapdick," he said.

"It has a name?"

He paused to ponder the phrase he'd coined. "That'd be the best one for it. We're the guys who got no jobs. The guys who maybe should just give up."

"Why haven't you?"

"I've got a judge up my ass about child support."

That made me laugh. It also made me think of the guy who's up my ass.

"Looks like this is the first one for you," he said.

"It's that obvious?"

"I get notifications on my phone of all the quarterback moves. It's part of staying a step ahead of the lady in the black robe's foot."

"How many is this for you?"

"I lost track at thirty."

"Any advice for a virgin?"

"Show them your stuff. Do what they say. Then you'll find out if you won the lottery."

I thought about what he said. It wouldn't be too hard to lose the lottery on purpose. A misfire here or there and it would be, "Thanks for coming out, take care." I decided not to do that.

Maybe I was being smart. Maybe I was being competitive. Even though I didn't want to be on that team, but I couldn't not do my best.

A whistle blew. One of the coaches started calling out names and telling us where to go. When I heard mine, I did what he said.

Out came footballs from a big bag and off it all went. I slipped into practice mode. It was easy, since it was all I'd done for the last four years. Before they made the season twenty games, I would've played in the preseason. That's long gone, because there's way too much money to be made in having more games that count. So, no, I'd never played in any type of pro game, real or exhibition. I assumed I never would.

The tryout moved fast. Some of the others ran routes. The quarterbacks dropped back and threw passes in the direction of where the balls were supposed to go. Most of the time, they ended up in the general vicinity.

It's a hell of a way to operate, throwing football to players I'd never met. I didn't know anything about how they run, or how and when they'd make their breaks to the left or right. I did what the coaches said, throwing short and long and out and in and anywhere and everywhere.

I had no time to do anything but make one throw and get ready for the next. Before long, I could feel sweat starting on my neck, under my arms, in the middle of my chest. I didn't pay attention to any of the others. It felt like we were robots, because that's basically what we were.

Do this. I did. Do that. I did. On repeat until the whistle blew, and that was it. No one said it was over. It just was.

The cyborgs went back inside to get changed and, for most if not all of them, get lost. I followed along, acting like I'd been there before. Hoping I wouldn't spend the rest of the season doing the same thing, week after week until someone decided they liked what they saw.

Nobody showered, since it really wasn't much of a workout. We toweled off the limited perspiration and changed back into the clothes we'd worn to the tryout. Walker and I did some catching up. It was nice to be around someone I knew. It made me not notice what a depressing scene it was.

A big van took us back to the airport. My plane wasn't due to take off until two. I texted Paul to let him know the workout was over. He said he'd call his contact in the front office and find out what they were going to do. Even if they wanted me, I'd still need to go back to Las Vegas and get my shit together.

I thought about all the money in the apartment. I couldn't take it to a bank. That would have sent up red flags, somewhere. I'd have to bring it with me or rent a storage unit. Or I'd just keep my place and leave it there.

I wished I'd thought this thing through a little better before ever agreeing to do it.

I went through security and headed for the gate. After Walker peeled away for his plane back to Atlanta, I turned the burner back on. It started buzzing right away. I let it go to voicemail. I checked the screen. Johnny Motts had called more than twenty times.

I kept looking at the burner. That urge to get rid of it was back.

What would he do if he had no way to get in touch with me? I stood by a window watching planes take off and land while I thought about that.

After a few minutes, I decided not to find out.

14

JOHNNY MOTTS

This kid is pissing me off. I knew he was going to Minnesota to look for work. He was still under orders to take my calls.

I should have sold burner phones. We buy so fucking many of them. Every week, me and all my guys get new ones. Just so I can get them on the phone whenever I need to.

Now this little prick decides he's gonna snub me? I could tell he had it turned off. My calls went straight through to that voice telling me to leave a message. As if anybody needs to be told what to do when someone don't answer and the fucking beep goes.

I know he needed to focus on the tryout. He needed to get another job. I also wanted to know what the fuck was going on. At some point, he should have been able to turn the phone back on. Even if he was only gonna check to see if I called.

I sure hope this ain't gonna turn into another Larry Ballentine situation.

I've been spending way too much time trying to find more athletes. The bar at the Waldorf hasn't been producing. I've been going to the Wynn. I can't just hang around, or they'll start eyeing me. I wander from table to table hoping I'll come across somebody who looks like a player.

I spotted one last night. Tight end from Miami. They got their bye this week; I always check to see who's off so I know who might be in town. He's big and he's loud and he's single, far as I know. He also comes off like he's dumb. I know better. He ain't dumb about blackjack. I kept looking for an opening to help out. He never gave me one.

After he doubled down on a hand and won, I told him good job. He shot me a look and turned back to his chips. I guess I felt like I needed to impress him, so I bought in for another five grand. He turned around and took another ten, even though he already had more than twenty in his stacks. Then he started betting a dime for each hand. So I did, too.

I was sitting to his right. He got his cards before me. He started hitting whenever he knew I was going to, even when he maybe shouldn't. He'd give me this little smile when he busted with a face card that would have given me twenty or twenty-one. It was an expensive way to tell me to fuck off.

I got the message after I lost my five large. He said something when I walked away. I didn't hear it. I wanted to get in his face. I didn't need to make no scene. I had to just take it. It still would have been nice to have Larry Ballentine's bat handy.

Thinking about that bat made me realize I need another baseball player to take the place of the one we put in plastic. I'd like to get a few more basketball players, too. Them are the easiest ones to spot. Huge, like they come from a different planet. Or maybe they just slid down a beanstalk.

Whatever, I know a basketball player when I see one. One of the few I got might be starting to give me trouble, too. So I need to get more of them.

Don't they say bad shit happens in threes? From Ballentine to Carson Jeffrey to this new thing that might be bubbling up with Jimmy King. Denver ain't all that far away. I figure they got landfills there, too.

It would probably take more than four or five trash bags with somebody that big.

I'm going too fast here. Jimmy King ain't giving me any real trouble yet. He was off with his information about the game they played last night. He thought the point guard would take a lot more shots than he did. I'll give him the benefit of the doubt, for now.

The kid who used to be in Vegas, he don't get no benefit of the doubt. I told him what's what, plain as I could. And now he's not gonna take my calls?

He better hope he gets that job in Minnesota. I ain't in the mood to fuck around. I'm still trying to kick the habit of sending messages. If I ever have to go see him in person, it's only gonna be once.

I still haven't told Carmine the kid got cut. Maybe he found out about it, since the teams always tell the world whenever they make a move. It ain't like Vegas letting go of its third-string quarterback was gonna make the front page. And it ain't like none of the assholes I work with know the full list of my guys. If they did, one of them would find a way to let Carmine or Bobo know I got a player who became a stray.

What if I don't tell Carmine at all? What if I just make the fucker disappear? If they ask me about it, I can say I don't know nothing. It won't be the first time I lied to them. I know it won't be the last, either.

It could work. I could drive over there on my day off. I could swing by his place. I could take him out, probably with something more than a baseball bat. He really is a big fucker.

I could also take his cash. I guarantee you most of it's still there. Guys like that don't know what to do with that much money. I figure most of them are just piling it up. I could rob all of them while they're on the road. It ain't like they can call the cops.

Sometimes I think too much. Sometimes, I think about some shit that makes sense. I pay these dumbasses for information to help us win more bets. And then I can steal it from them when they don't expect it? I wish I thought of that sooner. Maybe when everything calms down I'll do it.

I wonder how much we paid Jeffrey, in all. I figure somebody has the numbers. Whatever it is, I'll bet all of it's still there. In whatever hiding place he found in his apartment that wouldn't be too hard to find.

No, he don't know what to do with all that cash. Maybe he uses it at the convenience store or the strip club. He don't seem like the titty bar type. Maybe it's the haircut. He looks like a Marine, or something. No mustache, no beard, hardly no hair. Cropped close and squared off. His head is shaped like a fucking car battery.

Yeah, he seems way too straitlaced for strip clubs. Of course, he seems way too straitlaced for messing around in this world. Why did I think he'd be interested? Why was he?

I can't remember. Maybe I was drunk. I sure remember he was.

It don't matter. What's that saying? The die is cast? I still don't know what the fuck that means. Maybe it means somebody is eventually gonna die.

15

ALICE SMITHSON

I watched Roger McClelland brush the backs of his fingers against one of his lapels. If he was clearing away lint, I didn't see any.

"I appreciate the gumption it takes to engineer an interview with someone like Henderson Robertson," he said. "But that's a very aggressive move."

He wasn't telling me anything I didn't know. Besides, my immediate supervisor knew what I was doing. I wasn't going to blame him for not making sure Roger McClelland approved of my project.

"Justice is aggressive when it has to be," I said.

"Discretion is important. And you know the saying. You go after the king, you better not miss."

He wasn't getting the quote exactly right. Even if my effort to correct the king of the office wouldn't have missed, I let it go. "He gave us everything we needed today," I said. "He lied to us."

"Was he under oath?"

"No, but—"

"It would have been better if he was under oath."

I wanted to ask how I would have gotten Henderson Roberston under oath. Subpoena him for testimony at a grand jury we didn't want him to realize I'd already convened? Roger McClelland should know there's an art to setting a trap. An element of surprise. If I'd gotten a subpoena for Henderson Robertson to testify before a grand jury, the force field would have been far stronger. He might have invoked the Fifth Amendment in response to every question other than *state your name*.

"The nerds can show footprints to both Henderson and Rory Nicholas," I said.

"The nerds don't make great witnesses."

"I'll make sure the jury understands we're proving they used elaborate means to cover their tracks."

"They should have used burners," he said. "These rich folks think they're too good for tactics the common criminals rely on."

"Or they think they're too smart to get caught. Or that we're not smart enough to catch them."

"I just hope you know what something like this can do. You got under his skin today, because I spent forty-five minutes on the phone with his lawyer. And more than forty minutes of it was his lawyer yelling at me for not controlling my people."

"I'm sorry you had to deal with that."

"Not as sorry as I am. What a mouth she has."

"The goal was to make her client nervous."

"Do me a favor, since it looks like someone didn't see fit to keep me in the loop. That's not on you. I'll assume you dotted every 'i' on your end. Going forward, let me know what you're doing on this one. I need to know when to brace for another call."

"Email or text?"

"Text. Any time."

I didn't ask for his number. I didn't want him to think I didn't already know it. I wondered whether he wanted me to ask my boss for it, since that would make him aware of the fact that, moving forward, I'd have a pipeline to the man in charge. "Should I wait for approval?"

He shook his head. "I'm not going to micromanage you.

If I have concerns, you'll hear from me. I just want to know what's going on. We don't go after many people like Henderson Robertson. I don't want anyone to suggest there are political motivations, or that we're trying to harm his broader business interests. I'd like to avoid a malicious prosecution lawsuit, or whatever else his lawyer may cook up."

Everything he said made sense. It bugged me that concerns other than the pursuit of truth and justice and the fundamental difference between right and wrong would impact his willingness to move against someone like Henderson Robertson. I knew going in that, the bigger the fish, the harder the fight. I'd now have to consider what the man who could make me unemployed with a snap of his fingers would think about whatever moves I planned to make next against a man that, in my mind, was guilty and should face every consequence flowing from it.

I decided this would all be good experience for my secret plan to enter politics. I'd spent my entire career thinking like a lawyer. I would need to start thinking like a politician. I didn't appreciate the potential interference with my ability to do the job the way I thought it should be done. I welcomed what was an unexpected, and maybe inevitable, introduction to a world far different from the one I'd occupied.

"Where do you see yourself in ten years?" he said.

Holy shit he can read minds.

"I try not to think about that," I said, lying because I had to. "I just try to get through one day at a time."

He got up and walked toward the door. "That's a very good answer. I've always said the exact same thing, for twenty years now."

He left the room and pulled the door shut behind him.

I sat there. Thinking about what had happened. Replaying the conversation as best I could remember.

I decided not to work at home that night. I stayed in my office, grinding through everything I would've done in my apartment. If the stench came back, I didn't notice.

Maybe I didn't notice because I kept thinking about how this shift in my relationship with Roger McClelland could help get me where I wanted to be.

Along with how it might completely screw everything up.

16

CARSON JEFFREY

"I was starting to think you put me on the pay no mind list," Johnny Motts said right away.

"Hello to you, too."

"Fuck hello. I've been trying to tell you hello."

"I've been busy."

"You ain't so busy you can't take my calls."

"You told me to get another job."

I'd found a gate where the next plane wasn't due to leave for two hours. No one else was around, except for some guy working his way through two hamburgers in large bites while watching something on his phone.

"So did you get another job?"

"Not yet."

"What's the holdup?"

Guys get cut all the time. Is it my fault he's too damn stubborn or stupid to understand that? There was no point telling him again.

"I did my thing," I said. "Now we wait."

"What are you doing now?"

"Getting ready to fly home."

"Why are you coming back here?"

"Where else am I supposed to go?"

"There's more teams."

"This isn't like getting a job at Taco Bell. You don't walk in the front door and ask if they're hiring."

"Maybe you need a different agent."

"They're not lining up to represent guys who don't have jobs."

"I'm still not sure you appreciate the situation we're in here, paisano."

"I understand it completely, paisano. I'm doing everything I can. I flew all night. I hardly slept. I had an opportunity. I took it. If you weren't pushing me so hard, I wouldn't have done it."

"I never pegged you for lazy."

"It has nothing to do with lazy," I said. "Every team has their guys. I have to wait until someone is looking for a quarterback. And then I have to hope they want me."

"I thought you was supposed to be good. I remember you in college. You threw that touchdown at the end of the game against Texas. Covered the spread. Cost me a pretty penny."

"Am I supposed to apologize for something I did before I knew you?"

"I'm just wondering whether I picked the wrong guy to do business with."

"So am I."

"Nobody forced you to do this. You've made good money. I should know. I counted out all them bills."

"I wish I could get you to see I didn't do anything. The team made a decision. I didn't make them do it. I was doing my job, for them and for you. I was one of the last guys on the roster. They needed my spot. That's how it works."

"I wish I could get you to see the heat I'm taking. It's not like we got a bunch of guys doing this."

"Maybe you should get more."

"Maybe we'll start looking for somebody else."

"I won't be upset. We can go our separate ways."

"This ain't no normal job," he said. "You don't give notice and quit. Once you're in, there ain't many ways of getting out."

"What does that mean?"

"Wasn't you an academic All-American, or some shit like that?"

"None of the courses covered the inner workings of the mafia."

"Watch it with that word. You got this arrangement all wrong."

"I guess I do."

"You drop a bomb on me out of nowhere yesterday, and then you stop taking my calls? The people I answer to are going in my ass and down my throat at the same time. They think maybe you decided to flip."

"Flip?"

"If you don't know what that means, you really are fucking dumb."

"I'm no different than any of the hundreds of guys who aren't on teams," I said. "I have to wait for my next chance. There's a chance it'll take some time, if it even happens."

"That ain't good enough. It needs to happen soon. Can't your agent twist arms? All these teams and all those players? Only eleven play at a time. He can find somebody who'll let you get back to doing what you've been doing."

"I thought you didn't want me to tell him what I'm doing."

"You need to come up with a way to make him know how important it is without telling him why it's so important."

"Do you realize how that sounds?"

"I don't care how it sounds. I care about you getting on another team. When will you be back in town?"

I didn't want to tell him, but I knew that pheasant wouldn't fly. "Tonight. Whenever the plane lands."

"Call me as soon as you get home."

"I'll try."

"I ain't asking you to try."

The line went dead. I looked at the burner. I saw a trash can. I wanted to throw it in there.

I started to walk away. When I passed the guy who was finishing up his second burger, he looked up.

"Hey," he said with a full mouth, "I know you. You're Carson Jeffrey, right? North Texas?"

I shook my head and smiled. "I think you've got me confused with somebody else."

He shrugged and went back to watching his phone and chomping his burger.

17

JOHNNY MOTTS

Right after I hung up, I started to think about going over to his place and waiting. I could get Nicky No-Nose to come with me. This ain't somebody to handle by myself.

He's tall. He ain't real thick. He's got those long arms. Like one of them monkeys. Not the gorilla. The orange-a-tan or whatever the fuck. I don't need no wrestling match with the kid. And I don't wanna shoot him in his own place, because I ain't got the time or money to track down a silencer.

That's one thing people got wrong about this life. You get thirty years minimum if they pinch you with a silencer while you're doing a job. Ain't nobody in this world risking that just to make things a little easier.

I ain't never understood why the movies got so many guys with silencers in their guns. Like they grow on trees. I guess it's cleaner that way. You shoot somebody without making no noise. They don't wanna come up with other ways to kill somebody quiet when they're writing them scripts. Pull out a gun with a silencer and zing.

I'm getting too far down the line. But I need to be prepared for whatever. I already had whatever happen with Larry Ballentine.

This time, I'll be freelancing. Nobody told me to send a message. How could they? I still ain't told Carmine he got cut. Carmine ain't said nothing to me, either. I'm gonna assume that means he don't know nothing about it.

Unless he does, and they're testing me to see if I'll come clean. That wouldn't be good.

Why does this have to be so complicated? It makes my head hurt. Plus, I'm getting a twitch right above my lip, under my mustache. It comes and goes and comes and goes.

The kid really pissed me off this time. He could have taken one of my calls. He's supposed to take them all. I can't let that affect my thinking. My judgment. Carmine talks about having good judgment. I think I got good judgment. Well, I used to think I did.

It's easy to have good judgment when everything is going smooth. I had good judgment with Larry Ballentine. It ain't my fault he bent over and took a bat to the melon. He's the one that had bad judgment.

Maybe I got bad judgment for not telling Carmine right away the kid got cut. But I need him to think I can control my guys. If I run to him with every problem that comes up, is that good judgment?

I'll check in with a few of my other guys while I wait for the kid to get back. Minnesota ain't one of the teams we got covered. I sure hope he impressed them enough to get a job. That would be good. It would be simple. Silencer simple.

I got a weird feeling this one is gonna keep getting harder. I don't like where this kid's head is. I don't like his attitude. He's already thinking about finding a way out. I have to get him under control. I have to make him get a job before I have to tell Carmine.

It's Tuesday. If he ain't on a team before Sunday, it'll be too late to go to Carmine. I need to figure out when to tell him. He'll ask why I didn't tell him right away. What'll I say? What'll he expect me to say? I'll just tell him the truth. I didn't wanna put none of it on him until I knew it was a problem.

Then he'll tell me it was a problem the minute I found out the kid got cut.

I could tell him the kid didn't tell me. Maybe that'll work. Then he'd tell me to send the kid a message. I could try to talk him out of it. What would I say?

My head really hurts. I got Percocets here somewhere. I should go back to the Waldorf and start looking for more guys. I don't wanna lose any more at the tables.

I still need to try. Now that baseball's over, maybe I can line up one or two to take Larry Ballentine's place.

I need more guys, but I don't need more problems. I gotta do a better job of picking them. Ballentine was a mistake. Jeffrey is turning out to be one, too.

Maybe he won't be. If he just gets with another team, we can get back to business. We won't miss a beat. Maybe I need to start getting guys who got more job security than Jeffrey did.

For football, it helps to have guys who ain't playing. Any of them can get me the information I need before the games. The ones who are playing ain't in position to give me much during games. Backup quarterback is perfect. I need backup quarterbacks who are good enough to stick on the team but not good enough to play.

I thought I was doing a good job with this. If I start fucking up now, I ain't gonna get to where I wanna be. I wanted this. I need to figure out how to work through spots like this when they come up. It'd be nice to have the choice to make them disappear if they ain't working out.

I need to make it work with the kid. I need to keep leaning on him. I don't need to get rough with him yet. He needs to know the stakes. Words, not actions. I wish it was that easy.

I found them Percocets. I think they're working. My head feels better. That twitch is still there.

So here's my plan, I think. I keep telling the kid he needs a job.

If he ain't got one by tomorrow night, I'll ask to see Carmine. I'll tell him what's going on in person. That way, I can read him. I need to be careful he don't read me.

I hope it don't come to that. I need some luck, I guess. Ain't that what gambling is? That's what it is when you don't know what's gonna happen. That's what all of this is about with these jocks. Knowing enough so you don't need no luck. Knowing enough so you're getting free money.

We've been making a lot of free money. I can't forget that. Will there be some issues? Sure. Will that make it harder to keep making as much money? Probably. But the money we already made counts for something, don't it?

That's what I need to be ready to tell Carmine, if I have to. Count up the money this project has made with me running it. They can't expect it to be perfect all the time. As we get more guys, there will be issues.

I can tell myself that. Telling it to Carmine is gonna be different. Like I said, everybody wants more. What we already got don't mean shit if we ain't getting more. And if it's all of a sudden my fault we ain't getting more, they're gonna blame me.

My plan is shit. I know that. It's the only plan I got. Lean on the kid, and hope we get lucky. Hope I get lucky. Hope my luck ain't run out.

If it has, I won't be moving no higher. Hell, I could end up being the one keeping Larry Ballentine company in the landfill.

18

ALICE SMITHSON

I kept going. I lost track of time. No food. No caffeine. Just the remnants of the adrenaline rush that happened the instant the boss made it clear he wanted to talk to me.

I kept thinking about the meeting that started the day. It felt like it happened a week ago. Maybe a month.

Time didn't matter. The past is the past. And the past doesn't mean jack shit.

That was another one of my grandfather's sayings. It usually came out after two shots of whiskey. One he would swallow in one gulp. One he would sip.

Why do I drink? Because he did. I wonder if he would have quit, if he'd known that.

The past doesn't mean jack shit. I used to think it was some broad observation about human history. As I got older, I figured out it wasn't quite so profound.

It was about his own life. It was about everyone's existence. What you've already done means nothing. What you're doing now does. What you will be doing, even more.

Everything leads to something. Where you've been and what you've accomplished doesn't mean a thing. Nothing good comes from thinking about it. Regret. Pride. Satisfaction. Those things distract from what currently is, from what is to come.

I never knew whether I'd figured that out on my own, or whether his influence led me there. It didn't matter.

I also didn't know whether Roger McClelland's message was supposed to discourage or encourage me. I picked encourage.

I needed to be careful. I needed to be transparent. I knew I could do both. Henderson Robertson had broken the law. I fully intended to prove it. If forces beyond my control kept that from happening, so be it. My own sense of what was just and proper had never failed me before. As far as I knew.

Was there a chance every impulse I'd ever acted on was leading me to the kind of colossal mistake that would destroy my career? If so, it was too late to change course now.

Either way, the boss was paying attention. He was engaged. A man spread way too thin by the usual responsibilities of his job had decided to carve out some of his time to watch what I was doing.

What's better? The boss watching my work, or ignoring it? I told myself this was good. I believed I could navigate Roger McClelland. I decided that, if I was wrong, I'd deal with it.

When one door closes, another one opens. That was one of the sayings my grandfather hated.

When one door closes, Ally, kick the damn thing in.

I'd find a way to placate Roger McClelland. I'd find a way to keep building the evidence I'd present to the grand jury. I'd find a way to turn the indictments they would give me into guilty pleas or convictions. And then I'd move forward, forgetting what I'd done and focusing on whatever I would do next.

And so on. Until I retired or dropped dead. I wouldn't ever reflect on anything I'd done. That would be for anyone else who happened to notice. Would they? Autobiographies are written by those who didn't do enough to get someone else to write their stories. Someone, someday, maybe would write mine. All I need to do is give them enough to fill up the chapters.

I know how that sounds. It's one of the reasons I've never told anyone what I was planning to do with my life. It's why I would have preferred having the boss leave me alone. All I wanted to do was put another pelt on the wall, forget about it, and move on.

That Tuesday night, I tried my best to think about none of those bigger issues. When I left the office and slipped back into my car, my main concern was the traffic. I didn't know where it was coming from. Then I saw the cheap purple and black material flopping on white plastic sticks poking up from the windows of some of the cars surrounding mine. The local football team had played a game that night, and the parking lots had started to empty onto the streets.

It was another reason to hate everything about football.

19

CARSON JEFFREY

Johnny Motts told me to call as soon as I got home. As much as I didn't want to talk to him, I knew I needed to play along.

It didn't matter that I didn't have anything new to tell him. He said call, so I called.

He still didn't understand why my agent couldn't snap his fingers and get me on a new team. It was becoming a problem.

Johnny Motts dropped a few hints about where it could lead. I was getting a little nervous about what might happen. I didn't feel threatened, not yet. That was probably because he hadn't threatened me, not in the way people like him make threats. I wasn't sure whether he was smart enough to come up with the right words to get the point across subtly.

I wondered whether it doesn't work that way, that maybe it's all vague and fuzzy. Until it's not.

I couldn't control my lack of employment. To Johnny Motts and whoever he worked for, that didn't matter. They lived in a world that refused to consider why I wasn't on a team. It was on me to have a job. It would've been nice to know that before I got mixed up in this.

Right now, it was as simple as it could have been. Get a job, or else.

Again, that hadn't been said. It was a feeling I'd gotten. He kept pushing me to do it. He hadn't said anything about a deadline. Maybe that was coming next. If I'd owed them money, I could have tried to find a way to get it. There was no way I could have gotten a roster spot with a pro football team if there was nobody who'd give me one.

I couldn't stop wondering how much of this was his fault. A failure to communicate, not because he wouldn't. Because he couldn't. Maybe he was just some low-level numbskull who hadn't explained the situation to his bosses and who didn't want to admit he fucked up.

If this was just Johnny Motts being stupid, how high up the ladder did the stupid go? There was a way to find out, but going over his head wouldn't have helped me. Even if I knew who or how or when or where, talking to his boss wouldn't have made things any better between Johnny Motts and me.

After I finished talking to him, I turned on the TV and watched some of the Tuesday night game. Cleveland was playing in Baltimore. I wondered whether Johnny Motts had anyone on either team giving information during the game.

I couldn't focus. That world felt strange to me, now that I wasn't in it. I really needed to get back in it. And not just because Johnny Motts kept telling me to.

No one wanted me. Las Vegas did for four years. Then, they didn't. I was undesired. Unemployed. How long would it last?

I checked on the cash. It was still under the floorboards in my closet. The space down there was almost full. Yep, I should've asked for something bigger than twenties.

I had no idea how much there was. I also had no idea what to do with it, if I had to leave Las Vegas.

I'd have to move at some point. If I didn't find a new team, maybe I'd need to disappear.

I considered whether I could vanish, whether they'd have a way to find me if I did. It didn't help that I was six feet and five inches, and that I weighed two hundred and twenty pounds. It wouldn't be easy for me to go unnoticed. I found that out in the airport.

I'd thought about New York. Of course, I hated everything about New York. And if I still wanted to get on another team, how hidden could I ever be, wherever I was?

I'd never felt hopeless before, not even after my parents died. This was the first time I had a problem I couldn't solve, because the only thing that'd get Johnny Motts off my ass was something I couldn't control. I couldn't make a team need me. I couldn't keep Johnny Motts from doing whatever he might do if I didn't find one fast enough for his liking.

I thought about Minnesota. I realized I hadn't heard from Paul Templeton. I called him to check in, mainly to get out of my own head for a minute.

"How's my favorite out-of-work client?" he said.

"How many out-of-work clients do you have?"

"More than you know. It takes guys a little while to accept it's over."

"Is this your way of telling me that's what I should do?"

"You play quarterback, and you're young. It's a matter of time before someone wants you."

"I take it Minnesota doesn't."

"My guy there didn't have an answer for me yet."

"That's probably the answer."

"I'll see if they add anyone tomorrow. Nothing has leaked tonight. The agents love to break news of their clients getting signed during these night games. They want a mention on the halftime show, or maybe get the player's name on the crawl at the bottom of the screen. I think they haven't decided what to do. Remember, Minnesota doesn't play again until Monday night. So they won't practice until Thursday. Tomorrow's the day for them to make a decision."

"Tomorrow might not be good enough."

"You understand how this works, right? Besides, you didn't seem to be in much of a hurry yesterday."

"That was yesterday," I said. "Is there a way you can get someone to throw me on the practice squad? I'll take the minimum."

"You were already getting the minimum."

"Is there a team out there that wants to sign one of your other guys to a new contract? Can't you tell them if they sign me you'll cut them a better deal?"

"Maybe I should hire you whenever you're done playing."

"I can't afford to be unemployed for too long."

"I've seen your place, and I know you're still driving that piece of shit. Do you have a drug problem you haven't told me about?"

"You know I'm clean. I can't imagine sitting around here, waiting for a phone call."

"Then don't. Work out. Stay in shape. I have that guy out there you can throw with. Stay ready. That's all you can do."

I wanted to tell him why it wasn't that easy, but it wasn't time for that. Maybe that time would never come. If Paul Templeton ever knew the truth about my non-drug problem, he'd cut me loose in a heartbeat. Then what would I do? It was hard enough to get back in the game with an agent. Without one, it would be a lot harder. Possibly impossible.

"Fine," I said. "Let me know what you find out."

"Just sit tight. And don't forget my saying. There aren't enough bad quarterbacks to go around."

"I always appreciate hearing it."

"That's not what I meant."

"It might not be what you meant, but it's sure as hell what you said."

"The point is you play a position that makes it easier to find work. Teams need quarterbacks. There's three spots per team. You're good enough for one of them."

"Then the question is whether you're good enough to get me one of them."

Paul started laughing. "I wasn't kidding. You'd be a good agent."

"Here's hoping I have one."

"Ouch."

"That's not what I meant."

"That makes us even. Get some sleep. You've had a long two days. By tomorrow, maybe it'll all work out."

I thanked him and hung up. When I turned back to the TV, I saw Baltimore's starting quarterback getting lifted onto a cart.

It looked like he'd hurt his leg, bad.

20

JOHNNY MOTTS

I don't like how he's been talking since he got cut. Something about it's been rubbing me the wrong way.

Of course, everything about this kid's been rubbing me the wrong way. I guess it ain't no surprise he put me over the edge. It's that attitude of his. He talks like some redneck, but now he acts like he thinks he's smarter than me. Like he thinks he's better than me.

Maybe he is. He's a pro athlete. Out of work, but still. Here I am, a two-bit legbreaker. It pays the bills and then some. It ain't nothing to brag about.

Still, I don't need him acting like that. It wasn't any one thing he said. It was everything he said. It was how he said it.

So I did it. I changed my mind. After he called me, I grabbed my piece and found a big knife from the kitchen and got in the car and went over there. I decided not to get Nicky No-Nose involved. I can't trust him. I can't trust nobody but myself. And I ain't completely sure I can trust myself no more.

I don't know what I'm gonna do. Scare him, I guess. Scare him good. If things go too far when I'm scaring him, so what? Nobody's gonna miss him. Like Larry Ballentine. The kid ain't got no family that'll be wearing out the cops to crack the case. He's gone and that's that.

No news is no news.

I parked in the same spot I use when I bring his money, back by the garage. There ain't no cameras there. I've checked every single place where one could be.

I was tired when I got there. I don't know whether them Percocets did it to me or what. I wanted to think things through. I didn't want it to go sideways. I needed to have a real plan, something I'd follow to the letter, without getting carried away. Part of me just wanted to be done with him, for good.

Then what? Carmine would get suspicious. I'd tell him I don't know nothing. He'd start looking into it. He'd find out the kid got cut on Monday. He'd find out he had a tryout in Minnesota on Tuesday. He'd figure it wasn't a coincidence that one of my guys went away four weeks after one of my other guys went away.

I couldn't take this one out, not now. So why did I go over there? What was I trying to prove? How would I make him know what he needs to do without me having to do something permanent?

For as much as I hate sending messages, I guess that's what I was gonna do.

I'd have to send a message without hurting him. I need him working. He wasn't gonna get no job if he shows up with a busted arm or a broken knee.

So what was I gonna do? I kept asking myself that question. I kept thinking through all the ways it could go down once I knock on the door and say I'm delivering a pizza.

I told myself the kid probably don't have a baseball bat. Of course, he don't need one. He's big enough to snap my neck real quick, if he wants. Does he have that in him? I didn't wanna find out the hard way. Then again, if he took me out instead, that would have solved all my problems.

Them Percocets was fucking with me. I shouldn't have taken two. I was sleepy. I decided to take a nap before I went to the door. I liked the sound of that. Get some rest. Let them Percocets wear off. Wake up and go see him.

I told myself I'm just gonna talk to him. Nothing rough. I need him healthy. I need him alive. What if he makes a move? At that point, I'd do whatever I had to do.

If that's how it goes down, I'd own up to it. Tell Carmine the truth before he could figure it out. The kid lost his job. I leaned on him to get another. I decided I could handle it. I wanted to make sure he wasn't dragging his feet. I went to see him to let him know how important it was. He overreacted. I did what we do when somebody overreacts.

That would work fine, if I hadn't just done the same thing with Larry Ballentine last month. It'd look way too fishy if it happened again. And then I'd have to worry about somebody deciding I can't handle my job. That I'm the one who needs to go away, before I fuck everything up and bring the heat on everybody.

I needed to have a clearer head. I needed to get them Percocets out of my system. I set the alarm on my phone for two hours later. Then I'd go talk to him and nothing else. I'd make sure he don't try nothing. If he did, I'd make sure it don't get out of hand.

I decided that, after getting some sleep, I'll think clear enough to do exactly what needs to be done. And that's exactly what I would have done, if I'd set that fucking alarm before the curtains came down for me in the driver's seat of my Cadillac.

21

ALICE SMITHSON

I made my way to work on Wednesday morning. I welcomed the list of tasks for a day that potentially would be eventful, but hopefully not as much as the prior day. There were no interviews on the schedule with anyone like Henderson Robertson, no reason to expect an unexpected visit from Roger McClelland to cap the afternoon. I'd be ready for whatever else the day might bring.

It was another one of my grandfather's sayings. *Every day could be the day.* He also liked to say, *Destiny knows nothing of November.* I didn't know what he meant the first time I heard the second one. I still don't think I do.

I've always known this. Any day can be the day that makes all the difference. Every day, everyone needs to be ready for the possibility that this is the day everything changes.

I also knew he meant any day could be someone's last day, too. I never told my grandfather I'd figured out that part.

I spotted Will Goldstein as I got close to my office. I sensed he'd been hanging around nearby, waiting for me to show. He followed me inside and closed the door.

"Heard you had an interesting night," he said.

"I never have an interesting night."

"Well, not by my standards."

"It was a normal Tuesday. Apart from getting stuck in traffic on the way home, thanks to the damn football game."

"So it counts as a normal Tuesday night for Roger McClelland to drop by?"

I waved my hand. "That was nothing. A quick visit."

"None of us ever gets any visit from Roger McClelland, quick or long or in between. You did."

"How do you even know about it?"

"Surely you're not saying my sources are misinformed?"

"He wanted to talk about Henderson Robertson. Why wouldn't he? Who else in the office is going after someone like that?"

"Still, the boss was in your office. The big boss. I have to know something. How did he smell?"

"Seriously?"

"I caught a whiff of him once. It was a little vanilla and a lot of heaven."

"I think he's married."

"I don't want to date him. I just want to smell him."

"I was too busy focusing on what he said. And wondering whether he caught the aroma in here. Sometimes I'm not sure I can smell it."

"Well, that's not vanilla. Or heaven."

"Perfect. The boss thinks I stink."

"Stink is subjective. Maybe he likes *eau de corpse.*"

"You're not helping."

"So what did he want?"

"I just told you. He wanted to talk about Henderson Robertson."

"Is he on board with your plan to lock him up?"

"He's not not on board with it. He wants me to keep him posted on what I'm doing."

Will's lip curled, his head recoiled. "Well, it looks like our girl now has a direct hotline to the United States Attorney for the District of Maryland."

"It's no big deal."

"Look around this place. He doesn't even know who half of these people are. And now you're in position to communicate with him, whenever you want."

"It's not like we'll be trading recipes."

"Only because you can't cook for shit."

"He expects me to let him know what I'm doing with Henderson Robertson. We're not buddies now, or whatever. He wants me to text him whenever I plan to do something with the Robertson case."

"That's a lot more than the rest of us will ever have. Do you think he's asked me once about any case I've ever handled?"

"I thought you had a case going to the jury soon."

"We start at one. The defendant has to decide whether to testify."

"The defendant never testifies."

"And then the jury will get sent home until tomorrow. They'll love that. Drive all the way down here, show up for ten minutes, go back home. We'll hammer out the jury instructions after they leave, the judge will read them tomorrow, and then we'll do the closing arguments."

"Are you ready?"

"I will be."

"Well, good luck."

"You want me to leave? Is that why you said that?"

"I'm just wishing you luck. Would you rather I didn't?"

"I'd rather you tell me more about Roger McClelland."

"There's nothing more to tell. Why is this such a big deal?"

"He doesn't keep tabs on any of us. He's keeping tabs on you."

"I'd rather he let me do my job."

"He can keep tabs on me whenever he wants."

"Do you want me to tell him that?"

He smiled at that one. "What I'd want you to tell him wouldn't be appropriate for a text message."

"You made your point. I have to get my shit together. I have a hearing in a little while."

"Fine, Sally Slammer. We'll continue this discussion on Friday night."

"You're still planning on that?"

"Don't you try to wiggle out of it. You said you'd go."

"If you change your mind, I won't complain."

"Be ready. We're going to drink some drinks and have some fun and find some men."

"I'm not looking."

He opened the door to my office and started to go.

"That's always the best time to find one," he said.

22

CARSON JEFFREY

For me, sleep had always been a one-way ticket away from whatever bullshit I was dealing with. And I was dealing with plenty.

Sunlight woke me up. I powered up my main phone. The screen said it was just after seven. I'd put the burner in a drawer in the kitchen. It was the closest I'd come to throwing it away.

I remembered what I'd seen the night before. The Baltimore quarterback, on a cart. They might need somebody. I checked their depth chart on my phone. Maybe this would be the place.

I noticed a missed call from Paul. He was based in Charlotte, so it was already after ten there. I checked my texts.

Call me ASAFP.

I needed to piss out nine hours before I could do anything. As the last of it dripped, I called Paul.

"It's your lucky day," he said.

"I haven't been lucky any day this week."

"You're going to Baltimore."

"I don't want another tryout."

"You don't have to. They want to sign you. Flight leaves at ten. Get your shit together and go."

"Where will I live?"

"They'll put you up in a hotel, for now. Don't you know how this works?"

"I've only ever played for one team."

"You can find a place whenever. Phillips blew out his knee. They wanted to get you before Minnesota could."

"Minnesota was going to sign me?"

"I don't know, and Baltimore doesn't, either. They're ready to go. Which means you need to be ready to go."

"What about my place here?"

"Baltimore has a bye coming up in a few weeks," he said. "You can straighten it out then. You won't be the only guy in the league with two apartments."

The good part is I wouldn't have to worry about moving all that cash. It wasn't like I'd need it in Baltimore. The team would be paying me. Johnny Motts would be, too.

"I guess I'll be ready to go."

"It's not like you have a choice. If you hesitate, they'll find someone else. You want this, right?"

"I want it."

"You're welcome."

Paul hadn't really done anything other than take a call. I thanked him anyway.

"You can thank me properly by making that flight." He said he needed to get the other line. Which was fine with me. I needed to make another call, on my other phone.

A wave of hunger hit me right away. I went to the kitchen and got the burner. I opened the fridge. The carton said the eggs had gone bad two days ago. I assumed they built in some sort of grace period.

I started scrambling the seven that were left. I searched for some bread. The date on the bag came and went four days earlier, but I didn't see any green spots. I popped four slices into the toaster right before I dialed Johnny Motts.

"I hope this is good news," he said.

"They want me in Baltimore."

"Baltimore? Maryland?"

"Unless they have one in Ohio I don't know about."

"What happened?"

"Their starter fucked up his knee last night."

"Ain't that some shit."

"It's some good shit," I said. "I got a job. I'm flying out at ten."

He didn't say anything.

"You wanted good news," I said while working the eggs. "You got it."

"Baltimore's a long way from here."

"So is Minnesota."

"I got people who wonder whether you're thinking about running."

"You've been telling me there are plenty of teams. One of them is in Baltimore. They want me. It's not like I'm going there to hide. We can keep doing what we've been doing."

"This changes things."

"Things were always going to change," I said.

"How am I gonna get the money to you? I ain't flying to Baltimore every week, that's for fucking sure."

"Hold it for me. I'll be back at some point."

"I ain't no bank."

"We don't have many other choices. What did you expect?"

"I didn't expect you to find something so fast."

I pulled the pan from the fire and threw the spatula to the floor. "You've been hounding me for two fucking days to find something else. This is what you wanted."

"You've been getting a little mouthy."

"You wanted to keep this going. I did my job. Do yours. Unless you don't want to do this any more. I've already told you I'm fine with that."

"Life was just a lot easier when you played in Las Vegas."

"Make up your fucking mind."

"There's that mouth again."

"I mean it. You've been on me non-stop. I found a new team. Now you're going to complain about it?"

"I don't wanna do nothing but keep making money."

"I have a way to do it. It's up to you to handle the rest."

"How do you know you'll get what we need?"

"Don't worry about my end. I'll know what's going on. I'll make my report before each game. If they call me up for game day, I'll do exactly what I did before."

"What do you mean, if?"

I sighed, loud enough for him to hear it. "I don't know if I'll have a helmet. If I do, I can keep doing what I've been doing. If I don't, I can't."

"You need to be on the sideline for the next game. With a helmet. So you know everything that's happening."

"If I do, I do."

"It'll be better for you if you do."

"It'll be better for me if you find someone else to do this."

"It's too late for that. You go there and do whatever you have to do to be in a spot to let us know whatever's happening during the game."

"I don't make those decisions."

Johnny paused. I was about to ask if he was still there when he started again, in a voice as soft as it was hateful.

"You better fucking hope whoever makes those decisions makes the right one."

23

JOHNNY MOTTS

When I woke up, I knew I was in my car, but why was my car where it was? I remembered I was out behind the kid's place. I remembered what I was thinking about doing. I didn't know whether I was glad I didn't do it.

I wouldn't go to his door in the daylight. I didn't need nobody seeing me there. There's always a chance we could have a conversation that turns into more than that.

I was pissed at myself for not setting the alarm. Yeah, that might have kept me from doing something stupid. It was also stupid to be sitting in the car all night, sound asleep. Somebody could have seen me there. Somebody could have walked right up to the car.

I think I got lucky. Nobody knocked on the window. Nobody called the cops. Wouldn't that have been something? Cop shows up to check on somebody passed out behind the wheel? With a gun and a knife in the car, that could have gotten interesting.

I still wasted the whole fucking night on the kid. I could have been at the Waldorf or the Wynn. I shouldn't have taken them Percocets. Once I did, I should have just stayed home. Sometimes, I'm too fucking dumb for my own good.

I drove home, thinking way too much while I did. I need my problem with the kid to go away. Maybe Minnesota will sign him. If not, then what?

I gotta talk to Carmine, one way or the other. I hope it happens after the kid gets a new job. I hope that new job lets him know what's going on during the games.

How the hell did I get this far without having shit like this come up? We saw a way to grab more money. It was easy. It made me think it would keep being easy. All of a sudden it's getting harder with Jeffrey. I got others who are doing it in football. But the kid was a cash cow. Out of nowhere, the milk got choked off.

It wasn't my fault the kid got cut. I should have let Carmine know. I wish I would have figured that out on Monday. I guess I really do got shitty judgment.

The only way to fix it is for the kid to get a job. Once I got home, I decided to call him and see if he got that job in Minnesota. The phone rang before I could. He told me he's going to Baltimore.

How the fuck did Baltimore happen? I needed to get lucky. I guess I did.

I gave the kid a hard time anyway. It's part of getting him under control. We can make it work if he's on a different team. I need him to have a helmet for the games, so he'll hear what the coach is telling the quarterback. I know there ain't no guarantee he'll have one. I pushed him as hard as I could to make sure he does everything he can to get it.

He still has that attitude. I don't like it, but the good news is he's got a job to go along with it.

I called Carmine as soon as I hung up with the kid. I told him I had some information about my project. I liked the sound of that word. *Information*. It made me feel like not a dumbass when I said it.

He said to meet him at one. I asked if he needed me to bring anything. He said he didn't need nothing but somebody who was ready to give up whatever *information* he thought was so important.

I didn't like the way the word sounded coming back at me.

It made me feel like he already knew I wasn't planning on being straight with him.

I need to get smarter. I need to control my guys. I need to be damn good at telling Carmine what I need to tell him about our guy who was in Las Vegas two days ago and is now about to be in Baltimore.

Carmine already thinks something is up. What the fuck is wrong with me? Why didn't I call as soon as I found out the kid was cut? What was I afraid of?

Whatever it was, I got something bigger to be afraid of now.

There was that fucking twitch again. Same spot, under the mustache. There was that fucking headache again. I got some more Percocets. The last thing I need to do is take another one before I go to Carmine's place. I gotta hope Tylenol does the trick.

I was half tempted to swallow the whole bottle along with the rest of them Percocets and the Grey Goose I keep in the freezer. That would make this day a hell of a lot easier than what it could be.

I ain't serious about that. But if I fuck this up and Carmine decides it's time for me to go, whatever they do will hurt a hell of a lot worse than it would to just eat them pills and drink that booze and sleep a lot longer than I did in the Cadillac last night.

24

ALICE SMITHSON

I knew I'd regret agreeing to go out with Will on Friday night. He outsmarted me, asking on Monday. Knowing I'd be more willing to write a check I wouldn't have to honor for four days. A sense of dread built, all week.

I craved a few hours of relaxation, followed by eight hours of sleep. I had no choice. I wouldn't let him down, no matter how badly I wanted to.

I wanted to fake an illness. But I couldn't lie to him. I was willing myself to be sick. If I could truthfully say I was under the weather, I could avoid the whole damn thing. I didn't stop to consider how pathetic it was to welcome the flu over embracing the inevitable hangover.

The only way to get through the night would be to drink my way into the mood. I'd feel like shit, one way or the other. I'd already strapped myself into the ride. There was no way off, unless I somehow found myself throwing up in my bathroom when I otherwise would have been looking for something to wear. Something appropriate for my age and the plans Will had made. Even if they were simply, one, go to one bar after another, two, swallow a stream of drinks, and, three, be on the constant lookout for someone Will could take home.

I went with casual. Jeans that hadn't developed a hole in either knee. A simple blue blouse I buttoned up higher than necessary. A jacket more suited to sitting in the stands at a football game I'd never attend.

I applied a little more makeup than usual, mainly to kill the time until he showed up at my place, courtesy of what would be the first of several Uber trips. I heard him knocking on the door just after nine. I rubbed off much of the blush and most of the lipstick before walking to open it.

He made a face. "That's what you're wearing?"

"What's wrong with this?"

"I wanted a wingman. I didn't expect someone who literally looked like a man."

"I didn't agree to any dress code."

"You're wearing less makeup than I am."

I studied his face. "I don't see any."

"That's because one of us knows how to properly apply it. Are you ready?"

"Don't you want to come in?"

"Not unless you plan on changing your clothes."

I rolled my eyes, grabbed my purse, and walked out of the apartment. "Where are we going?"

"Where we're going doesn't matter. What we're going to do when we get there does."

I didn't respond to that, because I already got the gist. I also knew that, the sooner we got started, the sooner it would be over.

The vehicle had arrived by the time we got down to the street. The breeze chilled my face. I didn't care what the wind might do to my hair. If that made it less likely I'd have a line of strangers trying to buy me drinks, it would be a bonus.

The ride arrived at the first stop on Will's secret itinerary. I didn't even look at the name on the sign as we climbed down from the back seat of the black SUV and walked inside.

The music was loud. I'd have to yell to be heard, which would make it easier for me to say as little as possible. Will had a spring in his step. It made me somewhat less unhappy to see him so happy. I kept reminding myself he deserved to have a good time, that it would have been better if I'd canceled than to be a wet blanket. I looked forward to drinking.

He ordered a martini. I opted for an Old Fashioned, another way to keep the memory of my grandfather alive. The only difference was he savored them. I drained the first one. I asked for another as Will regarded me with wide eyes.

"Pace yourself, Sally, or you'll be the one who ends up in the slammer tonight."

"I just need a little kick start." I took the second one more slowly. He turned away from me and absorbed the room with his eyes.

"I always look first for anyone I know. It's important to know who to avoid."

"I usually avoid everyone."

"Not tonight. We're finding me a man, and we're finding you a man. But I get dibs."

I laughed at that one, already feeling the liquor kick in just enough to make me not constantly wish I was on my couch, in pajamas and slippers. "If we see a man that we both want, I'm willing to let him decide."

Will looked at me again. "I'd feel pessimistic about that if you weren't dressed for a midnight trip to WalMart."

"I'm only trying to give you a fair chance."

He clinked his glass against mine and drained his drink. I finished the second Old Fashioned. We each got another and Will settled up with the bartender.

We carried our glasses through the room. It wasn't crowded, yet. There was still enough movement and lights and sound to energize Will.

We found a place to sit and sip. Will kept looking through and around the bodies. I could tell he wasn't fully on the prowl, yet. That would come after a few more bars and a few more drinks. I'd been out with him enough times to know it took a certain amount of alcohol for him to be willing to make a move. I was more than content to watch his routine unfold.

He finished his martini and rubbed his hands against his pants. They were a shade of red that fell somewhere between stylish and flamboyant. His loudly patterned shirt was large enough to conceal the fact that he didn't go to the gym as much as he'd like. He wore a pair of glasses he could never pull off in the office, and definitely not in court.

"That rush of waiting for a verdict will never get old for me," he said, "no matter how many times I do it. All the uncertainty that builds to a crescendo, and then they say the word. Guilty. It's magical."

"Far more magical than not guilty."

"Some of us hear that far less frequently than others."

"I've heard it enough," I said. "Those stay with me a lot longer than the convictions."

"Well, tonight's an occasion to forget about hearing not guilty and being a little guilty. Or a lot."

"Maybe for you."

"For you, too."

"We'll see."

"Yes we will," he said, and he grabbed my arm and led me to the next destination.

25

CARSON JEFFREY

The plane landed just after six on Wednesday night. Another intern greeted me. This one didn't need a sign with my name on it.

The kid drove me to the facility. I was a little more talkative than I'd been in Minnesota. I felt better this time around. I didn't mind being in Baltimore. And I didn't mind having a job again.

Even with a bunch of new worries, I liked what was going on. Anything that would happen to me in Baltimore would be better than whatever would have happened in Vegas, where I was never going to get away from Johnny Motts.

Maybe being on the other side of the country would give me a way to break it off. Probably not, but it was nice having a glimmer of hope.

After the intern dropped me off at the team's building, things went fast. From the physical (passed with flying fingers) to signing the contract (minimum salary, no surprise) to getting measured for a uniform and a helmet (as big as anything they had), I became an official member of the team. Well, the practice squad. That would have to be good enough.

It wouldn't feel official until I showed up for work along with the rest of the team. I didn't meet any of the coaches the first night, even though they were still in the office, getting ready for the next game.

They had plenty of work to do. They'd played on Tuesday. They'd play again on Sunday. Who gives a shit about wear and tear on the players when there's so much money to be made?

On the way over, the intern said the players had Wednesday off. Everybody would be back on Thursday for two days of practice before the next game, at home against Cincinnati.

I also found out they'd foot the bill at the hotel until I found a place. Well, a second one. Maybe I'd take my sweet time, stretch it out for the rest of the season. If I lasted that long. After getting fired two days ago, I wouldn't ever take anything for granted again. Not that I ever had. All I did was let my guard down.

On Thursday, I showed up thirty minutes early for the team meeting. Back row, like always. The head coach, Garrett McGarrett (yes, his real name), introduced me to a round of applause that barely made it to lackluster. I didn't care. I preferred being in the background. It made it easier for me to get what I needed.

There was a real freedom in being so far away from Johnny Motts. Sure, he could get to me if he wanted. It still felt damn good to be on the other side of the country. It also felt pretty damn good to not have that bastard burning up the burner phone, pushing me to get another job, get another job, get another job.

When I finally got one, the dumb shit pushed back. He's a fucking moron, and I was a bigger fucking moron for ever agreeing to do this.

Easy money? No. Such. Thing.

Garrett McGarrett started going over the film from Tuesday night with the players. I could feel misery hanging over the room like a wet fart on a hot day. They all knew something bad was coming, for somebody.

"I'm gonna go out of order a little bit," he said. "Because we got no chance to do jack diddly shit if people can't be trusted to do their fucking jobs. We'll start in the third quarter. Five fifty-three on the clock."

As he said it, the screen filled with a picture of the field from high behind the Baltimore offense. I could see the starting quarterback whose knee got torn up standing in shotgun formation, waiting for the ball.

"Let's focus on the left guard. Perkins, are you watching?"

A voice called out a few spots down from where I was sitting. "I am."

"What's your assignment here, Perkins?"

"To block!" someone called out from the other side of the room, down near the front.

"Shut the fuck up!" the coach said, without budging his gaze from Perkins. "What's your assignment here?"

"To help with the under tackle unless the middle linebacker blitzes."

"Congratulations. We've established you're not a fucking moron today. Were you a fucking moron on Tuesday night?"

Jerry Perkins started making sounds I couldn't quite make out.

"Perkins? Were you a fucking moron on Tuesday night?"

"Yeah."

"Say it, then. For everybody to hear. In fact, stand up. C'mon, get on your feet."

I wanted to turn and watch Perkins. I didn't move. I heard him getting up.

"I was a fucking moron on Tuesday night."

"Louder!"

"I was a fucking moron on Tuesday night!"

"And why were you a fucking moron on Tuesday night?"

"Because the middle linebacker came on a delayed blitz."

"That ain't what made you a fucking moron, you fucking moron. What made you a fucking moron?"

"I—I don't know what you mean."

"Get the fuck out of my room. Now. Empty out your locker and get the fuck out of my building."

I looked straight down. I could sense everybody else was, too. Everybody except for the head coach and Jerry Perkins. I heard Perkins starting to gather whatever he brought with him.

"Did I tell you to do anything but get the fuck out?"

I sat there, listening to the large man heading for the door and opening it. After it closed, Garrett McGarrett was back at it.

"Who's the next man up?" he said.

I kept my head down. I realized I was holding my breath, even if I didn't have a reason to.

"God damn it, who backs up Perkins at left guard?"

"I do." The man who said it was sitting two rows in front of me.

"Stand up, Simmons. This is your big chance. Let's see if you fuck it up."

I glanced to see him climb to his feet. His back was wide and a thick bald head sat on top of shoulders, no neck in sight. "Yes, sir," he said.

"Why was Perkins a fucking moron Tuesday night and why is he unemployed today?"

"He didn't pick up the blitz."

"Bingo," the coach said. "And what happened when he didn't pick up the blitz?"

"Quarterback's knee got fucked up?"

"Don't say it like you don't know what happened. Yes, the quarterback's knee got fucked up. Because the guy who was supposed to block him had his head up his ass." The bodies on the screen started moving. The linebacker blitzed. Perkins didn't move fast enough. When he did, the hit made the linebacker fall into the quarterback's leg. And there went his knee.

"Now, Simmons, do you plan on having your head up your ass or someplace else?"

"Someplace else?"

"Goddamnit, don't say it like you ain't sure! I need you to be sure of every fucking thing you do, starting right now. You're my new left guard. Unless and until you cause the next quarterback's knee to get fucked up. You got it?"

"I got it."

"Louder, son."

"I got it!"

The rest of the meeting was far less eventful, even though the head coach was still pissed about the play that had caused him to lose his starting quarterback for the rest of the season. It was hard for me to feel too bad about that, because it was why I wasn't sitting in my apartment in Vegas.

Before the meeting, they gave me a tablet with the team's playbook on it. Most offenses are pretty much the same. The names of the plays are different enough to force new players to take a crash course. It's almost like learning a new language. I wouldn't need to know it well enough to play in a game. I'd still have to bluff my way through practice, or they'd find somebody else as fast as they found me.

I still wasn't sure why they'd signed me. I didn't know the coaches. The only guy I recognized on the entire roster was sitting down in the second row. He was a safety at North Texas when I was getting my feet wet as a redshirt freshman. We knew each other a little bit.

I planned to tug on that thread. It could help things go easier. It could help get me get even more information for my other job.

After the meeting, everybody split up for the rooms where smaller sessions would happen. Then, we'd practice. I wondered how much I could figure out in the next two days before the Saturday night call to Johnny Motts. It wouldn't be as detailed as before. Johnny Motts was probably too dumb to know the difference.

Then again, if he noticed I'd gotten less information than usual, Johnny Motts would be too stupid to understand why. The bigger challenge would be showing the coaches enough during practice so that I could stand on the sidelines during the game with a uniform and a helmet, listening to the plays and giving the secret signals.

The new starter was a backup who got signed not to push the starter but to help him. That's how it goes on most teams. All of a sudden, Rich Wettle was the guy. The team's playoff chances would ride on whether he could play like he'd never played before.

I didn't know how much experience he had. Whatever it was, it wasn't nearly enough, based on how wide his eyes got and stayed during practice.

The new backup quarterback was some rookie from Oklahoma. Baltimore took a flier on him with its last draft pick. Some teams think they should take a quarterback every year, because nobody ever knows where the next Tom Brady might come from. I could tell by looking at Willie McGill that Tom Brady wasn't hiding inside him.

Then again, how would I know? I'd never played in a game.

Maybe that helped me spot other guys who'd never play. Birds of a feather who won't ever fly.

That's when it hit me. Maybe I'd have to do it. Get in the huddle. Call plays. Take snaps. Throw passes. I would like that. Johnny Motts wouldn't. Which could make me like it even more.

They didn't expect much on my first day of practice. That was a good thing. I didn't know the playbook well enough to do more than throw passes during individual drills. They had McGill run the scout team. They tried to get Rich Wettle ready without freaking him out any more than he was. I tried to soak up as much as I could about what Baltimore would be doing against Cincinnati, so I could make my report.

I spent Thursday night going over the playbook and watching film from their other games. I felt more confident at Friday's practice. They still didn't expect me to do much. That made it easier to watch and listen, figuring out as much as I could for

Saturday night, and for the Sunday afternoon run-or-pass routine. If I ended up being in position to do that.

I was starting to make the shift from outsider to teammate. It'd take some time. Before I'd ever feel like part of things, I could be gone. With two guys in front of me who seemed more than a little shaky, that could get me on the field—or it could get me out the door in favor of somebody better suited than me to take the wheel.

Of course, there weren't a bunch of options at quarterback. That made me feel safer. Getting fired on Monday would make me never feel safe again.

By the time Friday's practice ended and they didn't tell me to turn in my playbook and check out of the hotel, I started to feel like I would make it through Sunday's game. Sitting on the chair in front of my locker, scrolling through my main phone, I heard somebody say my name. The sound made my heart skip a beat. I thought I was already being sent to the coach's office for the same message Jerry Perkins had gotten.

When I looked up, I saw Lefty Thomas.

"Been a while," he said. "Remember me?"

"North Texas pride," I said.

"North Texas guys need to stick together. Not many of us make it this far."

"You've made it farther than I ever will."

"I'm one of the old men now. There ain't much of an appetite in this league for thirty-year-old defensive backs."

"You're thirty?"

"Well, not until February. It's hard not to feel that old with all these youngsters around."

"You'll be here longer than I will."

"We're all temporary. I'm riding it out as long as I can. Beats working for a living, I think. I don't really know, because I never have."

"At least you'll be playing on Sunday. That's something I've never done. Probably never will."

"I felt the same way when I got here. And then Larry Gordon pulled a hamstring. They threw me into the mix at practice. I made a good decision to stay home on a play-action fake, intercepted a pass. That gave me a chance to show what I can do in a game. I managed to hold my own, somehow. So they decided they could trust me. Eight years later, here I am. If it happened for me, it can happen for anybody."

"Don't sell yourself short. I remember how good you were in college."

"Every guy in here was good in college. You were too, eventually."

"Not good enough for this."

"Maybe at some point. You've got an advantage. For me, thirty means I'm close to the end. For a quarterback, thirty can be the beginning."

"If I'm still around by then."

"Where's your confidence? Plenty of shitty quarterbacks have made a good living by showing the right amount of swagger at the right time."

"I'll work on it," I said.

"For now, guys need to get to know you. Some of us are going out tonight."

"It's been a long week for me."

Lefty shook his head. "It ain't no request. They put you up at that place near the stadium, right? Be outside around nine. We'll pick you up."

I wanted to try a little harder to get out of it, but I knew it wouldn't work. Besides, maybe Lefty was right. I'd get to know some of my new teammates, even if they wouldn't be my teammates for long.

I want to keep cramming as much as I could into my brain for the call to Johnny Motts. I decided he'd have to settle for whatever I'd deliver without a few extra hours of Friday night study.

It wasn't as if Lefty had given me a choice. Also, something about making that decision made me feel pretty good, for some reason.

26

JOHNNY MOTTS

I made sure I got to Carmine's place early. I knew to leave my phones in the car. Carmine thinks the government has a way to listen to us when we ain't even using them. That don't make no sense to me, but I ain't ever telling him that.

Bobo took me to the back room. Did he think I don't know the way? Or was Carmine just messing with me?

I was glad Bobo didn't hang around for too long after he brung me back to the leather couch. It was full of holes from cigarettes, maybe cigars. I started counting them. Then I started thinking about the kid.

He's on his way to Baltimore. I need to drop the money there. It'll cost ten points, maybe more, to get clean cash delivered by whoever runs things there. That ain't my concern. This project makes enough to make an extra ten or fifteen or even twenty percent no big deal.

I don't know whether Carmine will agree. But they wanted me to get guys all over the place. Nobody ever said we should only use guys in Vegas. If somebody ends up on a team someplace else, that's part of the deal. Cost of doing business. I think that's what they call it.

Plus, ain't it better to not have everybody in Vegas? If we have more guys in places far away from Nevada, maybe it never raises eyebrows.

That part is my concern. If somebody gets suspicious, my guys are on the front lines. If the cops get to me, I'm screwed. I'll be the one who keeps his mouth shut, goes up the river, gets forgotten. I can't even think about not keeping my mouth shut. If I do, somebody might sense I will. They might think maybe I'll squeal. They might make sure I'll never get the chance.

My guys got too much to lose. I got too much to lose. They won't run their mouths. They can't let no one know what they're doing. This is only the side hustle. They don't want to fuck up their main gig.

Are they stupid? I try to pick guys who ain't. I think they're smart. I don't want them being too much smarter than me. The kid in Baltimore might be. How many dumbasses play quarterback in the NFL? Not many. It don't matter. If we're gonna have a guy on offense who can find out what the plays are gonna be before they happen, we need a quarterback.

I hate waiting, even for Carmine. Even though I know that's how it goes. I don't need no extra time to think. Thinking don't do me much good. Thinking gets in the way of doing.

I need to be ready for whatever happens with Carmine. I'm gonna tell him the truth about the kid. Vegas cut him. Minnesota looked at him. Baltimore wanted him. Life goes on.

I can play it all out in my head. I'll tell Carmine what went down. He'll ask me why I didn't tell him sooner. I'll tell him I didn't wanna bother him until it was important.

Then what will he say? Thank you? He should. What if he don't? What if he says it was important for me to tell him from the start? That the kid not being on his team no more was a big deal? That I should be smart enough to know that?

What'll I say to that? Will I just repeat myself? Apologize? Promise to never do it again?

Will I tell him the kid is getting mouthy and I think he might be a problem?

I can't tell Carmine that part. I don't need another one of my guys becoming a problem. Not after Larry Ballentine. And not with Jimmy King possibly about to become my third problem.

That's all I can do. Apologize and promise to never do it again. I need to hope that's good enough.

I sure hope it is, because I ain't got many other moves to make.

Just as that happy thought occurred to me, in walked Carmine. And he looked not too happy, at all.

27

ALICE SMITHSON

Will dragged me through four different bars. Maybe five. I lost track. I also lost track of the number of Old Fashioneds sloshing around in my stomach, along with a lightning shot of cheap tequila (no salt or lime for me) and a slower sip of the same 1942 I kept at home. I paid more than two hundred bucks for a fifth at the liquor store. Tonight's double with three ice cubes cost more than a fourth of that. I was too tipsy to care.

It was the only good thing about ending up in that condition. The woman who usually obsessed over everything decided, for a little while, to not give a shit about anything at all.

I sat at the table we'd claimed in the latest place with a name I didn't know and if I did I wouldn't remember. Will's jacket was draped over one chair. Mine was on another. I sat in the third with both of my feet on the fourth. It didn't send a full-blown *don't-fuck-with-me* vibe, but it was close. And it was working. Between the clothes I'd picked for the night and the attitude I tried to project (even with a blood-alcohol concentration that would have kept me from pedaling a tricycle in a padded room), no one was bothering me.

I watched people milling around as I nursed the tequila, hoping I could stay in this glow of inebriation without it turning into full-blown intoxication. I sensed it might be too late to keep that from happening. I also knew it was too late to worry about it.

Will stood roughly thirty feet away. He was talking to a man whose looks fell short of the standard Will had set. Alcohol did a great job of nudging the bar lower, or of creating the impression it had been met. I could tell by the look on Will's face, by the way he used his hands as he spoke, that he'd found who he was looking for, at least for tonight.

I expected to be sliding by myself into the back seat of an Uber that would take me home. I hoped to be, sooner than later. I thought about checking the time on my phone, but I didn't. This rare state of not caring included not noticing that late Friday had crept into early Saturday. Part of living in the moment includes not knowing exactly when the moment is. That sounded like something my grandfather would have said. Maybe he did.

I smiled at the uncertainty. Did he? Or did my impaired brain just come up with it? Would I ever know the difference? I took another sip and looked up.

"What's so funny?"

A fairly tall and well-muscled man wearing a shirt more than tight enough to show it all off stood over me. He was flipping his chin, trying to act cool. I wanted to be disappointed I hadn't noticed him approaching. Again, by that point I didn't care.

"Nothing is funny," I said. "Not yet. Do you plan on telling me a joke?"

"I don't know any good ones," he said. He stood there flexing his pecs like a rooster on growth hormone. The polo shirt left very little to the imagination. I tried not to look at it, because it was obvious he wanted me to. I eased a foot from the chair to my left and swung it onto the floor. The other foot stayed where it was.

"Everybody knows a good joke."

He looked at the chairs, obviously angling for an invitation to sit. "Not me."

"Then you've never heard a good joke. If you had, you'd remember it."

"I've heard some good jokes. I don't remember how to tell them the right way. If you don't, they're not funny."

"How about this? You go learn a good joke, and you come back and tell it to me. If it's funny, I'll let you buy me a drink. But it has to be the drink I'm drinking."

He looked at my glass. "I've got a feeling that drink's not cheap. How about I buy you one now and we forget about the joke? I can afford it."

I pulled my other foot from the chair and sat forward. I took another slow drink before saying anything else. I didn't want to give him the satisfaction of asking how he could afford it, since that would be his opening to brag about how he makes his money.

"Sorry. Those are my terms. Learn a joke. Tell a joke. Make me laugh. Buy a drink."

"What's in it for me?"

I shrugged. "You'll finally learn a good joke."

He shook his head and walked away. I noticed someone else standing behind him. Taller. Thinner. He seemed to have no compulsion to wear anything that would accentuate his physique. He kept his hair in a blond buzz cut. It was just like the one I'd seen in the photographs of my grandfather when he was young.

The next thought came to me without thinking. This was the man I wanted to talk to. I hoped that, when his friend came back, he'd still be following. With that exact same demeanor.

The demeanor of someone who would have preferred to be anywhere but there.

Just like me.

28

CARSON JEFFREY

I was still carrying the beer I'd been nursing since we got to the bar. One would be enough for me, because a second would turn into a third. A third would turn into a fourth. Then a fifth and then however many more and then a fistful of Advil the next morning. I had too much to do to waste the first two hours of the day working my way free from a hangover.

Seven of us had gone to dinner, three from offense and four from defense. Lefty never said that would be part of it. One of the linemen joked about sticking the new guy with the check. I laughed at that until I realized he was me.

Lefty said it would be different if I was a rookie, and that ended any talk of me footing the bill. Based on what those guys drank and ate, Lefty saved me a nice little chunk of change.

After dessert, Lefty started talking about some bar he wanted to go to. I thought maybe I could pull off an Irish goodbye, once the others started talking about things they had to do the next morning. With everybody else leaving, I could, too. When I tried, Lefty cocked his head in a way that reminded me I would have been out five grand or more without him.

It ended up being me and him at a place where I felt uncomfortable and underdressed. I didn't know whether he was looking for a partner or a shadow. Whatever he wanted, that's what I was.

And he was on the hunt. Which was fine with me. The sooner he found a woman to spend some time with, the sooner I could slip out the door. I held out hope that maybe I'd be able to put some more time into the playbook before turning in. I was disappointed when Lefty didn't end up hunkering down with the first woman he targeted.

"Don't tell me you just struck out," I said as we walked away from her table. I hadn't really seen the woman Lefty had picked for his icebreaker move. It was clear he hadn't even put a crack in it.

"Not yet," Lefty said. I followed him to the other side of the room.

I pointed in the other direction. "Well, now she's all the way back over there."

"Tell me a good joke."

"What?"

"She wants me to tell her a good joke. If I do, I can buy her a drink. And then I'm in."

"There has to be an easier way to pick someone up."

"I guess I like a little challenge sometimes."

I looked around the bar. "I can throw a shoe and hit somebody who'd sleep with you. You've had eyes all over you since we walked in."

"I can do that whenever. I'd like to put in some work for a change. So tell me a good joke."

I thought about it for a few seconds. I remembered something that had made me laugh the first time I heard it. It made Lefty laugh, too.

"That's good," he said. "Now I'll tell it back to you."

Lefty butchered it. I made a face and shook my head.

"I told her I'm not good at remembering jokes." Then he brightened up. "Why don't you go tell it to her?"

"Me?"

"Tell her I sent you. If she laughs, ask her what she's drinking and I'll take one over."

"I'm not sure you noticed this, but we're not, you know, twelve."

"Maybe she'll like it. It's my only chance with her. She's smart. I can tell."

"All the more reason for you to go after someone else."

"Come on, man. We're teammates again, right? You need to prove yourself. You pull this off, and I'll make sure they all know Carson Jeffrey is a guy who can help you close the deal."

"I don't see myself closing any deals tonight."

"How hard can it be? It's not like you're the one trying to pick her up."

I took a longer drink of beer that was getting a little too close to room temperature. "If this works, that's it for me. I'm heading back to the hotel."

"It's a deal." Lefty gripped his palm on my shoulder and squeezed hard. When he let go, he gave me a shove. "Go get your hall pass."

I sipped from the bottle and started back to the table where Lefty had been chatting up the woman who had him acting like he was in middle school. Then again, maybe Lefty always acted that way.

I spotted her. She was still alone, nursing her drink. She was trying her best to be ignored. I noticed something in her face when she saw me coming. She looked past me for Lefty. She didn't seem to be upset when she realized Lefty wasn't behind me.

"My friend was just over here talking to you," I said.

"He doesn't seem like a guy who has many friends."

"I've known him for a long time."

"How long?"

"We went to college together, sort of. He was a few years older than me. I hadn't seen him since he left. I just got to town."

"I'm no expert in male relationships, but that seems to be stretching the definition of friend."

"He told me you want to hear a joke."

"I want to hear it from him."

"He said you wanted to hear a joke. He didn't say he had to be the one to tell it."

She tilted her head. Her eyes flashed. I wished I hadn't seen it. "I guess that's technically right. I should have done a better job of negotiating my terms."

"Does that mean I can tell you the joke?"

She pushed out one of the chairs with her foot. "If it isn't funny, the deal is off."

I took another drink from the bottle and sat. I hadn't expected to feel jitters. I put the bottle on the table and tried to look at her without staring.

"How tall are you?" she said.

"I wish I had a dime for every time I've been asked that."

"I know plenty of guys who would love to have that problem."

"I'm six foot five. And a half."

"That's tall."

"How about you?"

"If I had a dime for every time I'd been asked that, this would be my first dime."

I chuckled. I took another drink.

"You're supposed to be the one making me laugh," she said.

"Excuse me?"

"You're here on behalf of your friend. To tell me a joke. So let's go, Cyrano."

"Hey, how did you know that was my name?"

This time, she laughed. It was loose and natural. I liked the sound of it. It was something I could get used to. I pushed that idea away.

I stood up. "My work here is done."

"What do you mean?"

"I made you laugh."

"You didn't tell me a joke yet."

"I made you laugh. Isn't that what the joke was supposed to do?"

"Are you a lawyer?"

"God, no. I hate lawyers."

"Well," she said, "I'm a lawyer."

"I didn't mean you particularly. I just mean lawyers generally."

"It's fine. Everybody hates lawyers. Until they need one."

"I'm starting to feel like I might."

"That could be taken a couple different ways."

I felt myself starting to blush. I hadn't done that in years.

"I'm kidding," she said. "You win. Your friend can buy me a drink. You're released from your duties. You performed them well."

"So you don't want to hear the joke?"

"You can tell me some other time."

I wasn't sure what to say to that. I started to walk away. I stumbled just enough to feel like I was the one back in the eighth grade.

"Wait," she said in a firm voice that made me stop and turn. "I'm drinking Don Julio 1942. Double with three ice cubes. Tell your friend to bring one for me, and one for him."

I nodded at her. I'd pulled it off. I could leave.

I didn't feel as happy about that as I should have.

29

JOHNNY MOTTS

"Find something else while you can," Carmine said.

I tried not to look confused. I couldn't help it.

"Did I speak a different language or something?" he said.

"Different what?"

"Different language, Johnny. Italian, French, Spanish. Did I not speak English?"

"You did. I just don't understand."

Carmine went to his chair. He stood behind it and squeezed the top of the seat with his hands. "I said to find something else while you can."

"Something else what?"

"Not something else what. Something else."

"But something else what?"

He picked up the chair and slammed it down. One of the legs broke off.

"Look at what you fucking made me do."

I didn't make him do nothing. I knew not to say that. "I'm sorry," I said.

He gave me a dirty look. "What are you sorry for?"

"For making you break your chair."

"Did you make me do it?"

"You just said I did."

"That's just a way of talking." He tossed what was left of the thing aside. For an older guy, he was still strong. He crossed his arms and stared at me.

"You wanted me to find something?" I said.

"Find something?"

"You said to find something else while I can, or something."

"Right. I did. This whole thing is going to shit."

I didn't know what to say, so I didn't say nothing.

"You finally understand me, right?"

I nodded, only because I didn't know what else to do.

"So what am I saying?" he said.

"To find something else while I can?"

"What does that mean?"

"I don't know. You said it."

"I know I said it. I just wanna know if you know what it means."

I leaned forward and whispered. "I'm sorry but I don't really know what you mean."

He rolled his eyes. He took in a long breath and blew it out. "Never mind," he said.

"OK," I said, because I didn't know what else to say.

"OK what?"

I was getting more confused. "OK OK?"

"Why are you here?"

"You told me to come."

"I know I told you to come. I told you to come because you said you had something to tell me. Now, what do you have to tell me?"

I was afraid I wouldn't get the words out right. I was stuttering. Nothing was coming from my mouth. I could tell Carmine was getting upset. I stopped and took a breath and tried to focus on saying what I needed to say. I wasn't even sure I could remember what it was. I was nervous, way more nervous than I thought I'd be.

"Carson Jeffrey plays for Baltimore now." After I managed

to say it, I felt relieved, almost happy. I started smiling. Then I noticed Carmine looking at me.

"Who the fuck is Carson Jeffrey?"

"The quarterback. He played here."

"You just said he plays in Baltimore."

"He does. Before that, he played here."

"When was that?"

"Two days ago."

"So what happened?"

"He got cut."

"Like with a knife?"

"Like cut from the team."

"When?"

"Monday."

Carmine's head pulled back. He shook it back and forth. "That's two days ago."

I didn't know what to say, so I went with something obvious. "It was."

"Why am I just finding out about this now?"

That's what I was waiting for. Even if it took a while to get there, that was the question I knew he'd ask. I took in some air before I said anything else.

"I didn't wanna bother you."

"You didn't wanna bother me? Is that what you just fucking said?"

"I didn't wanna bother you."

"Why would you be bothering me with something like that?"

"I said I didn't wanna bother you."

"But why do you think it would bother me?"

"You got enough to worry about already."

"You're right about that, but this thing is part of that. If one of your guys loses his job, that would be something I need to know about."

"He got another job."

"Two days later."

"Only two days later."

"What did you do to make that happen?"

I didn't really understand the question. I wasn't about to say that again. "Nothing."

"Did it occur to you I might have been able to do something to make it happen?"

I skipped over just saying *no* and said, "Like what?"

"Like what don't matter. You don't know what I can do. You need to assume I can do anything."

"So you could have done something?"

"That ain't my point." He was getting madder. "I don't know. You don't know. I didn't get a chance. Because you didn't tell me. Why didn't you tell me?"

I slipped back into my plan. "I didn't wanna bother you."

"I swear, Johnny, if I hadn't already busted my fucking chair, I'd bust it right now over you head."

"Did I do something wrong?"

"What do you think?"

"I feel like I did."

"Trust your feelings."

"But what did I do?"

"You should have told me."

"It won't happen again," I said, almost saying the words the same way I rehearsed them.

"You don't know that."

I didn't know what to say. I wanted to ask how he can be so sure. I didn't know what his answer would be. I had a feeling that, whatever it was, the question would piss him off even more.

He was staring at me. He was still mad. I could tell he was thinking about what to say next.

"So he's on the team in Baltimore? It ain't no tryout or meeting?"

"He's flying there today to sign the contract."

"That ain't happened yet?"

"It's gonna happen."

"How do you know?"

"He told me. I got no choice but to believe what he tells me."

"I'll believe it when they say something official," Carmine said. "Just like when Las Vegas said something official about him."

I froze when he said that. My face gave me away.

"That's right. I know he got cut. On Monday. I know you didn't tell me on Monday. I know he worked out in Minnesota on Tuesday. And I know you got fucking lucky today."

"I don't feel so lucky."

"You should. But if that kid don't sign in Baltimore, you got a problem with me."

"He's gonna sign in Baltimore."

"You better hope it happens. And you better hope nothing else like this happens again. First it was Larry Ballentine. Now this. What else you got up your sleeve for me, Johnny?"

"I'm just doing my job."

"You need to do it better. You need to control your guys. If you can't do it, I need to find somebody who can."

And there it was. I already knew it. Hearing it made it seem more real. It also made me more nervous, even if I already knew what I had to do. I gotta control my guys. All of them.

Starting with Carson Jeffrey.

30

ALICE SMITHSON

The insult of a sunbeam made my eyelids flutter. I cursed myself for not completely securing the wooden blinds. When I woke up, I felt tiny daggers burrowing into each temple, an icepick at the base of my skull. I'd forgotten to drink a bottle of water before passing out on the mattress. It wouldn't have made much of a difference.

It was that last glass of tequila, the one I'd sipped with the moron who proudly allowed himself to be called Lefty. I vaguely remembered the goofy explanation as to how he'd gotten the name. Not because he was left-handed. Something else. Something stupid. Almost as stupid as he was.

I should have known what he was right away. I got a kick out of the admiring glances he drew from others while he sat there, flexing a thicket of muscles in his torso while he went through the same old paces that usually delivered the victory he assumed he'd already won. I liked that the women who were watching him with anticipation were also firing dirty looks my way.

He complained almost as much about the taste of the 1942 as he had about its cost. He drank it fast, just to get rid of it. The tequila made him babble even more about himself. I gave up and let him keep going, throwing in a word or two from time to time during what was an otherwise uninterrupted monologue of moronity.

I found myself looking forward to when he'd suggest we continue the conversation elsewhere. I was disappointed he never trotted out, *Your place or mine?* He otherwise filled every box on the shit-for-brains checklist, the stereotypically overconfident jock who had the self-awareness of a toddler on the wrong end of peek-a-boo.

At one point, he bragged about his skills at cooking breakfast. Scrambled eggs that he undoubtedly regarded as a rousing success if no pieces of shell were in the finished product, toast that was acceptable as long as none of the bread needed to be scraped clean with a steak knife.

I smiled as he went through his routine. I wanted him to think it was working. He was clueless he'd lost the moment he said he plays pro football.

I should have spotted it when he first approached. No man that age with a real job could manage to keep himself in that kind of shape. He talked about how weird it felt to be almost thirty, oblivious to the fact that his current target was more than four years older than him. I was wishing Will's bull's-eye would implode, that he'd come back and grab our coats and take us to the next stop on his Baltimore bar crawl.

When Will returned, he sported the grin of a conquering hero. He lifted his own jacket from the chair and excused himself, saying, "I'll let you two lovebirds get back to it." He was gone before I could say anything, primarily because Lefty kept rambling.

His words projected a presumption we'd be going back to the mansion he purchased with the signing bonus he received, after he was named All-Star or All-Pro or all-whatever. All-Meathead would be more like it. I toyed with finding the perfect time to burst his bubble. To witness his knowing glances and cheesy habit of winking at me every thirty seconds or so melt into the expression of a man who realized he'd misread the scoreboard all along.

Before I plunged a hatpin into the balloon he'd recklessly

pumped to full capacity, I asked about the man he had recruited to tell me the joke I hadn't been told. A football player, too. That ordinarily would have disqualified him immediately. I was willing to make a temporary exception. Until I knew his name, until I found out he was single. Until I learned he'd just arrived in town and was staying at the Lord Baltimore Hotel. I doubted I'd ever act on that information. I wanted to have the option.

I pulled my legs over the edge of the mattress and dropped my feet onto the floor. I frowned when I realized I badly needed a pedicure. I grinned at the memory of standing up and saying to Lefty, "Well, this has been fun, but I need to get going." His jaw dropped. His chest sagged. His shoulders slumped.

"You'll be missing out on one hell of a breakfast."

I'd opened a palm and gestured toward the rest of the bar. "I'm sure one of these other ladies will be happy to eat it."

"You know, those drinks cost me like a hundred bucks."

"Is that your way of getting me to change my mind?"

"I just wanted you to know."

"I'd already bought one for myself. I'm not sure I would have been able to multiply by two."

"Are you making fun of me?"

I slipped into my jacket. "As best I can tell, you do a pretty good job of that all by yourself."

"I should have known you were a bitch."

I smiled at him. "I tried to make that clear the moment you decided to bother me. Maybe next time you'll notice the signals before you waste a hundred bucks."

"I know why you aren't married."

He was pissing me off. I kept the anger under control. "You don't know anything about me. You can't. You spent this entire time talking about yourself."

"I know the type."

"So do I, Lefty." I reached into my purse and pulled out five twenties and slammed them on the table. "Here's the money for the drinks. You'll need it more than me. It's just a matter of time before they realize they can find someone a lot younger and cheaper."

I almost felt bad for feeling proud of myself. But Lefty needed a dose of reality. I had done him a favor. Maybe it would register that way, until he careened toward a far more willing participant for whom he was currently cooking eggs riddled with tiny pieces of shell. Maybe he'd reflect on the exchange. Maybe, some day, he'd realize he learned a lesson. Maybe it would help him deal with the inevitable realization that the thing that had become the foundation of his identity was gone forever.

The experience with the man named Lefty should have been enough to get me to not give a second thought to the tall man with a buzz cut whose lone contribution to the world was playing football. Still, he seemed different from his teammate. Maybe they all aren't like Lefty.

I told myself I didn't want to find out. I hoped that would be enough to do the trick.

31

CARSON JEFFREY

I got in a few hours of film study before climbing into bed. It wasn't long enough to hold my body, even after I turned myself from one corner down to the other. I set the alarm on my phone for nine. I was ready to sleep.

I couldn't.

There was something about that woman. Relaxed and loose. But she seemed smart. Brilliant, probably. I felt hypnotized when I was talking to her.

Lefty saw her first. Not that I would have done anything if Lefty hadn't made a move. I probably wouldn't have even noticed her. There's no way I would have gone up and talked to her. If Lefty hadn't sent me over, none of this would have happened.

I couldn't remember how long I'd sat with her. It was a blur. I wished it was longer than it was. I really wished Lefty hadn't planted a flag.

I didn't know what had happened with them. I knew I'd find out soon enough. The whole team would be checking in later. It was such a stupid routine. Keeping players under the thumb of the coach the night before a home game. As if we'd go out and raise hell. Everybody has a phone with a camera. Pro athletes aren't getting away with anything.

Thinking about the stupidity of curfew was enough of a

distraction from her to get me to fall asleep. The alarm woke me up. I ordered room service for breakfast. Even if the team wouldn't be paying for my food, I had plenty of money in my checking account. And more cash than I could count back in Vegas.

I kept trying not to think about how I'd get it. How I'd use it. It was pretty much an ATM for gas and groceries. What else could I buy with all those twenties? A car? A house?

It only made me worry. I had enough to worry about. I needed a way out of this business. The way I saw it, the two possible outcomes were prison cell or wooden box. For now, I'd keep going. I'd also end up with more cash I couldn't spend. Maybe it was time to ask for a different kind of payment.

The impulse took over before I could think it through. I grabbed the burner and called Johnny Motts.

"It's a little early for your report," he said. "Please tell me you ain't trying to get ahead of bad news."

"Bad news?"

"You know, like you've been cut again. Or you ain't been there long enough to know what they're doing. Or they ain't giving you a helmet tomorrow with that radio thing that lets you know the plays."

"I haven't been cut. I know what they're doing. I don't know if they'll put me in uniform tomorrow, but why wouldn't they? The rules let them use a third quarterback from the practice squad, and I'm the third quarterback."

"So why are you waking me up at seven in the morning?"

I didn't think about the time difference. "I can't get used to being on the other side of the country."

"I can't get used to you being there, either. You got no idea the steps my people had to take to keep this situation going."

It was up to Johnny Motts to make sure they'd be able to use whatever I fed them during games. Trying to get Johnny Motts to understand that would be a waste of time. I'd have a better chance teaching a squirrel how to skipper a speedboat.

"Is there another way to handle my end?" I said.

"What do you mean?"

"My package."

"We already have to figure out how to make the delivery in Baltimore."

"Is there a different way to do it?"

"What do you mean?"

"You know, electronic. To my bank account, or something."

Johnny Motts started to laugh. "Who do you think you're dealing with?"

"Hasn't every business moved past cash?"

"Not this one. We don't leave footprints. You get clean, laundered cash. That won't change."

"I've already got more cash than I can spend."

"Take it to the bank."

"You don't think that'll set off any alarms?"

"Once we pay you, it ain't our problem. That's for you to figure out."

"Can't you hold it, for now?"

"I thought I made that clear. We ain't no credit union. Your cut will be delivered to wherever you tell us. Every week. We ain't never been late."

"I don't know what to do with it."

"I don't care what you do with it. Once we count it, it's yours. And if you don't tell us where to drop it off, we'll just keep it."

"That doesn't seem fair."

"We made a deal. You agreed to this. It ain't for us to teach you what to do with the money. You're the one who chose to cross over to the wrong side of the tracks. It's up to you to figure out how things work over here."

I let it go. I was dealing with criminals; I knew that. Now I had to worry that, whenever I got back to Las Vegas, whatever I left there would be gone.

Really, how hard would it be for Johnny Motts to send someone in the middle of the night to rob my place? What could I even do about it? Call the cops and say someone stole all the cash I made by giving inside information to the mob? For all I knew, Johnny Motts already had somebody go there and take it.

"You need to let me know where this week's payment should go," he said.

"I'm staying in a hotel."

"Again, not my problem. If you do your job tonight and tomorrow, you'll get another bag on Monday. If they have to leave it at the front desk, they will."

"I guess I need to find an apartment."

"I don't care what you do, as long as you do what I need you to do. Now, can I please go back to bed?"

"I don't care what you do," I said.

"That's the spirit. Call me tonight and tell me what you know."

After the call ended, I looked at the burner. I'd grown to despise that thing. But I'd keep it until Monday, when it was replaced with a new one.

I opened up my laptop to start looking for a place to rent. I'd probably have to sign another lease. Probably for a whole year. Whatever. If I couldn't take that money to a bank, I needed to have a place where I could keep it.

32

JOHNNY MOTTS

The call from the kid made me jumpy. I guess I was already sort of feeling that way. The more I thought about the meeting with Carmine, the jumpier I got. It was three days ago, and I'm still looking over my shoulder wherever I go.

It don't help that Jimmy King fucked up again. He was supposed to say he had the stomach flu or food poisoning and leave last night's game early. We loaded up on the unders for all his stats—points, rebounds, assists, three-pointers.

I was in my place, with all my TVs on. Eight screens. On the nights when I ain't looking for new recruits, I keep an eye on the games where we got action. There was only three that affected us. Two basketball and one football.

I was mainly watching Atlanta and New Orleans. We got a running back in Atlanta who tells me shit before the games, and who also has a way of giving us a signal when he's getting the ball. He keeps one foot behind the other, just a little bit. It's hard to spot it if you ain't looking for it. He's worried somebody on the other team is gonna notice it. I told him it's too hard to see it when you're down on the field. I said it's something you gotta catch on TV. I don't know if that's true, but I needed to say something to get him to keep doing it.

It worked like a charm. He lined up. One foot was behind the other. Our guys locked in that it's a run or that he's getting the ball.

I stopped watching Denver after Jimmy King tapped out. During a commercial in the football game, I looked up and what did I see but Jimmy King back on the floor. I thought my eyes was fucking with me. He was out there playing like everything is fine.

I forgot about the football game and kept watching Jimmy King. He was getting closer and closer to the magic numbers. I hoped he knew what they were, and I hoped he knew what he had. I also hoped he knew what it would mean if he beat any of them.

He made me sweat it out, all the way to the end. He finished under on everything. One more bucket, and he would have been over on points.

Bobo tried to bust my balls about it, but I told him the unders hit and that's all that matters. Carmine didn't say nothing. That told us both he didn't care.

He didn't care about that one. He cares about pretty much everything else. Carmine is way smarter than me. He's always a step or two ahead. If I don't catch up soon, I'm gonna have a real problem.

I already got a real problem. Carmine knew about the kid getting cut. Carmine knew I held out on him. I'm surprised he gave me a pass.

Maybe he didn't give me a pass. Maybe it's gonna happen when I don't see it coming. Maybe that's why I've been so jumpy. I'm watching, everywhere I go. Even in my own damn house. When I wake up. When I get out of the shower. When I get off the commode.

When you least expect it, expect it. I know how that goes, because I done that plenty of times myself.

Maybe I'm worrying too much. In all the time I've been at this, nobody from the crew got whacked. One guy moved to

Florida. I never thought twice about that. Maybe he didn't move to Florida after all.

Maybe I'll be moving to Florida.

Things seem to be under control with the kid in Baltimore. He'll make the report before tomorrow. Will he have a helmet on for the game? I think I explained to Carmine that wasn't no sure thing. I hope Carmine understands I can't do nothing about it.

I need to focus on one problem at a time. I keep telling myself that, for most of my guys in sports, it's working fine. I think I heard somebody say they get ninety-five percent of their trouble from five percent of their employees. It sure feels like that's what I'm dealing with.

Larry Ballentine. Carson Jeffrey. Now Jimmy King in Denver. How am I gonna send a message to a basketball player?

There I go again, thinking about sending messages. I hate sending messages.

The only good thing about the last three days is I spent a bunch of time at the Waldorf, looking for more guys. I got a lead on three. Plus, I didn't lose too much money at the Wynn.

I need another baseball player. I'd like to get one from the local team. It's a lot easier when the guy lives in town.

The one I was talking to last night pitches for them. Middle innings. Just signed a new contract for three years. The money is ridiculous. He only works like once or twice a week.

For me, he'd be working more than that, for a lot less money. It would still be more than he's already getting. More makes the world go around. Like I say, everybody wants more.

The guy mentioned how Larry Ballentine is still missing. I didn't know how to act. There ain't no reason for me to seem surprised by it, since the story was in the papers. Still, I didn't want to come off like I knew too much.

I ended up getting his number. I'll let it play out for a little while before I hit him up. I got time. They don't start playing again until April. I'll see him at the Waldorf, and I'll get him to go back over to the Wynn.

Yeah, he'll be back. He fits the profile. No wife. No kids. It would be better if he didn't have parents, but it's hard to find orphans in their twenties. I got lucky with a few of these guys. Larry Ballentine didn't have nobody. Carson Jeffrey don't have nobody. Jimmy King got some family, but he cut them off when they started asking for too much money.

I wonder if I get too caught up in finding guys without ties that I maybe miss the signs they could be a problem. I know how to read people. That don't take smarts, not the thinking kind. I've been around enough people to know after spending a little time with them who'll be easy to deal with, and who won't. Did I miss that Carson Jeffrey and Jimmy King might be a giant pain in my ass, just because I really liked the idea that they was pretty much alone in this world?

Jeffrey don't even have a girl he was dating regular. Maybe he just kept that from me. Maybe he wants to protect whoever it is. Not that we'd mess with civilians. That ain't never been our way. Of course, it wouldn't hurt to bring up the possibility, if that's what it took to keep somebody in line.

You can't drop that kind of hint and not be ready to act on it. I can only say it if I know it'll do the trick. That the guy will stop fucking up. That he won't wanna play Russian roulette with somebody he cares about. If he keeps screwing the pooch and I don't do nothing, I'll look like a punk.

Maybe that's what I need to do with Carson Jeffrey. Find out if there's somebody special. Even if I didn't read things right on him not giving me attitude, I got him pegged as somebody who wouldn't wanna risk getting his girlfriend gone.

I don't spend much time thinking about shit like this. Usually, when I think too much I come up with bad ideas. This one might not be too bad. I'll dip into my own pocket. I'll call my buddy who used to work for the Vegas police. I'll have him find out whether Carson Jeffrey got anybody here in town. If there ain't nobody, I'll see if my friend can connect me with somebody in Baltimore. Maybe Jeffrey already found himself somebody there.

Sure, he only got there the other day. What better way to get comfortable in a brand new city than to find a brand new somebody to get comfortable with? If he has, maybe there's a way for me to get him to quit giving me so much lip.

Now that I got ideas that might not be all that bad, I should figure out whether Jimmy King got somebody, too. After the shit that happened with Larry Ballentine, I can't make a move on Jimmy King. Maybe I can make a move on somebody Jimmy King would miss.

I know that breaks our code. If it comes down to my own ass or some broad I never met, I might have to cross that bridge.

I've been telling myself I need to get a little smarter if I'm gonna survive in this life. Maybe I finally am. Maybe the way to get a little smarter is to get a lot tougher with these clowns.

What's that saying? Fuck around and find out? Maybe the only way I can get Carson Jeffrey and Jimmy King to stop fucking around is to get them to find out.

33

ALICE SMITHSON

I spent most of the day in my apartment, catching up on the last bits of work from the week that was and getting a head start on the days to come. I kept busy. Kept my mind occupied. If it wandered, I knew where it would go.

I thought about going to the gym, but I'd end up sweating out everything I drank the night before, stinking the place up while thinking about everything that happened. And where it might lead, if I let it.

I kept working. I kept finding more useful things to do. It felt good to have preparations in place for everything that was on the docket for Monday, Tuesday, and half of Wednesday.

By late afternoon, I wanted to take a nap. It would only make it harder to fall asleep that night, without drinking more tequila. Better to be exhausted and hit the bed and pass out. Better to not lay there fantasizing about the large body topped by close-cropped hair that I wouldn't mind joining me.

I started dinner instead. As the water was moving toward a boil, I checked messages I'd ignored. Will texted seven times. He wanted to brag about finding the man he'd end up referring to as the next Dr. Jekyll and Mr. Wrong. Infatuations burned bright for Will, making him almost believe it would last. Last it would, until the instant he lost interest or found the flaw or three that would make him limit communications until cutting him off completely, before immediately starting the search for the next Dr. Jekyll.

I opened a bottle of wine for the pasta dish I'd learned from my grandfather. "The Italians gave us the mafia and spaghetti," he used to say. "That's a pretty fair trade."

I went easy on the cabernet, even though it went perfectly with my meal. One glass became two became a vow to not drink more than half the bottle. I slipped into a glow. It was almost happiness. I realized I was enjoying the Saturday night I'd hoped to have on Friday.

Friday. That was the opening for the small battalion of memories to attack. Why did I think they could be sealed off for an entire day? Not the part about the lunkhead named Lefty. The other one. I knew his name was Carson Jeffrey. I knew where he was staying.

Before my bowl was empty, the screen on my laptop had propped open and radiated light into the darkened apartment. I typed his name in the browser. I put my finger on the button. There was a good chance I'd learn enough about Carson Jeffrey to make me not interested. That would be the best outcome.

There was also a chance I'd like what I found. The wine made the decision to press *enter*. What was the harm in checking him out? I'd end up doing it at some point. Why not just get it over with?

Carson Jeffrey. Born in Covington, Kentucky. My grandfather was from Kentucky, too. Not that town, but *shit*. Three-year starting quarterback at Holmes High School. All-State two times. State champions his junior year. He chose the University of North Texas over offers from better programs, because his mother had gone to school there. *Son of a bitch*. Second-team all-conference as a sophomore and junior. First-team as a senior. Academic All-American. *Fuck*.

He was undrafted out of college, whatever that means. He

signed a contract with Las Vegas. He was cut as a rookie but added to the practice squad, whatever that means. He was their third-string quarterback for three years and part of a fourth. He never played in a game.

I said the next part out loud. "Is he really a pro football player if he's never played in a pro football game?" I knew which way this was heading.

I kept searching for anything that would turn me off. Nothing. No evidence of arrests, for even the most innocuous of crimes. No disorderly conduct. No simple assault. No open containers or public urination. I checked the federal database, just to be sure. I ran his parents' names, too. I would have checked out his siblings, but he was an only child. Just like me.

I found videos of some of his interviews from college, along with a couple of grainy local news segments shot while he was in high school. He had a twang, more country than southern. My grandfather had some of that, too.

I recognized in the videos the man who'd sat at the table and charmed me without trying. He wasn't classically handsome. His face wasn't fully symmetrical. One eye seemed to be a little bigger than the other. When he spoke, the left side of his mouth pulled back to show a canine that was missing a chunk along the bottom, robbing it of the point the other one had. He wasn't self-conscious about that at all. He almost seemed to be proud of it.

If I were a psychiatrist, I'd think he was letting the world know he was slightly damaged, and he didn't care who noticed. An open book, without a thing to hide. Nothing I saw made me inclined to run and hide. I wanted to know more, more than the many things I'd been able to find. I also knew how to go about doing that.

All I had to do was call the front desk at the Lord Baltimore Hotel and ask to be connected to Carson Jeffrey. Would they want the room number? Would they want to know why I was calling? I'd made my way past plenty of gatekeepers who were far more aggressive than a hotel clerk would be.

I found the main number for the hotel. I punched it into my phone. I held my breath. My thumb hovered over the glowing green circle.

34

CARSON JEFFREY

I stayed in the hotel for the rest of the morning and all of the afternoon, watching more game film. Looking at the playbook. I decided not to waste time trying to figure out Cincinnati's defense. If I have to take the field as the third-stringer who showed up the other day, Baltimore will be up shit's creek without a paddle. Or a boat.

I needed to learn as much as I could about the offense. That'd help me make the report to Johnny Motts. Even if the last thing I wanted to do was talk to Johnny Motts.

It occurred to me at some point during the afternoon that I should get through the season and retire. Maybe I'd have an injury that would keep me from playing. Maybe I'd make one up. If Johnny Motts had six months to figure out how to replace me, that would be a lot easier for him. Also a lot easier for me.

What would I do if I couldn't play pro football? Well, I wasn't playing. I'd probably never play again. I could go to another league. But no kid grows up dreaming of playing in the CFL or the UFL or the Whatever-FL. There's only one place anybody ever really wants to play.

It became the plan, just like that. I'd finish the year and move on to something else. I read somewhere that Chuck Noll called the time after a guy stops playing football his *life's work*. I'd be taking up my life's work. And Johnny Motts would have to find another way to make his life's work work out.

What would I do next? All I knew was that my current work was coming a little too close to putting me in trouble. It wasn't worth it. I had a pile of money I couldn't spend. It was starting to feel like threats were being made. I didn't know whether to take them seriously. Deep down, I knew I should.

I kept going through the film and the playbook until it was time to meet up with the rest of the team for dinner. I went down a little early, waiting for them. When I saw Lefty, he gave me a simple hello. I didn't ask questions about her, even though I wanted to.

The herd moved into a conference room for a buffet better than I expected it to be, but not as good as what we used to get in Vegas. I went for the chicken, mainly because it's pretty hard for anyone to screw up chicken.

I found a spot with the other quarterbacks and several receivers. The guys who count on having footballs thrown their way are always looking to suck up. I focused on my food and listened.

Wettle seemed less nervous than he'd been at practice. Maybe he was just accepting reality. There's a comfort that comes from assuming the worst.

After a while, I saw some of the players walking out. We'd have our team meeting in a different room. I was curious to hear how Garrett McGarrett handled them. He started as soon as everyone's ass was in a chair.

"Gentlemen," he said. "We only get so many opportunities. The next one comes tomorrow. We'll be shorthanded. That makes it an even bigger chance to shine. And shine you will. There are no excuses for not having our best players available. When this game goes in the record books, there won't be an asterisk that shows we didn't have our best quarterback. The only thing that matters is did we win, or did we lose?"

It wasn't exactly the kind of thing that'd inspire guys to run through a cinderblock wall. But what else could he say? They knew what they were up against. They'd do their best, and they'd try to get through in one piece.

He went over the game plan again. He said the defense would expect us to run, so we'd flip it around and throw. He said it would be our only chance. I knew that was the idea. It helped to hear it again before I made my call. I also knew from talking to Wettle that he's got a comfort level with the tight end, Mike Adamston. If Wettle will be throwing, the ball will be going to Adamston.

McGarrett talked about the defense, too. We planned to take away their top two receivers and dare them to run. That would mean plenty of work for the tailbacks. Johnny Motts would need to hear that, too. By the time the meeting ended, I figured I had everything I needed.

I had no idea whether everything—or anything—I told him would register. It was pretty clear Johnny Motts is a lot dumber than I thought. I'd never pegged him for a genius. But I didn't think he was a moron, not until recently.

I got back upstairs just after eight. I took a little grief for having my own room, when the rest of them had to double up. I didn't mind. Little things like getting ribbed could help me fit in.

Besides, I'd found an apartment. I'd be moving in on Monday. Just in time to start looking for a place to stash the next bag of cash.

I decided to take one last look at the game plan before making the call. I needed to be sure I'd be giving Johnny Motts the best possible information. One thing I would never be accused of was failing to do either of my jobs to the best of my ability.

I was procrastinating. I'd gone from sort of liking him at first to not caring much about him to hating his guts. He was as stubborn as he was stupid. The best part was, after Sunday, I wouldn't have to deal with him for five days. Unless Baltimore decided to cut me as fast as they'd signed me. I wondered how many different apartments I'd end up with by the time the season ended.

It was part of the price to pay for messing around with something that felt like easy money. I went through my reasons for doing it, again. I told myself it's a victimless crime, again. I reminded myself the sportsbooks have inside information, again. I repeated the same question I always came back to: Why shouldn't the bettors level the playing field?

I still knew it wasn't right. All that cash I had in Las Vegas proved it, along with the next bag of cash I'd be getting in Baltimore.

I decided to just get it over with. I'd make the report to Johnny Motts. Then I could focus on getting a good night's sleep so I'd be ready for my first game with my new team. So I could listen to the calls and give the run-or-pass signal to whoever was paying attention, if I ended up getting a helmet. I had a pretty good feeling I would.

I didn't know how hard it would be to get in the right position. I had no idea who else had a habit of standing in the best spot for being in the camera aimed at the head coach. I needed to check the angles from other Baltimore games to figure out where to stand. I knew Johnny Motts wouldn't take any explanations or excuses for me not being seen by those who needed to see me.

I was glad I thought of that. Anything I could do to take away some of the uncertainty would make my life easier. I'd focus on that project as soon as I finished the call.

Just as I picked up the burner, the phone in my room started ringing.

35

JOHNNY MOTTS

I hope I can trust Lego Billy. He knows who I'm with. He's smart enough to know what'll happen if he runs his mouth. I don't wanna remind him. I like him. I don't like making threats to people I like, usually.

I called him from the burner. He didn't answer. He probably didn't recognize the number. I left a message. "It's Starsky. Call me back."

Lego Billy calls me Starsky because he thinks I look like that guy from the old TV show. The one with the cops who drove the Ford that was painted like a can of Coke, or something. I don't think I looked like Starsky. He didn't have no mustache. I guess I'd maybe look like him if I shaved it off.

I hung up and waited. I tried not to think while I waited. I've already been thinking too much. I sort of liked what my thinking had been about. I didn't wanna think some more and fuck it all up.

The burner rang. I checked the number to make sure it was him and not one of my guys. I hit the button and said hello.

"Did you get a new phone?"

"I use this one sometimes," I said.

"Bat phone." He said it all sly, like the light bulb just went off for him about why people might use a second line.

"I got some work for you, if you want it."

"Depends on what it is and what you're paying."

"I just need you to get some information. And I'm paying the usual."

"Local or out of state?"

"Both."

"You know how the out of town stuff goes. I might need help, depending on where it is."

"This ain't my first rodeo."

"You're looking for a cowboy?"

"What?"

"You said something about a rodeo."

I wanted to call him stupid. I needed him too much to piss him off that fast. "You gotta be careful with this one," I said.

"I'm always careful."

"Extra careful."

"I'm already careful."

"Just be more careful than careful. I've been doing business with some athletes."

"What kind of business?"

"Enough business that I need to give you business. Ain't that good enough?"

"I'm just curious."

"I only need you to be curious about what I'm asking you to do. Find out whether two of them have girlfriends."

"Who are they?"

"First one is Carson Jeffrey."

"Who the hell is Carson Jeffrey?"

"Backup quarterback. Played here for a few years. I need to know if he got someone in town. And in Baltimore. That's where he's at now."

"Why do you need to know if he got a girlfriend?"

"When does why I need to know what I need to know matter?"

"Just curious again."

"Stop being curious. Except when you're doing this job."

"You said there was another one."

"Jimmy King."

"I know who that is. Basketball. Plays for Denver."

"I need to know if he has someone up there."

Lego Billy got quiet.

"Got it?" I said.

"I got it."

"So why did you clam up?"

"You don't want me asking no questions."

"I feel like you got some."

"I thought you guys don't mess with women."

"Who says we're gonna mess with women?"

"Of all the times you ever asked me to find somebody, you never asked me to find nobody's girlfriend. Now you got me looking for them in three cities."

"Don't worry about why I need to know. I just do. And I need it to be right. No mistakes on this."

"So if they ain't got nobody, they ain't got nobody?"

"If I find out later that they do got somebody, that'll be something I have to share with somebody."

"Who?

"Who do you think?"

"Why him?"

"That's who I work for."

"That guy scares me."

"Join the club."

"I should charge more for this."

"You get the usual amount," I said. "Do I need to call Frankie Flag?"

"Fuck Frankie Flag."

"So you'll take it?"

"I don't know how much it's gonna cost in Baltimore or Denver."

"Whatever it is, pay it. You can mark it up fifteen points. I trust you not to put your thumb on the scale past that."

"Don't worry. I know Carmine would chop it off if I did."

I hung up the phone and stared at it. It's not good that people are more scared of Carmine than me. Yeah, Carmine is a scary bastard. I need to have people think that way about me.

Maybe I'm on my way to that. I'm cranking things up a little bit with Carson Jeffrey and Jimmy King. I'll get them in line by making them understand what'll happen if they don't. If I have to do it, I have to do it.

Why are civilians safe anyway? They chose to associate with guys who are connected. They take the risk. Even if they don't, there's plenty of bad luck in this world. Innocent bystanders get shot. Trucks run over little kids. People are in the wrong place at the wrong time, all the time.

If I'm ever gonna run things, I need to think different. Rules need to change. Starting with rules that never made no sense in the first place. Why give everyone who isn't in the crew a pass? I bet plenty of wives have put plenty of ideas in plenty of heads. Ideas that caused plenty of trouble. Why just assume they're all untouchable?

I need to make sure nobody knows about none of this. Yeah, I hope I can trust Lego Billy. If I can't, that'll be that. It would be a shame. Of course, he wouldn't be the first guy I liked that I got rid of.

It's way easier when I don't like them. I don't like Carson Jeffrey. I don't like Jimmy King. Because of Larry Ballentine, I can't do nothing to them. Why the fuck did Larry Ballentine duck when I swung?

I'm getting nervous again. Jumpy. Twitchy. Lego Billy could run his mouth before I take him out. If Carmine finds out I decided to go after civilians, I'll be done.

Or will I? Carmine wouldn't want whoever he works for to

know we crossed that line. I still think there's something above us that ain't like us. Carmine made that remark about finding something else to do. Something changed. He don't like how it is now.

I still don't know who he's working for. I got no way to find out, unless I start looking around. Maybe I will.

I really don't like all this thinking. Because now I'm thinking I should start snooping around into shit I shouldn't be snooping around about.

36

ALICE SMITHSON

I made it past the front desk. I only needed sixty percent of my courtroom voice to get the person who took the call to transfer me to his room.

The line rumbled, in the old-school way phones connected to other phones by actual wires do. In the middle of the fourth ring, I heard the receiver lift from its cradle.

"Hello?"

The voice made my knees wobble. I tried not to let my own voice sound quite so unsteady.

"Hi," I said in a perky tone that I hated but couldn't help. "You don't know me. Well, you sort of know me. I mean, we've met."

"That doesn't really narrow it down." I could already tell he was enjoying this.

"We talked last night. You told me a joke. I mean, you never told me the joke."

He started to laugh. "I thought you sounded familiar. Do you need to track down Lefty? Let me guess, he didn't give you his number?"

Hearing that idiotic name helped me get things under control. "Not him. That one ran its course right away. No love connection there."

"Love connection?"

"It's an old TV show. My grandfather used to watch it, for some reason. They'd set people up on blind dates, I think."

"Does Lefty agree with your assessment?"

"I think Lefty got the picture. He should have figured it out when I got up and left."

"So you leftied Lefty?"

"I did what?"

"That's why they call him Lefty. Not because he's left-handed. He's known for, you know, leaving after."

"After what?"

"After doing whatever he was trying to make happen last night."

"Does that make me the new Lefty?"

"Are you looking for a nickname?"

"I already have one."

"I can only imagine."

This time, I laughed. It might have sounded like a giggle. Oh well. "I'll tell you what it is when you tell me that joke."

"Did you call to hear a joke?"

"Jokes aren't as funny over the phone."

"What are you saying?"

"I'm not just stating facts."

"So when do you want to hear that joke in person?"

"Well, that's direct."

"You're the one who called me," he said.

"It's not like I can claim I buttdialed the Lord Baltimore Hotel and accidentally asked for your room."

"How did you know I was here?"

"Lefty was happy to share those details."

"Lefty might not be too happy to find out what you did with them."

"I assume Lefty found someone else he loved and leftied."

"I don't think love has much to do with it."

"I went with something a little less crass. Look, what are you doing tonight?"

"I'm sort of on lock down. No one said there's a curfew, but once we're at the team hotel the night before the game, we shouldn't go anywhere. And they usually frown upon visitors."

"Are you allowed to come out and play after the game?"

"You really are direct."

"God, I don't mean it that way. How about a nice dinner somewhere? You're new in town, I know that much. You need to figure out where some of the decent restaurants are."

"Let me guess. You're part of the Baltimore Welcoming Committee?"

"Just got the assignment this week."

"I'm not one to get in the way of somebody who's trying to do her job."

"I'll give you my number," I said. "Call me when you're free and I'll let you know where and when to meet."

"I need to know one other thing first."

"What's that?"

"I hate to be so forward, but it sure would be nice if I knew your name."

"It's Alice."

"Alice what?"

"Isn't Alice enough?"

"Only if you don't have a last name."

"So you can Google me, right?"

"I can only guess you've already done that to me. And I can only guess you didn't find anything that would make you not want to call."

"You win. It's Smithson. I'm Alice Smithson. And you're Carson Jeffrey."

"Nice to meet you, Alice Smithson."

I liked how it sounded when he said my name. I asked if he was ready to take down my number. I heard him open a drawer. He said he had a pen.

"I never do this," I said.

"You can't say you never do it if you're doing it right now."

"You know what I mean."

"Then I suppose I'm honored, Alice Smithson. Newest member of the Baltimore Welcoming Committee. I have a feeling I'll have a hard time confirming that online."

"Don't believe everything you read on the Internet."

"That's something people in my line of work usually say. But since you liked what you found, I'd say to go ahead and believe every last bit of it."

I laughed at that. Had I misread him? No, I had pretty much figured him out. If not, I never would have called.

"Good luck tomorrow."

"I won't be playing."

"I know," I said. "I just didn't know what else to say."

"Good night is fine with me."

"Then have a good night. I look forward to hearing from you after the game."

I both liked and detested the glow I felt after the call ended. Sally Slammer, smitten by a tall stranger whose most redeeming quality came from the fact that he reminded me of my grandfather. The conversation confirmed the feeling.

I spent the rest of the night wondering whether he'd call. I hated that feeling, too. Confidence in all things and at all times had become one of my strongest attributes. I wasn't about to let some dumb jock who had proven to not be very dumb at all—and, at his current level, not much of an actual jock—get the better of me. Then again, he already had. Otherwise, I never would have called that hotel.

I tried to do a little more work. There was no use. I did my best to fight through it before pouring another glass of wine and finding a sappy romantic comedy to watch on my laptop before settling into a bed that, by the next night, I might not be sleeping in alone.

37

CARSON JEFFREY

I didn't fully understand what had happened. The woman from the bar last night. The one Lefty went after. Calling out of the blue. I didn't know how I'd explain it to Lefty.

Maybe I'd never have to. I'd have a friendly dinner with her. Nothing more.

Did I want it to be more? That depended on whether she did. I learned the hard way in high school about getting twisted up in knots over someone who doesn't feel the same way. I'd never taken it personally, not since Barbie Lynn in the eleventh grade. There's no sense trying to make something happen if the other person isn't interested.

If Alice was, well, maybe I was, too. I kept shaking my head at the thought. But she'd called me. Had she been drinking a little? It seemed like she knew her way around the hard stuff. Maybe by Sunday morning she'd regret calling. Maybe by Sunday night she wouldn't even answer.

I sat there and wondered whether I would call. I wasn't meeting a bunch of new people. Besides, there was something about her. If I'd majored in English and not Parks, Recreation, and Leisure Facilities Management, maybe I'd know how to put it into words.

I had to push those thoughts away. Johnny Motts was waiting for the full report on Sunday's plan. When I called, he didn't sound as pissed. But he was short and abrupt, from start to finish.

"What do you got for me?"

"Where do you want to start?" I said.

"Where do you always start?"

"The running back had ice on his knee all week."

"Which one?"

"Left, I think."

"No," he said, "which running back?"

"Richardson. The starter."

"He took all his reps in practice?"

"As far as I saw. He's just icing it a lot."

"Anyone else more hurt than what they're saying?"

"Not that I've seen."

"OK, next."

"They're gonna cut it loose with Wettle."

"The backup quarterback? Bullshit."

"That's what they're saying. They think the defense expects running plays. They're changing it up."

"Might have something to do with Richardson's knee," he said.

"Either way, that's what they're doing. Also, he likes the starting tight end."

"Who?"

"Mike Adamston."

"No, who likes him?"

"The new quarterback. Wettle."

"How do you know that?"

"How do I know anything?" I said. "I talk to them. I see them on the practice field. I hear what Wettle says in the meetings. I think he'll be throwing to him a lot."

"You think or you know?"

"I said I think. So I think."

"Think don't win."

"Think is better than nothing. I've only been here three days."

"Next."

"They plan to take away the top two receivers and force them to run it. Which means Cincinnati's running back should have a big day."

"Unless they throw to the receivers anyway."

"That's always how it goes. This is never going to be perfect. But it's more than ninety-nine-point-nine percent of what the rest of the world knows."

"That stuff you get during the game is pretty close to perfect. Are you gonna have a helmet with a speaker inside?"

"They haven't said I will. They haven't said I won't."

"Have you asked?"

"Don't you think that would raise a red flag?"

"Not if you ask it in a way that don't raise a red flag."

"How should I do that?"

"That's for you to figure out."

"I'll know in the morning," I said. "I can't imagine I won't have one."

"Call me when you know."

"You want me to take the burner to the locker room? I'll have to leave it in there when I'm on the field."

"You can't carry it with you?"

"Where in my uniform would I put it? Besides, it's against the rules to have phones on the sidelines."

"So you're telling me I'll find out when the game starts?"

"As long as I can get in the TV shot."

"You better get in the fucking shot. Same spot as always."

"I don't know if I can do it."

"If you have a helmet, we need to see what you're doing."

"I'll do my best."

"As long as your best means you're in the shot, that'll be good enough."

"Are we done?"

"You know, I noticed something. All that time you was in Vegas, you'd say *we*. Tonight, you're saying *they*."

"I just got here."

"You won't be there for long if you don't start thinking of *they* as *we*."

I didn't argue with him. I just wanted to get it over with. Besides, he was right. The best way to stick around for more than a week or two would be to get myself thinking and talking like I'm part of the team.

The call ended. It didn't take much longer than usual. It made me think maybe things were getting back to normal. Normal as they could have been, since I was on the other side of the country and I had no idea how long I'd be here.

I wanted to stay a little longer. Because of her. I guess that was enough to get me to think of *they* as *we*. If that helped me have a chance with *her*, it was worth it.

Alice Smithson.

I pulled up the browser on my phone and thumbed in her name and the word *Baltimore*. My mouth fell open.

I was not messing with some run-of-the-mill ambulance chaser. She was a prosecutor. A federal prosecutor.

It looked like she was a pretty good one, too. Plenty of convictions. In big cases. Words like *corruption. Malfeasance. Obstruction of justice*. She liked to go after folks with money and power. I found two articles that said she was an expert in making complicated cases simple for a jury to figure out.

I could tell she was smart from talking to her. It looked like I was dealing with some sort of a genius. Maybe smarter than a genius, whatever that would be called. Somebody with a brain, who knows how to use it. She's made people face the music with it.

That made me think about what I'd been doing. I'd told myself it was fine. It was fair. It was no different than what the sportsbooks do. Did it break the law? I didn't know. But I knew enough to know that, because it felt wrong, there was probably a law somewhere that made it illegal.

The more I learned about her, the more I felt the heat spread on and around my face. I felt it along my hairline. Beads of sweat were starting to form and slide. I thought back to the two times I talked to her, tonight on the phone, last night in person.

This wasn't some gold-digging fan looking for followers or a reality show or eighteen years of child support. I was dealing with somebody who had no reason to waste time on a turd like me. I was dealing with somebody who'd take a real interest in my second job.

I thought about the dinner plans. I'd need to talk to her; I couldn't just sit there and chew. Would she pick up on something I'd say? I knew I shouldn't see her. I shouldn't call her.

What would she do about that? Would she move on? Or would she get curious? Would that take her to places that could become a problem for me?

I tried to go back to the playbook, to the film, to forgetting about this brand new complication that might make my life a lot more complicated than it was. I had a hard time focusing on the work. I didn't have a hard time focusing on her.

Fucking Lefty. He talked me into talking to someone who was too much for him to handle. Why didn't he just give up? I kept going back and forth between deciding not to call her the next night to realizing I should.

I'd just be careful. I'd think about every word before it came out. I'd think about every face I might make, like I was playing poker. If I only knew how to play poker.

My best move would be to come off as boring enough to get her to decide to get on with her life. To get her to focus on finding bad guys. To not wonder if she might be sitting right across from one.

I sat there and thought about it. *Is that what I am? A bad guy?* I wasn't feeling like much of a good guy. I thought about what I'd already done, about what I'd be doing the next day, if they ended up putting me in a uniform and giving me a helmet.

I couldn't stop now. I was in way too deep. Alice the person seemed to be interested in me. Alice the fed could be a lot more interested in me, and everybody I was working for.

I got on the mattress that barely held my body. I stared at the ceiling. I wished I could sleep. I kept hoping for it, right up until I started seeing gray corners of daylight coming around the edges of the blinds.

Gray corners of daylight coming from a world that seemed to be getting more dangerous for me, all the time.

38

JOHNNY MOTTS

Lego Billy said Jeffrey ain't seeing nobody in Vegas. Lego Billy was still trying to get somebody to help with Baltimore. I told him to try harder and faster. I know it takes some time. There ain't no harm in keeping a foot in someone's ass.

In Denver, Lego Billy had better luck. He already knew somebody. It didn't take long to find out Jimmy King got two women there. They think one don't know about the other, and vice-versa. Also, one of them has a kid.

That ain't horrible news. Maybe I can just threaten to blow up his love nests. That'd be a lot better than having to blow up one of his women.

I booked a flight to Denver. It'd be nice if we had a plane of our own. I heard one of the crews in Chicago got one. A real one, too, not one of them puddle jumpers. I bet whoever Carmine reports to got a plane. Maybe two. That'd be nice. Maybe when I'm fifty. First, I gotta make it to thirty.

In this life, birthdays ain't guaranteed. That's the way it is for everybody, I know. But we got a few more ways to not make it to the next cake than everybody else.

I bought a first-class ticket. If I'm paying anyway, I might as well enjoy myself. Have a little hooch. Maybe they'll give me a hamburger. I'll sit up front with the rich people. Maybe I'll get lucky and end up next to an athlete who just visited town and lost a shitload of money and might be looking for ways to make some of it back.

They didn't give me no burger. I also didn't end up next to nobody worth talking to. It was some old lady with a stick up her ass. I tried to make conversation, just to be nice. She didn't want nothing to do with me. Maybe it was obvious what I am.

I like it that way. There ain't no misunderstanding when you start talking to me. You'd be amazed how many people it draws in. Like I say, moth to a flame.

After the plane landed, I found a place to rent a car. I asked for a Cadillac, and the kid behind the counter made a face. I told him to give me the closest thing. He said he didn't have nothing close to a Cadillac. I asked for the nicest American car.

That ended up being some brown piece of shit Ford. I wasn't gonna see nobody I knew, which meant I didn't need to worry about how it'd look for me to be inside something like that. Besides, it was probably good for me to keep a low profile.

Once I got in the car, I called Jimmy King from the burner. They got a home game tomorrow night, so I knew he'd been in town. He knows I know his schedule, and he knows when I'll know to expect him to answer right away. Even though he's been fucking up lately, he's still smart enough to answer, fast.

"I was planning to get you the info later," he said.

"That ain't why I'm calling. I'm in town on business."

"Do you wanna hang out?"

"I got time to kill."

He got quiet. I could tell he was thinking. I let him.

"Should we be seen together?"

"I didn't think of that," I said. I kinda like lying about shit like this. I figure it's good practice when I need to lie to Carmine or somebody else important. "You don't have some place quiet you go where nobody would raise eyebrows?"

"Everywhere I go raises eyebrows. I'm nearly seven feet tall. Even if they don't recognize me right away, they assume I play basketball."

"Well, that's a problem then." I waited some more after I finished to let him get back to worrying.

"I'd invite you over, but I'm not exactly by myself."

"I thought you lived alone."

"I did. I mean, I do. I have a friend over."

"When's your friend leaving?"

"Whenever my friend leaves."

"Does your friend have an open invitation to stay as long as your friend wants?"

"What do you mean?"

"I ain't never had trouble getting people to leave my place when I want them to."

I had him in a box. I could feel him squirming.

"Fine," he finally said. "Give me an hour."

"I'll see you in an hour."

"I didn't give you the address."

"I don't need it." I hung up before he could say anything else.

I put his address in the phone for directions. His place was twenty minutes away. I found a place to get the burger they didn't give me on the plane. Ordered it rare. There's nothing like a little bloody meat to get me in the right frame of mind for one of these meetings.

The first bite made me think of Larry Ballentine's head busting open. Maybe that shit would bother me if I was a normal person. I ain't been normal in years, if I ever was. Times like that give me a nice reminder I ain't getting soft.

I got to Jimmy's place maybe ninety minutes after I called. It was getting dark. I parked on the street. He has a big fucking house. So big he don't need to be trying to make extra money.

But everybody always wants more.

I'd like a house like that someday. The house first, then the plane. Would I ever make that kind of dough? Alls I could do was keep trying.

I brung a baseball cap with me. I pulled it down low. I figure there's cameras all over the place. What's he gonna do? Turn me in? I ain't here to send a message. I ain't here to do nothing but talk. I don't really care if his system would have pictures of some guy in black pants and a black shirt with the green hat I took from Ballentine's house pulled low on my face.

He opened the door when I got to the porch.

"I assume your friend is gone?" I said.

"Hello to you, too."

I walked by him and went inside. "Nice place you got here. Too bad I wasn't a foot taller."

"You play basketball?"

"I was a foot taller, I sure as shit would've learned."

I went through the front room. He had art on the walls. I wondered how much it cost. I wondered if he even knew. I spotted a couch. I went and sat down. I don't care how nice somebody's place is. The way to take control is to act like you own it.

"Did you play baseball?" he said.

"I've used a bat in my day."

"You're wearing a baseball hat."

I kept it on. Kept it pulled low. "I got this from an old friend."

He stood there, looking at me. I could tell he was pissed I made myself at home. Good.

"Can I get you something?"

"I'll have whatever you're drinking."

"I'm not drinking tonight."

I looked past him to the kitchen. There wasn't no pots on the counter. No dishes. No glasses. All I seen was a brown bag with a white piece of paper on it, like he ordered in.

"Maybe you should be drinking tonight," I said.

"Why should I be?"

"You got a night off. You should relax. Take the edge off a little."

"I don't drink to do that."

I could smell a hint of weed in the air. That's even better than if he had booze in his system. If things went sideways, he'd be slow to react. I reminded myself I ain't here for nothing like that.

"Sit down," I said. "Listen to me. I'm the one inviting you to sit down in your own place."

He got inside a big chair across from the couch. I could tell it was made special for someone his size. I would've gotten lost in the damn thing, like a little kid trying to wear his dad's clothes.

I waited for him to settle in. I stared at him. Even with however much he smoked before I got there, I shook him up. Good.

"You realize these mistakes you're making need to end. The other night, when you came back in the game? That was not good."

"I didn't hit the numbers."

"You was close."

"I didn't hit them."

"I had to fucking sweat the whole game that you might. You was supposed to go out and stay out."

"The doctor was looking at me weird. I think he thought I was faking. I got nervous. I decided to just play but keep my numbers under control."

"It still ain't good. Besides, you've been giving me bad info lately."

"I'm trying."

"Try harder."

"I am."

"If you ain't giving me the right shit, you ain't trying hard enough to get it."

"There's only so much I can do."

"Do more."

I could tell he wanted to start giving all the reasons why it was so hard. I could also tell he knew I wouldn't give a shit.

"I will," he said.

"Sometimes, people need a little extra incentive to try harder."

"Are you offering more money?"

I laughed at that, and not in a way that should have made him think I thought it was funny.

"So what's the incentive?"

"You know who you're dealing with, right? We've got ways to give people reasons to do what they need to do when they ain't."

He got a little stiff in the chair. He was looking at my waistband for the kind of bulges a piece would make.

"Relax, Jimmy. I didn't come to your house to shoot you."

He got even more stiff when I said that. Good. I stared at him and waited.

"So why did you come here?"

"The biggest part of my job is to know things. That's why we're in business together. You know things. So then I know things. That's the arrangement."

I went back to staring at him. After a few seconds, he nodded a little bit.

"I know more things than the things you tell me," I said. I waited again.

"So what do you know?"

"I know plenty."

"Plenty about what?"

"For starters, I know you don't live alone." I didn't know that for sure, but what I found out from Lego Billy and what Jimmy said during the phone call helped me piece it all together. Jimmy King was living with one of his two girlfriends.

"She has her own place."

I threw out my arms and looked up. "I bet it ain't as nice as this. I also bet she ain't slept in her own place more than two nights this month."

"Fine. You know I don't live alone. I don't know why any of that matters."

"It matters because you told me when we got started that you live alone, and you ain't never told me no different. So either you wasn't being truthful then, or you didn't bother to tell me once your girlfriend moved in."

"I didn't think it was important."

"When you're doing what you're doing, everything is important. I told you nobody can know about this."

"She doesn't know anything."

"If she did, I wouldn't expect you to tell me."

"She ain't my wife. We ain't even engaged. She just sleeps here."

"That means she's here when you call me. You don't know what she might've heard when we talk on the phone."

"I never call from the same room she's in."

"Again, I wouldn't expect you to tell me nothing different."

"I'm telling you, she doesn't know a thing."

"I'm telling you I got no choice but to take your word for it. Even if I can't help but wonder whether you're telling me the truth."

"Am I supposed to bring her over here so she can tell you she doesn't know anything?"

I looked past the room to the rest of the house. "I got a weird feeling you wouldn't need to bring her very far."

"Her place is like ten miles away."

"I got a feeling she's still here."

He was getting even stiffer. He started looking around, too. "You want me to take you room by room to show you she's not?"

"I'm just telling you I got a feeling she's here. I get feelings sometimes. Don't you?"

"I got a feeling right now."

"Tell me about it."

"I got a feeling you're not gonna accept anything I tell you."

"See? Sometimes when we have a feeling, it ends up being one hundred percent accurate."

"What do you want from me? Just tell me so we can get this over with."

"I already told you what I want. This is about how to give you the right incentive to do it."

"What is it?"

"I don't think you want me to say it out loud, in case she can hear what we're talking about."

"I don't follow."

"I think you do. I think you follow me perfect. Like I said, I know things."

I stared at him some more. I didn't expect him to say nothing. I just wanted to make sure he got my drift. I watched his face. It was wrinkled up with his thoughts. Then the muscles relaxed and the eyes widened.

Once that happened, I got up and walked out.

39

ALICE SMITHSON

I can't remember the last time I watched football. Are they even on TV anymore? I think it's all streaming.

I figured it out an hour before the game started. I signed up for a seven-day trial. I'd cancel it the next day. My GS-14 was already stretched to the limit.

I'm not sure why I wanted to see it. He wouldn't play. If he did, it probably wouldn't go very well. I guess I just wanted to see him.

I assumed I wouldn't, not much. I'd be looking at pictures of the sideline (I think that's what it's called), searching for the man wearing a purple jersey with the number eighteen on the front and back.

There he was. Standing behind the head coach. Wearing a helmet and watching the field with those eyes I'd managed to not gaze into two nights earlier. The screen had an options menu in the upper corner. I cycled through the choices. I realized I could pick the angles, up to four different views at once.

I had full control of the cameras. That's not the way it was the last time I'd tuned in. It was probably a Super Bowl. Possibly before I started law school.

I divided the screen between the game on one side and the shot of the coach on the other, since that's where Carson stood. I didn't care about the game, but I would have felt like a stalker if I only watched the angle that included Carson. I did it anyway, ignoring the other half of the monitor.

I had a crush. So what? It was normal. Still, I wondered if I'd spend time the next day scribbling his name over and over on a legal pad, like some high-school girl. Would I then write *Alice Smithson Jeffrey*? Would there be a hyphen? *Alice Smithson-Jeffrey*. Would I keep my name? Would I submit to *Alice Jeffrey*? Whatever I'd pick, Sally Slammer wouldn't be going anywhere.

Sally Slammer. Coincidence or not, that's precisely when her skills were unleashed.

He was fidgeting. Before every play, he'd grab at the bars in front of his helmet. It made it harder to see his face. It was the whole point of picking that camera angle.

Sometimes, he'd move the hand away. Other times, he wouldn't. There was a strange sort of rhythm to it. His eyes stayed focused. The rest of his body barely moved. That hand kept coming up. Sometimes, it would stay briefly. Other times, it would remain there longer.

I found myself paying less attention to his face and more attention to his hand. I could see the coach. He was talking into the small microphone connected to the headset that was wrapped over a purple hat with a black logo on the front. Before every play, the coach would talk into the microphone. Carson would then start working his hand. Something about all of it seemed very weird.

"What is he doing?" I said.

I made a mental note to ask him about it that night, if he called. I assumed he would. If he didn't, maybe that would be the end of it.

I thought it through. If he calls, we'll go to dinner. We'll talk about various things. I'll mention, hopefully with the right amount of nonchalance, that I'd watched the game. I'll ask what he does during the game. I'll let him tell me what he was doing with his hand, without specifically asking him the question. If he ever thinks I'm cross-examining him on our first date (I hated thinking of it as one), there wouldn't be another.

Fear of alienating him didn't make me less curious. That's who I'd always been.

Curiosity. My grandfather used to say curiosity doesn't kill the cat; it keeps the cat alive.

I sort of felt alive in a way I hadn't, not in years. I stumbled across a man who made me curious. Why wouldn't everything about him make me curious? Why shouldn't I allow that curiosity to fuel our conversation? People love to talk about themselves. I'll let myself indulge in my curiosities. If that scares him away, so be it.

I could tell the team was having a rough time without its normal quarterback. I knew that when a football team throws the ball, the quarterback needs to do it accurately. I knew enough to notice the home team's quarterback wasn't doing that, not well enough to help the team move the ball toward the end of the field where it could score points. Six for a touchdown, three for a field goal. I've picked up that much.

I didn't know much beyond that. If this new thing continues, I'll be learning a lot more about it. I'll be learning a lot more about him.

So what's wrong with wanting to understand exactly what he was doing while he was standing on the sideline during the game?

40

CARSON JEFFREY

In the locker room after the game, I sensed right away the difference between playing for a team that kicked the shit out of everybody and ending up on a team that regularly takes the kicking. Nobody was talking. The only sound came from players hurrying up to shower and change so they could get the hell out of there. Nobody made it through the big doors with the *NO ADMITTANCE* sign before the coach walked in and let loose.

"Well, that was a fucking disgusting display," Garrett McGarrett yelled. There was a box on the floor with peels from oranges some of the guys ate at halftime. Compostable refuse, or something. He kicked the box and it zipped right across the floor. It hit a locker and orange peels flew everywhere, like fireworks. One of the guys went to clean up the mess.

"Leave those fucking things where they are! You see those oranges? That's how many of you I'm gonna dump if we don't straighten this shit up, fast. You got me?"

What he said didn't make much sense, but no one said a word.

"Do you fucking got me?"

"Yes, coach." The words came out as a shaky and muffled chorus.

"I can't fucking hear you!"

"Yes! Coach!"

"Get your asses cleaned up and go home. I don't wanna see or hear any of you went out gallivanting tonight. We got a lot to go over tomorrow. I want everyone to be fresh and rested for it, in case any of you get the same orders Jerry Perkins got last week."

It took me a few seconds to understand the message. He was telling us to stay in tonight. There went my dinner plans.

Then again, I didn't play. He couldn't be mad at me, except by association with the rest of them. Yeah, *them*. They're the ones who fucked up, not *we*. Not *me*.

It felt weird to be on the receiving end of something I wasn't responsible for. It hadn't happened since I was in college. There, I was the best player on a bad team. Sometimes, the coach would let me have it, to make the others think I wasn't above the rest of them.

Before losing their QB1, Baltimore had won as many games as they'd lost. Losing to Cincinnati as bad as they (we) had wasn't a huge surprise. Cincinnati had their top quarterback, they (we) didn't.

It's about throwing the ball and scoring points. A team that can do it with its best quarterback will almost always beat a team that can't.

After McGarrett left in a huff, I did what I'd always done. I kept my head low and my mouth shut. I watched and listened. I was still learning what I could about this team. I'd learn plenty more in the next few days about whether the coach's bark would be backed up by any bite.

I figured that, for now, not much would happen. At this point in the year, making major adjustments would be like trying to change the tire on a moving car. I planned to do my best to stay tucked away in the trunk, for as long as I could.

I spotted Lefty. He'd let a receiver get behind him for a long touchdown, so he was keeping a profile almost as low as mine. Which made it easier to avoid him. I doubted Lefty would say anything about the woman he struck out with on Friday night. I still didn't want to chance it.

I slipped out without anyone noticing me. I drove back to the hotel in a car I was renting by the day. I didn't want to buy one. I had a perfectly good Wrangler in Las Vegas.

I scanned the card to my room at a few minutes after seven. I checked my phone. My dad used to call after every game. Win or lose, he said the same thing.

I'm always proud of you, no matter what.

I wish I'd saved one of those messages. I'm sort of glad I didn't. He wouldn't be too proud of me now, if he knew what I've been doing.

I was on my own. I was pretty much used to it. The only child of two only children. With my parents gone, I had no one. Not until I found someone. If I ever did.

I thought of her again. It was way too early to wonder whether she could give me the things I didn't have. Any relationship I started at this age might end up being permanent, or something that would head that way until it didn't. What was wrong with thinking it could be possible?

Really, why waste time with somebody where there's no potential? Get acquainted, see how it goes. If it goes one way, move in. If it goes the other way, move on.

There was only one way to find out. I thought of what McGarrett said about staying in. I decided again that it doesn't apply to me, and that I'd take my chances he'd find out I ignored a direct order that didn't directly apply to me.

I stared at the number I'd scribbled on the notepad the night before. I thought about texting her. She said I should call. I wanted to show her I'm smart enough to pay attention. That I can do what I've been asked to do.

I dialed. She answered. I felt a smile starting.

"Well, hello," she said. "I was starting to wonder about you."

"I got back a little bit ago."

"I assumed you were coming up with a good excuse. The only one I know you can't use is you got injured during the game."

"Ouch."

"Maybe you did."

"That's the best thing about not playing. When you don't play, you never get hit."

"What about during practice?"

"They put the quarterback in special jerseys. Nobody can touch us."

"When was the last time someone tackled you?"

"I haven't seen live action since my last game at North Texas."

"They call it live action?"

"That's what it is."

"It sounds so official. And dangerous. Are guns involved?"

"That would increase the TV ratings."

"It would have helped today."

"You watched?"

"I support the local team."

"Can you name five players on it?"

"I can name one. Two, actually. Carson Jeffrey and some guy who goes by Lefty but not because he's left-handed."

"Forty percent. Still an F."

"You get an A for math."

"We're not all dumb."

"Remember, I looked you up. Academic All-American."

"What's that old saying? In the land of the blind the one-eyed man is king?"

"You're not so bad for a cyclops."

"You're not so bad for a lawyer."

"You don't know me very well. You've got a chance to learn a little more tonight, if you still want."

"I called you."

"Indeed you did. We'll see if you show up for dinner."

She gave me the name of the place. I made sure it was a casual thing. I didn't pack much of my wardrobe. Not that the rest of it would be good for anything much fancier than Burger King. We agreed to meet at half past eight.

I showered and shaved, brushed my teeth thoroughly. I managed to floss most of them. I found some cologne down in a pocket of my bag. I was careful about how much I put on. I picked through my stuff for something that might work. I ironed out the wrinkles as best I could.

I kept telling myself I needed to be careful. Was it worth it? I was willing to risk it.

I hoped like hell I was making the right decision.

41

JOHNNY MOTTS

I made it to the last plane from Denver. Maybe I'll get in a few hours at the tables. It makes for a long day. I'll take something to give me a bump if I need it.

I didn't have no luck finding partners or associates or whatever I should call them. It was stupid to think something like that would happen. It's a lot easier to find them at the Waldorf or the Wynn. If they're hanging around places like that, they're halfway to where I need them to be.

Did I get Jimmy King halfway to where I need him to be? I made my point without doing nothing. Was his girlfriend at his house? I was only guessing when I said it. The way he acted made me think I guessed right.

That's why I decided to drop hints about the other woman, in case his girlfriend really was listening. He was smart enough to get my meaning.

He didn't say nothing about it when I called from the airport for info on the next game. He told me what he knew and nothing else. All business, the way it should be. We ain't friends. He tells me shit and gets paid for it.

Hopefully what he told me tonight ends up being worth a damn. If not, I'll call him after the game and make sure he knows what's next.

When the plane landed and I turned the burner on, I seen a missed call from Lego Billy. I hit him back from my car, after I talked to Jimmy King.

"What do you want?" I said to Lego Billy.

"That ain't very polite."

"What the fuck do you want? That any better?"

"Remind me why I deal with this?"

"It pays good."

"Money ain't everything."

"Not getting a bullet between your eyes is pretty important, too."

"What does that mean?"

"What would it mean other than what it means?"

"I was just having a little fun. I didn't want this to turn into something. We go way back."

"How much longer we go forward might depend on whether you tell me what you want pretty soon."

I could tell he wanted to keep it going. He thought better of it. I was just fucking around when it started. Then I was getting pissed off. It probably had something to do with Carson Jeffrey and Jimmy King and the ghost of Larry Ballentine.

"I found somebody in Baltimore."

"It's good to know you can do what you're told to do. What did he find out?"

"It's a she. Former city cop."

"She, he, we, they. I don't care. I just wanna know if our guy ends up with a woman in town. Or a guy."

"It ain't if," Billy Lego said.

"He already got somebody there and your woman knows about it?

"He had dinner with her last night, after the game."

"Well, well. Do we got a name?"

"She didn't get a good look. They didn't leave together."

"Then how does she even know he had dinner with somebody?"

"She talked to a guy at the restaurant. He sat them down."

"How much did it take to get him to talk?"

"Two hundred."

"Which means it was a hundred and she added another hundred for herself."

"We ain't in a position to do nothing about that."

"I ain't saying I got a problem with it. Tell her to keep eyes on him. He ain't too hard to spot. He'll be going back and forth to work pretty much every day."

"You want twenty-four hours on him?"

"I wanna know the name of the woman he found, and I wanna know where she lives. Whatever it takes."

"That ain't gonna be cheap."

"Did I tell you to make it cheap or did I tell you to find out who she is?"

"Should I let my gal know who she's working for?"

"What do you think?"

"No?"

"Alls she knows is she's working for you. If you feel like mentioning that the people you're working for don't fuck around, maybe it won't cost me a new Mercedes to find out what I need to know. And maybe it won't cost me another new Mercedes to take care of your new friend in Baltimore."

"That's a lot of Mercedes."

"Just make sure it won't cost me a third new Mercedes."

"A third new Mercedes?"

"I'll let you figure that one out by yourself."

I hung up the phone. I liked what I heard. It wasn't everything, but it was a good start.

It started to put me in a better mood. I needed it after the day I had. Maybe I wouldn't need to find a little coke or whatever to get through the rest of the night. I think I maybe even started to smile a little bit.

That smile went away when the burner started to ring and I found out who was calling.

42

ALICE SMITHSON

I got there twenty minutes early. I picked a place in Little Italy. I'd been there a few times with people from the office. I wanted a place where I'd be comfortable, since he had the ability to make me feel so uncomfortable.

I asked for a table tucked away from the handful of groups in the heart of the room, working through their meals and letting the wine and/or whiskey increase their volume. I wanted him to be able to hear me. I wanted to be able to hear him.

I asked the host to make sure no one would be sitting near us. I gave him a twenty-dollar bill as I said it. He made a face at that, like he was confused. I gave him another twenty. His expression shifted to compliance. He put the money in his vest and wished me a pleasant dinner.

A waiter offered me a glass of wine. When it arrived, I tried to sip. I wanted to land in the sweet spot where I'd be both relaxed and fully in control of my faculties. I was used to staring down criminals, fighting with lawyers, placating judges, sometimes pushing them beyond the limits of their patience.

This was different. I was feeling anxious on our first date. I still didn't want to think of it that way. I wanted to take off just enough of the edge so that Sally Slammer would let her hair down and live a little.

Or maybe a lot.

I could never stop being the prosecutor I'd become. It came from that basic curiosity. Curiosity combined with the ability to ask questions aimed at getting real answers. Which would lead to more questions and more answers. I wished I could turn that part of me off. Alcohol was the only thing that would slide the dimmer switch down from full blast.

He walked in, impossible to miss at a full head taller than anyone else in the place. With his perfectly imperfect face and the haircut that looked like old pictures of my grandfather. The feeling in my stomach intensified. I took a very long drink of the wine and waited for the host to deliver my date. Once I saw him, that term stopped bugging me.

He nodded to Carson and swept a hand toward the table. The host gave me a look with a raised eyebrow, as if to say he now understood why I was willing to give up forty bucks for some quiet time. Carson seemed confused by the interaction.

"Have a seat," I said. "I wouldn't want you to bang your head against the ceiling."

He looked up to see he had several inches before the top of his skull would strike wooden beams arranged in clean, tight lines. "I think I'd have to jump first," he said.

"That can be arranged."

He pulled back a chair and eased himself into it. "How do you figure?"

"I have my ways."

"You'll have to do something other than get me drunk. When I get tipsy, I get tired."

"They serve coffee here."

"I don't drink coffee."

"Who doesn't drink coffee?"

"I just said I don't."

"Have you tried it?"

"My parents drank it when I was growing up. In my mind, it was something old people do."

"Now you're old. You can drink coffee."

"I'll have some later. Just for you. We can be adults together."

I flashed a devilish grin without trying to stop myself.

"That's not what I meant," he said. "I'm sorry."

"I'm not complaining about it."

I could see sweat forming along the top of his forehead. "So what's good here?" He picked up the menu and looked at it. A bead began to trickle toward his brow.

"Do you like spicy food?"

"How spicy?"

"Spicy enough to make you sweat."

"All I know is I'm starving."

"Didn't they feed you at the stadium?"

"They had stuff around after the game. But I didn't play. It'd feel weird to take food meant for the guys who had worked for it."

"How many on the team didn't play?"

He dropped the menu and started thinking. "Well, we have fifty-two in uniform. Eleven start on offense. Eleven on defense. There's another five or so who rotate in and out all the time. Then there's the kicker, punter, long snapper. Special-teams players, basically second- and third-stringers. At quarterback, only one played. There's the main backup, and there's me."

"So how many didn't play?"

"Well, since the main backup is also the holder for field goals and extra points, I'd say everybody played at some point but me."

"I saw you on the sideline during the game."

He lifted his napkin from the table. Instead of placing it in his lap, he patted it against his face. "How did that happen?" he said.

"You were standing right behind the coach. That was the coach, right?"

Carson lifted a glass of ice water and took a long drink. "That was him."

His eyes began to jump from the menu to me to the menu.

"What do you do during the game?" I said.

"I watch. I listen to the plays that are being called."

"How can you hear the plays? It has to be loud down there."

"There's a radio. A speaker in my helmet. All the quarterbacks have one."

He squirmed in his seat before taking another drink of water.

"So who calls the plays?" I said.

"Sometimes the head coach. Sometimes the offensive coordinator. Here, it's the head coach. But he talks to the coordinator about it."

"Where's this coordinator?"

"Some are on the sidelines. Some are up in a booth, where they see the whole field. Ours is in the booth."

I sounded out what he told me, more monologue than conversation. "So this coordinator is upstairs. The coach talks to him. And then the coach calls the play. The quarterback on the field hears it in his helmet. And the other quarterbacks who aren't in the game hear it in their helmets, too?"

"You figure things out fast."

My eyes strayed away from the table. Then they came back to him.

"Yes," I said. "Yes, I do."

43

CARSON JEFFREY

I'd gotten back a little after eleven. I didn't know what to make of any of it. She'd grilled me about what I do during games. It seemed like she'd put a lot of thought into it. When the topic changed to something else, she seemed different than she'd been.

She kept drinking wine. She ordered a bottle for both of us. She had a lot more than me. She warmed up again, between the time we finished sharing a fancy salad and the meals showed up.

I tried to keep the conversation going. I asked where she was from. Where she went to school. She could tell I was asking questions I knew the answers to. Isn't that what lawyers do?

She kept giving me really short answers. It forced me to come up with more questions.

The wine must have been kicking in. She got more talkative. She started asking more questions. She wanted to know a lot more about me. I could feel her attitude soften some when I told her both my parents had died, and that I had no brothers or sisters or cousins or really any other family. I couldn't tell whether it was pity or something else. I also couldn't figure out whether she liked me the way I thought she did.

She had called me. I kept reminding myself of that.

By the time dessert and coffee had shown up at the table, I was starting to think she was interested in me again. I was still feeling cautious.

Before the night started, I didn't know whether I'd end up at her place or she'd come back to the hotel. I wasn't all that disappointed when neither happened. It would, if we kept spending time together. Something was holding her back. I kept wondering whether she was onto me, whether she'd figured out what I'd been doing. I told myself over and over that it couldn't have happened. I had no idea whether what I'd been telling myself was right.

After dinner, I kept thinking about how we left it. We didn't talk about another date. We didn't really talk about anything going forward. I left while she settled up with the waiter. Not because I wanted to. She told me good night when the check came, so I got up and walked out.

Maybe it would be for the best. The whole thing started out of the blue. If it ended just as fast, that would have been fine by me.

I wasn't looking for a girlfriend or a wife. I had no idea how long I'd be in Baltimore. I had no idea where I'd end up next. I'd pretty much delayed any of that until my football career was over. I'd have the rest of my life to pick a place to live and settle down and meet someone and see how it all played out.

Isn't that how it always goes? In any of the cities or towns I could choose after I'm done playing, I'd find somebody. Spouse or soulmate or whatever. It'd be half geography and half luck. Anybody could find somebody pretty much anywhere. It's how the human race continues.

It'd be better if this one doesn't keep going. She was older than me. And by more than a year or two. I tried to do the math. I was twenty-seven. She was somewhere between thirty and thirty-five. That wouldn't have been enough to scare me off, if it turned out she could be the one. It was enough to not force it. The possibility of ending up on her radar screen for different reasons made that feeling even stronger.

I had enough shit going on. I was moving to a new apartment the next day. I'd keep learning more about my new team. I'd keep trying to prove myself in the meetings and the practices. I'd try to get a chance to stick around for the rest of the season. I didn't want Johnny Motts constantly up my ass again.

Johnny Motts. I wished I'd never met him. I wished I'd never listened to him. I wished I'd never let myself get caught up in that stupid idea of easy money, with all of it paid out in cash I couldn't use.

I wished I had a way out. I would have given all the money back to just end it. I wondered if that could be the ticket? Give it all back to Johnny Motts, and he'd agree to pretend we never met. I hoped there would be a way to bring it up.

I felt tired, more tired than I'd been all week. I also knew I wouldn't be able to fall asleep. I decided to get my stuff together for the move I'd make after I went to the facility for meetings and film review. I'd be bracing for the same news I got last Monday. I wouldn't be surprised if it happened again.

My mind started to clear while I organized my stuff. I wasn't feeling as messed up and confused as when I was sitting at the table with her.

That's when my phone started to ring. I picked it up. I looked at the screen.

It was her. I didn't want to answer. I kept looking at the name I'd punched into my contacts with her number.

ALICE BALTIMORE.

I mumbled *fuck* before taking the call.

44

JOHNNY MOTTS

It was Jimmy King on the burner. "You got more for me?" I said.

"More what?"

"Did you leave something out?"

"Yeah. I forgot to tell you I quit."

"Quit playing basketball?"

"I quit doing this. It ain't for me."

I started laughing. "You can't quit, Jimmy."

"I did. It's done. I'm out."

"That weed is fucking with your brain."

"You're the one fucking with my brain. You show up here tonight out of nowhere. Acting all tough. Next time you show up, you better be packing."

"I will be."

"You think I don't have firepower?"

"I think you should think about this. Did you not get my point from before?"

"I got your point, mutherfucker. You know I got two women. What you don't know is they know it, too. Money goes a long way toward getting them to deal with it."

"Then you won't care if I make sure they know?"

"This ain't no bluff, Motts. Tell them. She's here. I can put her on. You can tell her right now."

"So she knows about me?"

He got quiet real fast. I waited for him to keep going. "She knows I got somebody else. It don't matter who tells her."

"You really fucked up this time."

"You're the one who fucked up. I don't appreciate some goombah coming to my house and telling me what to do."

"Somebody needed to tell you what to do, Jimmy. You know what you signed up for."

"I didn't sign up for getting strong armed by somebody I could rip into pieces with my bare hands if I wanted to."

"Are you saying you wanna try?"

"I'm saying I want out."

"It don't work that way. But I'm done trying to convince you otherwise. You already pulled the pin on the grenade."

"You pulled the pin on the grenade, Motts. This is the grenade going off."

"Keep thinking that. While you do, you need to be thinking about something else."

"I'm done thinking."

"Is she there, Jimmy?" I said. "Is she in the room with you?"

"I'm in the garage. I can go get her if you wanna tell her what she already knows."

"What I'd be telling her now would be something very different."

"Look, man, do whatever you gotta do."

"I don't need your permission, asshole."

"Take out an NBA player and see how that works out for you."

"I ain't talking about taking you out."

He got quiet again. "You wouldn't."

"I wonder which one you would miss more."

"I thought you guys don't fuck around with women and children."

"You've been watching too many movies, Jimmy. Maybe I'll just flip a coin or something. Or maybe I'll just pay a visit to both of them."

"Bullshit."

"You're right, Jimmy. I'm just talking shit. That's what I do. I ain't gonna do nothing. I'm just trying to change your mind, and I got no other way to do it."

He shut up again. This time, I could hear him breathing. "So that's really it? You didn't mean none of that?"

"That's it. You win. You're out. I need to let my people know, and then I'll have to find somebody else to do what you've been doing."

There was more breathing. I could tell he didn't know what to think.

I sure as hell knew what I was thinking. I also knew I wouldn't be going to the Waldorf.

45

ALICE SMITHSON

I nearly hung up as soon as I heard the ringing in the line. I could blame it on the wine. But I knew this was no half-drunken impulse.

I wanted to talk to him. I didn't like how the evening had gone. I needed him to hear me say that. I had allowed Sally Slammer to take over just enough of the conversation to screw everything up.

Yes, I had real suspicions about what I'd seen while watching the game. His explanation made me more suspicious. I now understood how it worked. He was getting information from the speaker in his helmet. It was almost as if he was signaling something to someone after he learned what the play would be.

I needed to think it all through before things could ever progress the way I thought I possibly wanted them to. Even with my misgivings about whatever he was doing, I liked him. I was attracted to him. Am I not allowed to be attracted to someone?

I also felt bad for him. He was too young to have both of his parents gone. And he was too young to be messing around with someone my age. I wondered whether he figured out that I'm seven years old than him. If he did, it didn't stop him from coming to dinner.

I told myself it would be better to make a clean break. That didn't keep me from making the call. It was barely an hour after I'd seen him. I was hoping he wouldn't answer. That'll be the test,

I thought. If he doesn't answer, we shouldn't talk again. I won't even leave a message. I'll just move on with my life. It's all up to—

"Hello?"

"Did I wake you up?"

"I'm just packing for my big move."

"I didn't know you had so much to pack."

"I like to pace myself. All that standing around today really wore me out."

"I wanted to thank you again for coming to dinner."

"I should be thanking you. You picked up the check. Smooth move to have it all worked out before I even got there. I'll have to try that some time."

"I also wanted to apologize if things got weird."

"I didn't notice anything weird. I had a nice time."

"I did, too. It was odd we didn't talk about maybe doing it again."

"I have your number. You have mine. One of us was bound to call or text."

I felt relieved to hear that. I was still keeping some distance. I had to. I needed to figure out what he was doing during the game and why. If I didn't keep telling myself that, I'd end up giving him my address and asking him to come over. I could feel my mouth trying to formulate those very words. He spoke before I could.

"How about Tuesday night? That's our day off."

"I need to see what I have going on this week."

"You don't eat dinner?"

"There's a difference between going out to a restaurant and wolfing down whatever happens to be in my apartment while I'm working."

"Well, I won't be working on Tuesday. If you want to get together, call me. Or text."

My thumb shook as I pressed it against the screen to end the call. I was glad I'd have a little time to figure out what he's been doing. Assuming I could make time to do it, given everything else I needed to do on Monday.

I decided I would. I'd gotten a head start on much of my work for the week. I had to do whatever I could to understand why he was doing what he was doing.

I was tempted to get started right away. The wine was still lurking in my bloodstream. My eyes were getting heavy. Besides, if what I eventually learned would be enough to scare me away, I wanted to enjoy one night of thinking there might have been a possible future, short-term or long-term or any term.

I got ready for bed in the warm haze I continued to feel. I caught myself wishing he was with me. Maybe it would happen Tuesday night. Maybe I'd do my due diligence and everything would be fine. Maybe my instincts, usually razor-sharp and ultra-reliable, had been hyperactive and temporarily miscalibrated.

It was enough to allow me to settle in for what I hoped would be six straight hours of sleep. I'd figure it all out on Monday. Maybe it would be fine. Maybe he wasn't doing something he shouldn't have been doing. Maybe it wouldn't be something I'd have to prosecute him for.

I sat up in bed. I hadn't really thought about that angle. It was one thing to know he was doing something that required Alice Smithson to keep away.

What if he was doing something that forced Sally Slammer to get involved?

46

CARSON JEFFREY

I slept better than I thought I would. I forced myself to stop worrying about her, about what she might know or suspect or believe. I wouldn't obsess over something I couldn't control.

The Monday move to the new apartment would have to wait until after I watched film with the rest of the team. I didn't know how long it would take. All I knew was the coach wasn't happy after the game. Not that Garrett McGarrett should have acted any differently. But why should he have expected anything other than what he got? Backup quarterbacks are backups for a reason. I was living, breathing proof of that.

The rent for my new place seemed high. That didn't really matter. I could afford it. Maybe I could try to pay with some of the cash they'd be dropping off on Tuesday. (Yes, I somehow got Johnny Motts to wait a day.)

At first, the building manager was impressed to hear I play pro ball. After I told him my name again, the look on his face said he thought I might be lying.

That's how it works for players like me. Some people, like the guy eating burgers at the airport in Minnesota, learn our names and faces from college. When we don't play in the NFL, it's just a matter of time before we're forgotten.

I wished I could be forgotten. By Johnny Motts, and by everyone else.

Eventually, I would be. By everybody. The sooner, the better.

I drove to the facility and parked in the lot. Just like in Vegas, I had the worst car of them all. They'd want that money later. I already knew more than a few guys who wish they'd bought a used Ford instead of a new Ferrari with their signing bonuses.

I went through the front door. Before I could catch a whiff of lingering gloom from the loss, the quarterbacks coach grabbed my arm just above the elbow and yanked me down a hallway. His last name was O'Shea; I knew that much. I couldn't remember whether his first name was Greg or Gary.

"Come with me," Coach Greg/Gary said.

Here we go, I thought.

"Where are we doing this?" I said.

"In my office."

"I don't even get to see the coach for this one?"

"He's too busy."

"The head coach is never too busy to cut somebody."

Coach Greg/Gary stopped and spun around. "Who's getting cut?"

"I thought I was."

He turned and started walking again. "You're not getting cut. We need you."

"Need me?"

"Didn't you hear?"

"I just walked in."

"The backup dropped a thirty-pound weight on his foot this morning. That dumb son of a bitch."

"Is he OK?"

"You ever drop a thirty-pound weight on your foot?"

"No."

"Don't do it any time soon. We need to keep you healthy and get you ready."

"Ready for what?"

"You're the new next man up. I've got to make sure you can play if we need you."

I was thrilled. And also terrified. I'd gone from bracing to get fired to being more important than before, in one fluke slip of a chunk of steel. I'd now be first in line behind the man who shit the bed against Cincinnati.

I was still a long way from getting on the field. I was also the closest I'd ever been to doing it since I took off my North Texas helmet for the last time.

Coach Greg/Gary opened the door to his office. "Get ready for a crash course."

"I know the playbook."

"Not like you need to."

"Is there a game plan for next week?"

"You'll get that tomorrow. For now, I need to be sure you know all the plays so that you'll be able to run the ones they pick for Sunday. That's our job for today. We'll go over all of it. Every play. One at a time. You need to know them inside and out."

I thought about my plans for the rest of the day. "How long will this take?"

"You got someplace better to be?"

"I'm moving into a new apartment today."

"Call whoever you need to call and tell them you'll do it tomorrow. You'll be busy for the rest of the day. I'll get us some coffee."

"I don't drink coffee."

"There's no day like today to start."

I took a seat in the chair across from a desk overloaded with notebooks and papers and other clutter. The burner was in the car. At some point, I'd need to call Johnny Motts and let him know what was going on.

I called the building manager and told him something came up. He thought it meant I didn't want the place. He started yelling about how he had three other people ask about it since I said

I'd take it. I told him I still wanted it, but that I couldn't make it there today. He laughed while saying he thought I'd already been cut. I promised him that hadn't happened, not yet.

Given what being so close to playing could mean for my second job, I had a feeling I'd soon be hoping it would.

47

JOHNNY MOTTS

I went straight home and started thinking about my next move. Jimmy King didn't just cross the line. He jumped over it with both fucking feet.

Do I tell Carmine? Do I handle it myself? Do I take out one of King's women? Do I do both of them?

I've got another headache. Maybe I should just put a bullet in my skull and be done with it.

I sat down at the table in the kitchen. I needed to try to think this through, step by step.

First, should I tell Carmine about Jimmy King quitting? That'll make it look like I can't control my guys. So, no, I can't tell Carmine.

Second, should I take out Jimmy King? Not after what happened with Larry Ballentine. I don't need another guy to disappear. Besides, he won't go away quiet like Ballentine. One of King's girlfriends will make a stink. Maybe both.

I'd bet the one he lives with knows all about his side gig. She probably told him to stop doing it.

Third, should I take out his girlfriends? If one of them ends up dead, he'll play ball again. If he don't, I'll get the other one. If that don't do it, then maybe he goes away.

I don't need the heat from Carmine. It all goes back to Larry

Ballentine ducking his head. That whole thing screwed me up. Then Jeffrey gets cut and I decide to handle it myself because I don't want no more trouble. Now I got this thing with Jimmy King and I don't know what the fuck to do with it.

I hope none of my other guys start screwing up. It's like that thing where a bunch of dominoes is lined up and once they start falling they just go and go and you can't make it stop.

I can stop it. I can get it under control. I need to get it under control with Jimmy King. I'll be able to keep it under control with Jeffrey once I know more about his new friend in Baltimore.

Am I willing to cross that line? Can I take out one of Jimmy King's women? Didn't I already decide I could? The way this shit is going, it could come down to them or me.

The one that don't live with him got a kid. What would it be like for that kid to grow up with no mom? I'm pretty fucked up as it is. I'd be even more fucked up if I had to grow up without my mother, God rest her soul. The kid needs a mother. She lives.

It won't be easy to take out the one that lives with him. I need somebody watching his place. I don't know whether she travels with him to road games. Ain't that kind of shit frowned on? It ain't no tour bus, with friends and family hanging around everywhere. Or is it? I'll have Lego Billy see if she stays there the next time Jimmy King hits the road.

This shit is about to get way more expensive. Between paying somebody in Baltimore to watch Jeffrey and paying somebody in Denver to watch Jimmy King, I'm gonna end up buying a whole fucking fleet of Mercedes. Maybe when this shit is over, I'll finally go out and buy one for myself. A nice one. That big ugly box that costs like four hundred large.

If I do, it means I'll still be around to do it. That's my goal. Stick around long enough to spend my money. Life's too short to not enjoy what you got. This line of work can make it even shorter.

Eat, drink, and be merry, because tomorrow you'll be dead. For everybody else, it's a figure of speech. For me, maybe it ain't.

That word stuck in my head. Tomorrow. That's when I'll call Lego Billy and tell him to watch Jimmy King's place starting the day before Denver's next road game. If he goes and she stays, I'll go back and make sure he has one hell of a surprise when he gets home.

I liked that plan. I felt as good as I could, with all the shit that's been happening. That's when the fucking phone rang again. I looked at it.

What the fuck is Carmine calling me this late for? There wasn't no way I could pretend I didn't see it.

I took a breath and answered. I tried to sound happy to hear from him.

"When was the last time you talked to your guy in Baltimore?"

"Which guy in Baltimore?" I knew it was a dumb thing to say as the words came out.

"How many guys you got in Baltimore?"

"You mean the guy who just went?" That was dumb, too. I guess I was buying time.

"Again, how many guys you got in Baltimore?"

"I talked to him the night before the game. He delivered, right? Before the game and during the game. He was solid, like always."

"You don't know what happened there today?"

"I ain't heard from him."

"I thought you had these guys under control."

"Did he get cut again or something?"

"Are you playing dumb with me, Johnny?"

"I ain't playing nothing. I ain't heard from him."

"Then that ain't good. After what went down today, he should have called you."

"It's almost morning there. Maybe he'll call when he wakes up."

"If he don't, you got a problem with your guys. You do a

good job lining them up. I ain't complaining about none of that. But lining them up is just the start. It's on you to make sure they always let you know when shit happens that could affect our arrangement."

"They always tell me."

"Yeah, that's right. Whether you tell me is a different thing."

I noticed I was sweating. Real sweat, running down my face and all through my mustache.

"I apologized for all that."

"You apologized because you had to. I'm gonna assume you ain't holding out on me again. But that means your guy is holding out on you. Either way, it ain't good."

"Whatever it is, I'll handle it."

"Like you handled Larry Ballentine?"

"I told you that was an accident."

"We don't need no more accidents. I hope you learned from the accident you had that nothing gets handled that way unless I know what you plan to do."

"We're on the same team here."

"Same team, huh? Well, just like your guy in Baltimore, people can get cut from teams if they fuck up enough times."

"I swear, I don't know nothing about whatever happened today."

"The sooner you do, the better off you'll be."

He hung up on me. I looked at the burner. I checked the time. I don't care if the kid's asleep. I need to know what in the fuck is going on. And I need to know why I'm finding out about it from my boss.

48

ALICE SMITHSON

I tried to sleep. Three different times, I closed my eyes and counted backwards from two thousand, like my grandfather taught me to do. Every time I made it to ten and nine and eight, I was still wide awake. I didn't want to do the math on how long I'd spent trying to fall asleep.

I found out when I looked at my phone. It was after two. I admitted I wouldn't have any chance at falling asleep until I did what I had to do.

I opened the app on the smart TV. I called up the football game. I fiddled with the options until I matched the camera aimed at where Carson had been standing on one side of the screen with the game on the other. I pulled a legal pad and a pen from the top drawer of the old wooden desk my grandfather had given me. I started charting the connection between Carson's hand signals and whatever happened next. The pattern became obvious. I stopped what I was doing after the first quarter.

My instincts had been accurate. As usual. He was letting someone know whether the next play would be a run or a pass. I didn't know much about football, but I knew that much. The quarterback gives the ball to another player, or he throws it.

Carson was providing information to someone. They were doing something with it. Probably making bets in real time.

Every time, he knew. Every time, they knew. I had no idea who they were. He did. It was whoever he was working with. Whoever was paying him, most likely.

There could be other reasons. Maybe he was being blackmailed, threatened. Maybe he owed someone money. Whatever it was, he was breaking the law at the behest of someone else.

I turned off the TV. I stared at my notes. Why would he ever talk to me, about anything? Why would he meet with me? Did he not realize how obvious this was?

I had plenty of things to figure out. I couldn't ignore what I knew. I couldn't look the other way. I couldn't abandon my duty, my oath.

The easier path would have been to forget what I'd seen. Forget him. Steer clear. Ignore all of it. How had no one else noticed this?

I opened my laptop and reminded myself of his work history since leaving North Texas. Three-plus years with Las Vegas. If I went back through every game, I'd figure out when this started. How long it had been going on. How deeply he had stepped into quicksand that was now starting to pull me into it with him.

I wished I hadn't gone out with Will. I envied the oblivion I could have had. Knowledge is power, they say. Knowledge also complicates lives, creates dilemmas, forces people to do things they'd rather not do.

It wasn't really a dilemma. The law was being broken. When he was working in Las Vegas, it was out of my jurisdiction. Now, this man I couldn't quit thinking about had brought his illegal scheme into my district. I wouldn't ignore it.

I checked the upcoming schedule. Their next game was on the road, in Kansas City. After that, they'd be back in Baltimore. Maybe he'd stop. Maybe the fact that he knew who I was, what I did for a living, what I could do about it would get him to quit.

It didn't matter. He'd already done it. I already knew about it. I had to do something. I had to tell someone. Right was right, wrong was wrong. It was wrong for him to do it. It would be wrong for me to do nothing about it.

I shoved the lid of my laptop shut. I'd finally tripped across a man who made me think like a woman, and Sally Slammer was about to screw everything up. Or perhaps make everything right.

I never dreamed I'd be in a predicament like this. Not with anyone I cared about. Every criminal I'd ever prosecuted had been someone I didn't know, someone I never would have known. I hadn't considered what would happen if someone I knew was into something that landed on the wrong side of the line I'd spent my life guarding.

The only way out of this would be to quit. To walk away from my obligations. I laughed that the idea even crossed my mind. It was too late. I knew what I knew. I couldn't pretend I didn't. Even if I resigned the next day, I'd have to share what I'd found with someone who would deal with it instead of me.

Could I make it any better for him if I was the one to deal with it? I could confront him about it. I could tell him what he needed to do. To basically turn himself in, strike a plea deal before it was too late. To cooperate with the effort to bring down whoever it was that had him doing whatever he was doing.

If they're doing it with him, they're probably doing it with others. It was likely a broader operation. He could be the key to bringing it all down, if he was willing.

I had the ability to make him willing. The power to persuade him. The authority, courtesy of the federal government, to tell him there was only one way out of the turmoil he'd created, regardless of why or when or how long it had been going on.

I'd be doing him a favor. Someone else would figure it out, at some point. Someone else wouldn't be so careful to engineer the best possible outcome for him.

That's the power of being a prosecutor. I could find a way to balance doing the right thing generally with doing the right thing by him specifically.

Before any of that, I had to figure out how to raise it with him. How to set aside my own personal desires or urges or instincts and do the right thing. I'd then have to persuade him to do the right thing.

The first part wouldn't be easy, the second part would be even harder.

49

CARSON JEFFREY

I got back to the rental car after dark. I sat in the driver's seat and looked at the burner. I needed to tell Johnny Motts I'd been bumped to second string. It wouldn't make much sense to rehearse it. The only approach with a dumbass like Johnny Motts was to dive head first into the conversation and hope to swim to shallow water.

I looked at the burner again. Just like that, I decided not to call him. I didn't really have a reason. If I didn't feel like talking to him, why should I? He'd find out soon enough. There was no rule that he had to find out from me.

When I got back to the hotel, I thought about Alice. I thought about calling her. I decided to think about it some more. I ended up thinking about it while I was lying on that tiny bed. Before I knew it, I was asleep.

The phone rang in the middle of the night. I grabbed for it.

"Don't tell me you got fired again."

I was still coming out of it. "Who's this?"

"Who the fuck do you think it is?"

I started to wake up a little. I realized I was talking on the burner.

"Sorry. I was asleep."

"Did they cut you already?"

"Not yet."

"I know something's going on. And I know you should have told me by now."

"The backup dropped a barbell on his foot. I'm the backup now."

"You're still on the team, right?"

"It's different now. I have to be ready to play. I can't just hang around on the sideline and make hand signals. I have to be ready to go if something happens to the guy who's playing."

"You're either in the game or you ain't. If you ain't, you keep doing what you've been doing."

"I'll be more involved now. I'm the backup. I have to be paying even more attention to what's going on. If anything happens to the guy who's playing, I have to go in."

"I don't see how that changes anything. You'll still have that speaker, right? You'll know the plays before anybody else?"

"You don't get it. I need to be locked in. I need to know the flow of the game. I need to pretend I'm on the field, because I never know when I might be."

"Fuck the flow of the game," Johnny Motts said. "You got two jobs. You've been doing both of them just fine. Keep doing them."

"What happens if the quarterback gets hurt?"

"Not my problem."

"I'll have to play."

"You better hope that don't happen."

"If the guy who's playing gets hurt, I have to go in."

It sounded like Johnny Motts threw the phone down. I waited for him to pick it up.

"If you're playing, you just do the same fucking thing," he said. "You make the same signals."

"You don't get what it means to play quarterback. I'll have fifty different things to worry about."

"Consider this thing number fifty-one."

"Think about this, Johnny. I'm in the huddle. I get the play from the sideline. I tell it to my teammates. I go to the line of scrimmage. When do I make the signal?"

"You just answered your own question."

"You want me to make the signal standing in the middle of the field before the play, with everyone watching?"

"What's wrong with that?"

"The coaches are smart. They'll figure it out. They'll be all over whatever we do."

"Alls we need to know is whether it's a run or a pass."

"Everybody else will know."

Johnny Motts got quiet for a little while. "Maybe we need a different signal."

"Whatever it is, somebody will figure it out. It's one thing if I'm standing on the sideline. If I'm out in the open, whatever I do, they'll all see it."

"I never figured you'd play."

"I didn't, either."

"Can't you shit the bed in practice or something? Get knocked down to third string?"

"If I do that, wouldn't they just cut me? Then we'll be right back where we were."

"You never said nothing to me about playing."

"I never thought I'd be playing. I never even banked on being the backup. Quarterbacks don't get hurt like they used to. Everything is set up to keep them healthy."

"Keep them healthy, huh?"

I cringed a little bit at how he said it. "I can still do the signals as the backup. But if I get on the field, there's nothing else I can do."

"If you get on the field, there's nothing else I can do, either."

"What does that mean?"

"Whatever it means."

"I'm not following you."

"I have a feeling you are. This business has risks, my friend. You already knew that. If you didn't, you do now. Shit happens, right? In this life, the shit has a real specific smell."

I tried not to listen to what he was saying. I didn't want to think about what it meant. It was too late for any of it. I should have known. Maybe, deep down, I did.

I'd always wanted to play. I never thought I would. Now, for the first time, I was one step away. And if that next step ever happens, it could be the last step I take.

"I'll keep taking care of my end of this," I said.

"You'd better. And you'd better make sure you let me know what to do with this money. I hate to see someone take so much risk without getting his reward."

The call ended. The threats he made seemed even louder in the silence.

I needed a plan. I needed a way to escape.

I thought about Alice. What would she say if I told her what's going on? What could she do?

What would they do if she tries to do something?

I'd spent too much time thinking about what could happen to me if she finds out who I'm working with. I hadn't thought about what could happen if who I'm working with finds out about her.

I decided to start doing that.

50

JOHNNY MOTTS

I can live with the kid being the backup quarterback. Will he have other shit to worry about? Sure. He can still do both of his jobs.

I don't get why Carmine acted like it was such a big deal. The kid is one step closer to playing. So what? It happens. Quarterbacks get hurt. If we're gonna have quarterbacks on the payroll, some of them will play.

I got spoiled by the kid being third string as long as he was. I also got lucky. I didn't know it, because he was our first quarterback. I need to expect it once we get more. That's something I also gotta do. Get more.

Knowing the plays before they happen is a real bonus. It's one thing to know who's hurt and who ain't and who's gonna get the ball and who's gonna be just standing there with his dick in his hand. Knowing what every play is gonna be before it starts makes a difference. Our people see it, they lock in the action, and we win.

Carmine tells them to fuck up once every four or five plays. The house always get suspicious if it loses too much. That's why we're always making new accounts in phony names. Or maybe it's real names of people who don't know they got accounts. I don't know, and I don't care. That ain't my part of it.

I sort of wish it was. I wouldn't have so many fucking headaches if I was dealing with that end.

I hope Carmine knows that. Maybe he's just giving me a hard time to keep me in line. Same as I do to the people I need to keep in line. I hope he never has to do to me what I might have to do to keep some of my people in line.

This Jimmy King thing ain't gonna be easy. It also ain't the first thing I ever dealt with that wasn't easy. Yeah, I'm crossing a line. So what? What's he gonna do? I'll make it look like she left and never came back. He'll know the truth.

What's he gonna do, turn state's witness and blow the whistle? He'll be pissing away his entire career. They'll kick him out of the league for good. Besides, he won't want his other woman to end up going away, too.

I need to read people in this job. My read on Jimmy King is he don't get what he's dealing with. Once he does, he'll get in line.

It would be easier if I didn't have the Larry Ballentine thing on my record. If I make Jimmy King disappear without Carmine's blessing, Carmine won't be so understanding.

Maybe he will. I'm the guy on the front lines, making shit happen. Without me lining up the players, this thing goes nowhere. They need me to keep doing what I'm doing. I ain't sure of much, but I'm pretty damn sure I can't keep doing what I'm doing if I'm dead.

Carmine answers to somebody. I still don't know who. I don't know if I'll ever get a chance to figure it out. I do know Carmine won't wanna get squeezed, same as I don't wanna get squeezed. If Carmine don't have somebody who's doing what I'm doing, he's gonna get squeezed. So, yeah, he needs me.

I wish this shit was easier. But this is how I prove myself. Not to them but to me. If I'm ever gonna be what I wanna be, I have to solve problems. If I can't, why am I even trying?

I can't be a foot soldier my whole life. I want Carmine's spot. I wanna be more than Carmine. I don't know how or when that can happen. I do know that taking care of my own shit is the best way to take the next step, whether the next step gets offered to me or whether I just grab it.

That might be the answer. I don't like thinking about it. It wouldn't be the first time somebody who was trying to get ahead took out the boss. Plenty of guys in this world have done it. It's probably one of the reasons Carmine is trying to keep me down. He don't want me coming to the conclusion that I can get where I wanna be a lot faster and easier by just making him go away.

That's why they harp on loyalty so much. They want guys who'll do their jobs, sure. They also want guys who won't get ideas. Ideas like the one I might be starting to get. Here I am, thinking about doing something that breaks our stupid code to leave civilians alone. I should be thinking about doing something that fits with what we do. Not all of us, only the ones who get to the point where they don't feel like waiting for what they want.

I still ain't ready to make that kind of move. If you fuck something like that up, you're done. For every guy who pulls off a mutiny, there's another five or ten or maybe twenty that tried and failed and ended up cut into pieces and thrown in a lake or buried in the desert.

For now, I need to stick to my plan. Do whatever I have to do to get Jimmy King in line. Do whatever I have to do to keep Carson Jeffrey in line. And figure out who Carmine is answering to. Because that's the person I'll be answering to, if I decide at some point that the only way to deal with Carmine is to put an end to Carmine.

I'm a soldier in a different kind of army. I'll march and take orders. I'll do whatever I need to do to make sure I'm following the orders. And then, at the right time, I'll make sure I'm the one giving the orders.

51

ALICE SMITHSON

My office stunk again. I didn't care. Will sat across from me. The look on his face told me he didn't feel the same way. But he wasn't going to go searching for fresh air, not after I told him the news.

"You met someone?" he said.

"I met someone."

"When did this happen?"

"Friday night."

He now looked more confused than repulsed. "I know I had plenty to drink. But I have a pretty clear memory of you leaving alone."

"I still met someone."

Will considered it a riddle to solve. "Right before you went, you were talking to the one in the tight shirt. Incredible skin. Shiny face. Too much moisturizer. An athlete. I know that look, all too well. You didn't seem to be interested. I know your body language all too well, too."

"You're getting warm."

Will moved his palms toward his cheeks and worked them up and down, kneading the thickening flesh. His eyes bulged. "The overwatered Marine?"

"Another athlete."

"There's no basketball team around here."

"He plays football. He's a quarterback."

Will stopped moving his hands. He squeezed his fingers into where his jawline once resided. "That's not like you."

"He reminds me of someone I used to know."

"Sounds like he's someone you want to get to know."

"I checked him out. He's from Kentucky. Went to school in Texas."

"Good ol' boy. Shit kicker. Made in America."

"How many other clichés do you have?"

"I work in threes. It's a trial tactic."

"There's another adjective that applies. One that doesn't fit the profile."

Will put his hands together. He rolled his fingers against his fingers as he considered my words. "That sounds like it's not good," he said, "which makes it even better."

"The adjective would be criminal."

"That bohunk with the buzzcut? I can't imagine he's ever jaywalked."

"He's connected."

"To what? A plow?"

"Connected connected."

"Bullshit," he said, practically spitting the word at me.

"He's feeding information to someone during games. Inside information. What we would call in an insider trading case material, non-public information. For gambling."

Will jumped out of his chair. "He told you that?"

"I figured it out on my own."

"How in the world could you figure out something like that?"

I shot him a look.

"I know," he said. "I learned a long time ago to never doubt your instincts."

"It's not instincts. I watched the game on Sunday, before I had dinner with him."

"How was dessert?"

"There was none. And there won't be any."

"You, my dear, need a big, fat piece of cheesecake more than anyone I know."

"I'm serious, Will. I picked up on it while I was watching the game. When I got home, I couldn't sleep. I went back and confirmed it. He knows what the plays are going to be. He's giving signals to someone."

"Who?"

"I don't know that part. Someone who's taking that information and betting with it, I assume. In real time. Locking in whether the next play is going to be a run or a pass."

"I thought you didn't know anything about football."

"I know enough to know that's how it works. The team with the ball—"

"The offense."

"Thank you. They can run it, or they can pass it. He has a speaker in his helmet. He knows what the play is going to be. When he finds out, he makes a signal."

"What does he do?"

"He puts his hand on his helmet. Those bars in the front. He takes it away when it's a run. He leaves it there when it's a pass."

"Sounds like a high-tech operation," he said.

"I can't believe no one has figured it out."

"You're sure it's not a coincidence?"

"He did it every single time. Every single play. The entire game."

"Well, this really is interesting."

"I can think of plenty of other words for it."

"What are you going to do?"

"I know what I'm not going to do."

"Did you break it off?"

"There's nothing to break off. We had one dinner."

Will paced around on the carpet. "You know, it really does stink in here."

"I can't act like I don't know what I know. I have to do something."

"I need to see this for myself."

"It's happening. I can't just let it keep happening."

"When's the next game?"

"Sunday. They play in Kansas City. They're not here again until the week after."

"So you have some time."

"I still can't let it happen, even if it's not happening in our territory. I feel like we need to let someone in Missouri know."

"What would they do? Go to the locker room before the game and tell him not to do it?"

"I don't know what to do. That's why I'm telling you. We need a good plan."

Will's head jerked toward me. "We?"

"You got me into this mess by making me go out on Friday night."

"Well, then, we don't have many options here. I can already tell letting this one go won't be one of them."

"One of the reasons I'm telling you is to make sure I won't do that."

"The Alice part wants to," he said. "The Sally Slammer part would never let that happen. And it's the right thing to do. However you found out about this, I agree you need to do something."

"So what do we do?"

As I finished, there was knocking. Crisp and sharp. We both flinched.

The door pushed open. Roger McClelland stepped inside. I noticed his reaction to the assault on his nose. He raised an eyebrow at Will. I fought back a laugh.

"Can you come see me when you're done here?" McClelland said.

"I'll be over in five minutes," Will replied.

"I meant her. Not you."

"Silly me. Her office. Not mine. Mine smells much better than hers."

I glared at Will. "I'm sorry for the smell," I said. "I don't know what it is. It comes and it goes."

"I'll make sure maintenance looks into it right away," McClelland said.

I didn't want to tell him maintenance had already been there, several times. Maybe when the boss tells maintenance to do something, it'll finally get done. I liked the idea that, once maintenance got a direct request from the man in charge to fix an issue in my office, they'd take future requests from me more seriously.

"Thank you," I said. "I'll be over in five minutes."

"Take your time, the rest of my morning is open. Besides, it looks as if the two of you were about to crack a case wide open."

"There's a look for that?" Will said.

"No," McClelland said. "It was something to say. But if you are, then by all means get back to it."

Will stared at the closed door after Roger McClelland was gone. When Will turned back to me, a dopey smile littered his face. "I'd give my left testicle to see that man in a Speedo for five seconds."

"That's a lot to give up for only five seconds."

"A memory lasts forever."

"I need your brainpower for other things. I'm too close to this. I need good advice on what to do about this predicament."

"There's my favorite word," he said. "I knew you'd say it. You always do, eventually."

"You really need to grow up. Besides, it's not the only word in the English language that has a 'dick' in the middle."

"But it's my favorite one that does."

52

CARSON JEFFREY

I spent part of Tuesday taking my stuff to the new apartment. I also got a new bag of cash. More bills I couldn't use for anything big without setting off alarms. Of course, those bells and whistles might already be making noise, given the questions I got during my dinner date.

I hadn't thought much about Alice since Sunday night. Monday had been a whirlwind. The next day ended up being the time to do everything I couldn't get to on Monday. I still had to make time to learn the offense well enough to run it, if the next man up ended up being the next man down.

She said she'd call if she had time. I didn't realize I'd be the one who was too busy. But it was good I wouldn't be sitting around, wondering if the phone might ring.

Coach Greg/Gary (I still didn't know) hounded me all morning and into the afternoon about coming back to the facility. It was technically our day off, but guys at the bottom of the roster shouldn't be quoting union rules.

I promised him I'd get there as soon as I could, and I did. It still wasn't early enough for Coach Greg/Gary. I ignored his bitching and got to work. I showed him I'd pretty much mastered the offense. I fired off the names of plays and concepts and checks and adjustments. He was impressed enough to quit complaining. By the time we wrapped up, all he could say was, "Let's see how you do on the practice field."

Sometimes at practice the backup quarterback runs the scout-team offense, playing the part of the quarterback the defense will be facing. This week, we (not they) didn't have that luxury. I need to know our offense. The free agent we brought in will play the role of the Kansas City quarterback. I sensed from my meetings with Coach Greg/Gary that I'd get some of the reps with the starting offense, if only to show I could do the job.

I was trying not to think too much about the possibility of playing. I kept telling myself it wouldn't happen. The game has changed. No, quarterbacks don't get injured like they used to. They kept making new rules to protect them. During practice, the quarterback never gets touched, not intentionally. It's the safest job on the field, because it's also the most important.

I knew all of that, very well. It was one of the reasons I'd never come close to playing. And that's what made my current situation even more uncomfortable. If the one player most protected from injury gets injured again, my football job might keep me from doing my non-football job. Which would put my safety at risk in a very different way.

I wished I could get Johnny Motts to understand. I knew that was impossible. If I ended up playing, Johnny Motts would expect me to come up with a way to signal run or pass. If I didn't, there would be consequences.

Consequences would come, either way. If I signaled the plays while playing, someone would figure out what I was doing. Then what? Alice was already throwing too many darts that were landing too close to the bull's-eye. If I were to tip plays while playing—with the face mask routine or something else—someone would figure it out, sooner or later and probably not later than sooner.

Hell, my own coaches would probably be the first ones to see it. They'd tell me to stop. Then what would I do? Keep doing it and say it's a nervous habit I can't control? Claim to have a very specific form of Tourette's syndrome? Maybe I should start shouting *fuck* and *shit* and *piss* from time to time to make that excuse more believable.

I was standing on the sideline of the practice field on Wednesday. I was trying to force myself to focus on the fact that I'd soon have to show them I could be trusted to perform. It was the one thing I'd wished for, for years. I was praying it'd be the last thing they'd ask me to do.

I didn't hear the coach calling for me to get out there. I didn't hear it the second time, either. I didn't realize what was going on until one of the offensive linemen, whose name I didn't know, grabbed the top of my shoulder pads and told me to get my ass moving.

That snapped me out of it, even if my expression wasn't making things any better. I could hear some of the others behind me laughing. The guys on the field who were waiting for me seemed pissed. The new guy became in the blink of an eye the most unpopular man on the team.

"Jeffrey!" Garrett McGarrett shouted. "Are you waiting for an engraved invitation? Let's fucking go!"

When I tried to fasten my chin strap, I realized it was already in place. I heard more laughing. I ran too fast onto the field, tripping over my own feet and nearly falling down. The sounds of even more laughter filled the inside of my helmet. I could feel my cheeks glowing.

I ignored the voices of the men in the huddle. Insults, complaints, whatever they were, I wouldn't let any of it register. At that point, nothing they said would have made me feel any worse.

If anything, I felt some relief. I was surprised. After that display, they'd never let a schmuck like me play in a game. They'd just put a running back out there to hand the ball off over and over.

A weird kind of calm came from the idea that maybe I wouldn't have to play, after all. That no matter what happened, I'd still be on the sideline, able to do everything I need to do.

I was too frazzled to notice it working like a reset button. It settled me down, letting me do what I was supposed to do. McGarrett, who also runs the offense, yelled out the next play to the entire team. So much for the defense not knowing what's coming.

It was a pass. I was supposed to look to the receiver to the left. He was running a post route, straight at first and then on a diagonal toward the middle of the field. Since the defense knew the call, they knew who the primary receiver was. The cornerback played to the inside, and the safety (Lefty) cheated over that way. I could tell they expected somebody to make an easy interception.

I didn't throw it there. The next step in the play was to look to the receiver who'd been lined up on the far right side of the field. That one was moving on a slant toward the middle. It didn't help that the defense already knew he was the second look.

So I skipped straight to the third option. The tight end had started from my left, three players down from the man who'd snapped me the ball. The tight end had run straight down the field. With Lefty cheating over toward the first guy in the pattern, the tight end was all alone. I fired a sharp, clean spiral. It hit him in stride. He sprinted to the other end of the field.

The other offensive players got quiet. Lefty cursed. I smiled.

And then I heard Garrett McGarrett's voice from behind me, getting closer and louder. "Goddammit, Jeffrey, what's the progression on that play?"

My smile was gone. "Post on one side, slant on the other, then the tight end," I said. "They jumped the post."

"Why the hell didn't you throw the slant?"

"I knew the tight end would be open. The safety cheated that way."

"That's not the fucking play," McGarrett said, tiny drops of spit hitting my face. "These plays are designed to go a specific way. First read, second read, third read. You only get to the third read if the second read is covered."

"The third read was open," I said. "I knew he'd be open."

"This ain't about who's open. This is about figuring out whether you know how to run the plays I've designed and called. I need to know you know my offense. We're not playing on a sandlot here, son. This is professional football."

I wanted to keep arguing the point. I knew I'd get nowhere. I also knew I should've done things the way they'd been drawn up. But I wanted to prove myself to my teammates. If I ended up playing, they needed to believe in me. Even though I had the head coach up my ass, I had a feeling the guys who might be counting on me to perform liked what they saw. The safety tried to get cute. I made him pay.

We ran several more plays. The defense always knew what was coming. The defensive backs didn't get as cute. Through it all, I showed that I understood what the combination of words and letters and numbers required me to do. I proved I can run the offense the way McGarrett wanted it. Although he didn't offer any compliments, he didn't have anything bad to say, either. That counts as a win in this league, especially with this coach.

I felt some satisfaction once it was time to leave the field for the quarterback who'd be playing in Kansas City. It seemed like my teammates on offense trusted me, and that my teammates on defense were pissed at me for getting the better of them.

Maybe that's why the defensive players got a little more aggressive during the next series of plays. Maybe that's why one specific player pushed a little too hard against the man who was trying to block him. And maybe that's why, even though the defenders knew to never touch the quarterback during practice, there was no way to keep an offensive lineman who'd been overpowered from losing his balance and falling down.

When he fell, he fell hard. Right into Rich Wettle's knee.

My head jerked back to the field when I heard the screaming. I saw Wettle grabbing his knee in a way that told me everything I needed to know, and that showed me the last thing I wanted to see.

53

JOHNNY MOTTS

I got to Denver a day early. I packed my piece in the suitcase I checked. I stuck my laptop in the bag I carried onto first class.

Yeah, I sprung for first class again. I don't care no more. This whole thing is sucking up too much of my money. I might as well piss it away in style.

I wanted to get to town early so I could get my shit together. It'll all end up being a waste of time if Jimmy King takes her to Dallas with him. I still don't wanna fly up there the same day I do it. I need a decent night's sleep before something like that.

I don't know nothing about her. That bothers me a little bit. I don't even know what she looks like. I don't know how big she is. She might be taller than me. Can she handle a gun? Would she use a shotgun or a pistol? Jimmy King acted like he's got some kind of an arsenal in his house. Will he have her ready to grab one of them and use it?

What about a knife? Or a hammer? Or something like an iron? I got hit by one of them fucking things once. It's one of the main reasons I ain't never getting married again.

I don't even know her name. I just know she lives with him. What if somebody else is there instead? His sister or his cousin or her sister or her cousin or just somebody who offered to take care of a really nice house for a day or two?

If Jimmy King took me serious, he ain't dumb enough to set somebody up like that. Maybe he is. I already know he's dumb. Hopefully he ain't completely dumb.

I told him at the end of the call I didn't mean none of it. Did he really believe me when I said that? I wouldn't believe somebody like me, not right after I said it's coming. It's way better for me if he believed it when I took it back. It's way better for whoever is in that house if he didn't.

I need to be ready for whatever. I always am. Whatever you don't expect is always what happens.

I stayed at a decent hotel, not some fleabag. Any day could be my last day on this fucked-up planet. Any day I try to make it someone else's last day on this fucked-up planet increases the chances.

I never killed a woman. I sort of wish I had. It'd make it easier now.

Fuck that. People is people. Meat is meat. Man, woman, kid. All the same. If somebody has to go, they have to go. If this one don't go, Jimmy King might not get in line. And then I might be the next cow that gets sent to the slaughterhouse.

The hotel has some fancy name. I ain't even sure how to pronounce it. I just want a big room with a good bathroom and a comfortable bed.

This place got all three. After I christened the toilet and rolled on the mattress to test it out, I ordered a steak and a bottle of wine. I checked in with a few of my guys while I waited for the food.

I passed along the info to Frank. I don't know whether he's in Vegas or someplace else. He never says nothing but *yep*. Even when it makes no fucking sense to say *yep*. If I asked him if he wants a bullet between the eyes, he'd probably say *yep*.

Right after ten, I heard from Lego Billy. His person in Denver said when Jimmy King left that day, nobody was with him. I should've told them to watch more than today. Knowing Jimmy

King is gone don't tell me for sure who's still there. I assume it's his woman because I don't know who else it would be.

I rented a BMW this time, one with tinted windows. I complained about how expensive it was. The girl behind the desk said they got a nice selection of Fords. I told her there ain't no such thing as a nice Ford. But this project is already costing me an arm and a leg. I might as well add another toe to the pile.

I stole a license plate off another car at the hotel and put it in the trunk. I found a place to swap it out for the tag on the BMW before I went over there.

I got a decent breakfast. If you get hungry on a stakeout, you get sloppy. I wasn't really on a stakeout, but it was the same idea. I was gonna be waiting for the right time to make my move.

I'd need to do some guessing. I know from my last visit there ain't much cooking going on in that kitchen. I figure she'll order food at some point before the game starts.

Is there a chance she's got leftovers in there? People with real money don't eat leftovers. It's one of the best parts of having real money. Just get more food, even if it's the exact same food you'd pull out of the refrigerator and stick in the microwave.

My laptop was on the seat across from me. I pulled it over and opened it up. It was time to use some of them two years I wasted at that fucking computer school.

Everybody's got a network in their house. Plenty of them don't have passwords. The ones that do usually got something easy enough to tell somebody who's trying to use it so that they can post a video on whatever social-media bullshit people use these days to show off where they are and what they're doing and what they got.

Ten choices popped up right away. KingMe was the obvious pick. It showed a lock next to the name. I clicked on it. It asked for a password. I sat there and thought for a second or two. What would be the easiest password to tell somebody who was at his house and wanted to know how to get on the KingMe network?

I typed *KingMe123*. I clicked the button. It worked.

Maybe I ain't such a dumbass after all.

I tried to remember what I needed to do to get inside and find the list of websites. It took me a while to get all the steps right. I almost gave up a couple times. It was making me sweat. I was getting a little claustrophobic in that car. The fact that I knew I couldn't get out and run around made me wanna do it even more.

I finally got in. I started scrolling through the websites. There was one type of thing I was looking for. I kept searching. She'd been using the network. She'd been buying a ton of shit on Amazon. If nothing else, he'd save plenty of money once she was gone.

I kept looking. More Amazon shit. I didn't look at what she bought. I should have.

That's when I saw the word I was looking for. Door. DoorDash.com. She was going straight to the website and not using the app. All in all I didn't feel too lucky, but I'd take whatever chunk of luck I could find.

I found an order from the night before. I kept looking. There was another one that morning. Another one from the day before. I finally put it in as a search term. They had so many DoorDash orders that Jimmy King should have just bought the fucking company.

It showed me what I need to know. Now I know what this day will be. I brung a bottle to piss in. If I need to do more than that, it'll have to wait. It ain't too hot or too cold out, so I won't need to put the engine on. I cracked the window a little for some air. I didn't bring no cigarettes. I got a cigar. I don't want that smoke coming out of the car, and I don't feel like hot boxing myself with it.

I'll have it after. A victory cigar. It's a win I really need. I'm already halfway there.

54

ALICE SMITHSON

Will and I didn't finalize anything after Roger McClelland left. I couldn't really focus, not after hearing he wanted to see me. I knew what to do about Carson. I didn't like it, but it had to be done.

The boss's visit made me very curious. Nothing had happened with Henderson Robertson, as far as I knew. Maybe Roger McClelland had heard something.

Whatever it was, it had gotten him to personally show up at my office again. And he wasn't looking for a stapler.

Walking on the carpeted hallways that led to his office, I wondered if I'd done something to accidentally get myself in trouble. If that's what had happened, I was about to find out.

Mrs. Maxwell sat outside the main door. She was large and solid and everyone in the building was afraid of her. She'd take a bullet for Roger McClelland, if anyone could ever muster the nerve to pull the trigger after hearing her speak.

"He's expecting you," she said with a voice deeper than most of the men I knew. "He told me to tell you to go in."

"Thank you," I said. She didn't look up.

"He seems to be in a pretty good mood, for a change. Let's try and keep it that way."

I was afraid of her, too. All I could muster was, "I'll do my best."

He invited me in before I could knock on a door that wasn't

completely shut. I pushed it open and walked inside. I'd never been there before. I didn't know what to expect. I glanced around the room without being too obvious about it. His office wasn't anything special. It was just bigger than the rest.

He could tell what I was doing. "You expected something nicer," he said.

"Someone once told me an office is a workplace, not a showroom."

"Sounds like someone I'd like to know."

"My grandfather says it. He helped raise me. He has a lot of sayings that sort of stick with me."

"I hope you tell him I don't have a showroom."

"He's passed on."

"I'm sorry. You spoke of him as if he's still with us."

"I do that all the time. I know I shouldn't."

"You should. It honors him. It keeps him alive."

As I thanked him and smiled, a flutter of emotion tried to push a drop out of my left eye.

He gestured to the seat across from his desk. That gave me a little rush, enough to keep my tear ducts under control. This was one of the most powerful men in Baltimore. Yes, mayors and council members and judges have juice. The local federal prosecutor trumps them all, because he can turn anyone's life upside down with a single indictment—and because he has the ultimate authority to decide who does, and doesn't, get charged with crimes.

"I had an interesting conversation about Orson Fredericks today," he said. "Do you know him?"

"I know the name." That was true, even if I had no idea how I knew it. I put my memory banks into overdrive. My eyes bulged when the name registered. "He owns the football team."

"I didn't know you were a football fan."

"I wasn't. I mean, I'm not. Baseball for me. My grandfather loved the Orioles."

"My dad took me to more of those games than I can remember," he said.

"We used to listen on the radio. He liked to sit on the porch and take it all in. It reminded him of the days before it was such a big business."

"Indeed it is. Nowadays, it's football much more than baseball."

"That's one of the reasons he hated football. He said they only ever cared about making as much money as they could, once they realized how much money they could make."

"And look at what it is now. Biggest sport in the country. Maybe one of these days it'll be the biggest sport in the world. They say it'll never catch soccer. You know, there was a time when most thought it would never catch baseball."

My curiosity short-circuited the smalltalk. "Has Orson Fredericks done something?"

"He could be the key to someone else who has done something. Someone bigger."

"I've already got a pretty big fish on the line. I'm not sure I can handle another."

"If what I heard is accurate, it's all connected."

I felt another surge of adrenaline, along with intrigue. It made me lean forward.

"Henderson Robertson may not have been sharing inside information about the RabbitRun cryptocurrency with just his staff," McClelland said. "He may have been giving it to someone who then passed it to Orson Fredericks. And he's worth a lot more money than Robertson. Fredericks is worth so much that he'd have no reason to waste his time trying to make a quick score like this."

"Why would someone like that do it?"

"Why does anyone ever do it? No matter how much they have, they love to get something for nothing."

"You said there was someone else. Someone even richer than Orson Fredericks?"

Roger McClelland shook his head. "Not richer. The other one has something more important than money, for our purposes."

"Fame?" I said.

He touched the tip of his nose. "That's right. It's amazing to me how many people think being famous insulates you from scrutiny. We know it's the exact opposite. What better way to keep the average person in line than to take down someone everyone has heard of?"

I couldn't stop myself from being blunt. "So who is it?"

"This one could reach all the way to the very top of the game."

I didn't follow the sport well enough to know whether anyone famous was at the top of the game of professional football. He could read that on my face.

McClelland spun in his chair. He reached for a football on the shelf. One of the four brown panels had been replaced with smooth white leather that had a Baltimore logo and Roger McClelland's name written on it. A gift from the team. He flipped the ball toward me.

I threw my hands up. The last thing I needed was to take a football to the nose. It felt solid when it struck my palms. It bounced off and headed toward the floor. I surprised myself by getting it under control before it landed.

I looked at it. I looked back at McClelland. He said nothing. I spun it around until I found the big shield in the colors of the flag under thick, white laces stitched into the leather. I saw a signature over the word, *Commissioner*. I looked at the autograph.

"Penny Charles?" I said.

McClelland laughed. "Wow, you really don't know much about football. It's Perry Charles. He's the head of the league. The biggest man in the entire sport. The biggest man in any American sport."

"The RabbitRun tip went to Orson Fredericks and then to Perry Charles?"

"I believe it went to Fredericks and to Charles, and maybe to a few others."

I kept looking at the name. I rubbed a finger over it. I resisted asking how he knew this. I knew he'd tell me when he was ready.

"I'll do whatever you need me to do," I said.

"I know you're already working harder than anyone in here, me included. I don't want to overwhelm you."

"I can do whatever needs to be done. And this one feels like a big deal."

"It won't be easy. You've handled yourself well with Henderson Robertson. This one will be even trickier. They'll come at us with everything they have, if we make a move. And we can't make a move unless we know it's going to work."

I nodded as he spoke. I started to flip the ball back to him.

"Hang onto that. Keep looking at that name. Do some research on who he is, how he got the job. How long he's had it. How he's been able to keep it."

"We'll need to find the electronic footprints," I said.

"That might not be necessary."

I shook my head. We could only nail them with technology. None of them was ever going to admit to doing it. That's when it dawned on me.

"Orson Fredericks is flipping," I said.

"That's an ugly word. Let's just say he's a concerned citizen, at best. Maybe an unindicted co-conspirator, at worst."

"If he acted on the information, he's just as responsible."

"I never said he acted on it. I only said the information was shared with him."

Something about the way he said it made me wonder whether it was entirely accurate. I didn't care. Roger McClelland was right. We had a chance to catch a much bigger fish.

"I'll set a meeting with Orson. You can do a formal interview. Get his full statement."

I held the football in front of my face. I thought about my other problem. I had an impulse to confess, then and there. I thought better of it. I wanted to have a plan in place before saying anything about it to anyone other than Will.

"The stakes are pretty high," McClelland said. "One false move could bring both of us down. You realize that, right?"

"I wouldn't have it any other way."

"I'm sure you've already done more than enough in your career to make your grandfather extremely proud. If we pull this one off, he'd be busting his buttons."

That tear came back. I felt it spill onto the top of my cheek. I kept looking down at the name on the football, hoping he wouldn't notice.

Perry Charles, whoever he is, was about to have his life get a lot more interesting.

55

CARSON JEFFREY

I felt like a stranger in my new apartment. The hotel room had a few knick-knacks and stray pieces of art or something close to it. This place is empty. Furnished, my ass. It seemed like I'd been sent to Russia. That wouldn't have been so bad.

In Moscow, I'd be safe from Johnny Motts. It'd put me farther away from her, too. Maybe I didn't want that part.

Random memories from both Friday and Sunday night popped into my mind. I had plenty of other things to keep me occupied. I kept finding myself occupied with thoughts of her.

I couldn't let myself dwell on her. I was due to be the starter for Sunday's game. Somehow. Me, playing. Me, starting. Just like that, I went from never playing at all to preparing to be the guy who'd play from start to finish on Sunday. Unless I got injured, too.

I hadn't told Johnny Motts. There was no way he'd find out otherwise, because the team hadn't said anything about Wettle's injury.

They'd try to keep it under wraps until Friday, to keep Kansas City from knowing what's coming. That gave me a little time to tell him. It also gave me a chance to come up with a plan for trying to play well while making the signals before each play.

I'd get through maybe one game without anybody picking up on the tell. Maybe I'd come up with new signals each week. Would that work? I had no choice but to give it a try.

First, I'd need to do enough with one game to get them to give me another.

After practice ended, I worked again with Coach Gary/Greg. We went over the game plan for Sunday. I wouldn't need to run the whole playbook. I'd only have to know the plays that'd be used during sixty specific minutes of football.

That would mean fifty or sixty, at the most. Some plays might get used more than once. It never made sense to me why most coaches won't use the same play twice in the same game. If it works the first time, why wouldn't it work again? If it didn't work the first time, maybe they'd run it better the next time. It would make sense to try that approach when the quarterback doesn't know the plays like he should.

Regardless, I'd be comfortable with the plays picked for the game in Kansas City. That part would be easy. The other part was what had my stomach in knots. I tried to get comfortable on the crappy chair at the crappy desk next to the crappy bed, staring at my phone and thinking about calling her.

It was after eleven. I didn't want to wake her up. I wondered whether she's somebody who silences her phone when she goes to bed. If she set it up for only certain numbers to get through. If she already made my number one that would ring whenever.

I wanted to talk to her. To anyone. Johnny Motts was the only choice, other than my agent. I already called Paul Templeton on the drive home. Now that I'd be starting, Paul was treating me like something more than the low-level slappy I'd always been. I didn't need more smoke up my ass, more catch phrases to make me believe in myself even though I could tell from his questions that Paul doubted I could pull it off. I couldn't really blame him for that. I was skeptical, too.

Screw it, I thought. I found her number and pressed the button.

It rang twice before she picked up. It seemed to take longer than it should for her to talk.

"Carson?"

"Did I wake you up?"

"Not really."

"That's a strange way to answer a yes or no question."

"I was just lying here. Unless this is a very realistic dream."

"I hadn't heard from you since Sunday."

"I hadn't heard from you since Sunday," she replied.

"I still wasn't sure how we left it. And I've been busy. I know you've been, too."

"How do you know that?"

"I assume someone like you is always busy."

"That's a pretty good guess." She sounded distant and careful. I already regretted calling.

"I didn't want to misinterpret anything," I said.

"What's to misinterpret?"

"Anything. Everything. I'm not very good at being subtle. Football players usually aren't."

"Maybe that's one of the reasons I usually avoid them."

"Isn't life easier when people are direct?"

"Yes and no," she said.

"Exactly."

"I'm sorry. I have had a busy week. Some unexpected things have come up."

"That makes two of us."

"See? You're already learning how to not be so direct."

"I'll be more direct. I'm playing on Sunday."

"I thought you were on the third string."

"On Monday, the backup dropped a weight on his foot. Today, someone accidentally caved in the new starter's knee. So it's me. That's not public information yet."

"Dang, I just posted it."

"I had to say it. They want to keep it quiet. It's one of the games they play. They don't want the opponent to know it'll be me. Like that will matter."

"What do you mean?"

"I've never played in a game. So it's not like they'll know what to expect. They won't expect much. They'll look at my college games. That won't help them. It's a completely different offense here. Besides, I've been a career third-stringer for a reason."

"You've still been on a team. You wouldn't have been on a team for the past four years if you stink."

"There are degrees of stink. Plenty of guys who have spots on teams wouldn't do very well if they had to play. I'll probably be the latest example of that on Sunday."

"You strike me as more confident than that."

"If you're not confident plus realistic, you're delusional."

She laughed at that one.

"How is that funny?"

"You sound like someone I know. Or someone I used to know, I guess. You just need to believe in yourself. There's nothing wrong with believing in yourself."

I considered what she said. I waited a few more seconds. "Can we get together before the team goes to Kansas City?"

"When is that?"

"We'll have a walk-through on Saturday and then fly out."

"That leaves tomorrow and Friday," she said. "Won't you be busy getting ready for the game?"

"I can take a break at some point."

"I need to take a closer look at my schedule. I really do have a lot going on at work."

"You weren't busy last Friday night."

"That was before things came up."

"I have a feeling you can't talk as openly as I can about the things that have come up."

"I appreciate you understanding that."

"If you decide you've got a couple of hours on Friday night, let me know, and we'll figure something out."

"I will," she said.

I wanted to ask whether that meant she'd call, or whether that meant she'd only do it if she had time. I decided to show her I'm able to not be quite so direct.

"Again, I'm sorry if I woke you up. Or whatever I did. Have a good night."

"You, too," she said as the call ended.

I looked at the phone for a long time. I wondered whether I'd hear from her before Friday night. I also wondered whether I'd ever hear from her again.

56

JOHNNY MOTTS

I plugged the laptop into the outlet in the BMW and watched three movies. A comedy about talking dogs. A sappy drama about some mom and her kid who both had the same kind of rare cancer. And a mob picture that will hopefully get me ready to do what I was about to do.

Not that I ever need that. I've done this enough times to know how to turn off my brain and get to work.

There's a switch. You flip it on, then you flip it off. Sometimes, it's hard to flip it off. I've never not been able to flip it on.

Still, I've never done it to a woman. A little extra kick from watching a few people getting whacked can't hurt.

The piss bottle was starting to fill up. My stomach was starting to make that sound like trapped farts going off. It was stupid to not bring food. I thought about driving over to a convenience store for a candy bar or some peanuts, but I didn't wanna miss what I was waiting for. The more time I spent there, the more I felt like I had to stay where I was.

Carmine called near five. I didn't say where I was. The closest he came to making me nervous was asking if I'd be around the place later. I told him I was planning on it, after going to the casino. He asked which one. I blurted out the Wynn without thinking whether he'd send somebody over there to look for me.

That's the kind of stupid shit I need to quit doing. Little things like that can fuck everything up. Alls I had to say was I ain't decided yet. Or maybe I'll go here, maybe I'll go there. But, no, I painted myself into a corner like a dumb son of a bitch.

I kept checking the network. She bought more shit from Amazon. It still didn't dawn on me to see what it was. I can't say I was stupid not to do it, but it sure would have been smart to wonder.

That's my biggest problem. I don't give a shit about stuff. I don't wanna know more than what I know. Is that something you can teach yourself? You either are or you're not. I can try to be. If I do it and it works, maybe I'll do it some more.

Don't they say curiosity killed the cat? I don't know how they came up with that one. I never really asked. That's what you get when you ain't curious.

Besides, I gotta worry about more than curiosity killing me. First, Carmine. Also, whoever opens Jimmy King's door, if she's holding whatever gun he taught her how to use. Maybe she won't even open it. Maybe she'll just blast a hole right through it. And me.

I was worrying too much. She wouldn't have no reason to shoot through the door. Alls I needed was for her to open it, and I'd take care of the rest.

She must have spent all damn day on Amazon. She had to be getting hungry. I needed to be right with my guess that she's too good for leftovers. Carmine calls it used food. He's got the money to not have to eat used food. She does too. I wish I did.

I saw it right around six. DoorDash. Order placed. I put the computer on the seat and waited for the car to get close. They carry that red bag. I got a rough idea of the kind of car somebody who drives food to people's houses would use. Something like a Ford. Whatever it is, it wouldn't look nothing like the cars I seen going up and down this street, that's for sure.

I'll need to move quick. Not too quick. I don't need the driver to get suspicious. That could force me to do something I don't wanna do. Maybe whoever it is heard about curiosity killing cats, too.

After about fifteen minutes, I went back and forth between looking straight ahead and checking the side mirror to see if anything was coming. It was dark, so I had to make a guess from how fast or slow it was going, or whether it was missing a headlight. If the driver ain't been there before, the car will go slow. If the driver is a regular, the car will just stop.

I was thinking too much again. That's what happens when you get curious. I just needed to trust my gut, like I always do. Then again, trusting my gut is what got me mixed up with Larry Ballentine, Jimmy King, and Carson Jeffrey.

I kept checking both directions. A couple cars came my way pretty fast. I decided not to make a move. Neither one stopped. My gut wasn't fucking with me, yet.

I saw another one rolling from the front. Moving slow. One of the front lights was a lot dimmer than the other. It was time to go.

I brung two hats. I wore the baseball hat to his house before. This time, I went with a black fedora. It's a little bit too big on my head. It makes me look even more like I'm in the line of work I'm in. My gut said it was the right hat for this job.

I grabbed it, put it on, got out. I left the BMW running so I could take off when it was done. I walked fast but not too fast to the spot in front of Jimmy King's house.

The car was still coming. I probably got started a little too early. Better too early than too late. I was getting nervous that it was taking so long for the car to get there.

It stopped. I walked over. The guy inside put the window down. He looked like he wasn't much older than nineteen.

"Delivery for Jimmy King?" I said.

"The name on the order is Stacy Johnson."

"This is Jimmy King's house. He's the basketball player. I work security for him."

"He lives here?"

"I just said it's his house."

"I'm supposed to take it to the porch and leave it there."

"I ain't supposed to let nobody on the porch."

"That wasn't in the instructions. I'm supposed to leave it on the porch and ring the bell."

"The instructions changed. Nobody goes on the porch but me. You understand how security works, right?"

"If I screw this up, it comes out of my pay."

"If I screw this up, I lose my job." I made myself smile and nod like we was just a couple of working stiffs trying to get by. I pulled out a twenty and dropped it on top of the red bag he had on the passenger seat. "That should cover whatever misunderstanding there might have been." I thought about slipping him a hundred, but that might have made him more suspicious. Which wouldn't have been good for me. Or maybe for him.

"Is Jimmy King in there?" he said.

"Road game. I watch the place when he ain't here."

"That's the kind of gig I need. Beats driving food all over town."

"Somebody's gotta do it," I said.

He didn't know what to say to that. He also was getting the impression he should just take the twenty and go, I could tell. He kept eyeing me. I hoped the hat was pulled down far enough so that whatever description he tried to give when the cops tracked him down wouldn't be worth a shit.

"She already put a pretty good tip on the order," he said.

"Consider this a bonus. It's way better than what anyone who sets foot on that porch tonight is gonna get."

I heard the door to the car unlock. I opened it and took the bag before he could say something else.

"Stay safe out there," I said. I pushed the door shut and turned to the house.

I walked slow. I listened for the sound of the car pulling away. At first, I wasn't sure he was going. Maybe he was checking his phone for the next order. Just as I was about to look back, I heard it roll off. That engine needed a tuneup, bad.

I started going faster to the porch. I pulled the hat down as low as it would go. I moved the bag to my left hand and checked to make sure my piece was where I needed it to be.

57

ALICE SMITHSON

I had another day to decide whether to see him. Or, I should say, to change the decision I'd already made.

I shouldn't see him. I wouldn't see him. The sudden possibility of prosecuting the Commissioner of professional football had forced my professional dilemma onto the back burner. As to the personal dilemma, well, there wasn't one.

I shouldn't see him. I wouldn't see him. I shouldn't have answered his call.

I couldn't help what I was feeling. That was the problem. Alice Smithson versus Sally Slammer. It was a fight Sally had won with a one-punch knockout. Alice had managed to let Sally believe she'd prevailed. As Sally raised an arm in the center of the ring, Alice slipped under the bottom rope.

It made no sense. I knew that. Half of me refused to see him. That same half was also oblivious to the fact that the other half would agree to the plan, before completely disregarding it. It's why I answered the phone when he called, even after telling myself I shouldn't. It's why I was considering the possibility of seeing him on Friday night, even after promising myself I wouldn't.

I had a glass of wine with dinner before switching to slow sips of tequila. Like most nights, the first glass gave me clarity. Like most nights, the second gave me peace. Unlike most nights, I poured a third. While that wasn't nearly enough to get me drunk, it was enough to give Alice an opening. To send Sally to bed. To tuck her in with a kiss on the forehead. To tiptoe from of the room and close the door. And then to sneak out for a night on the town.

I grabbed the phone before I could talk myself out of it. I pulled up the list of received calls and pressed the spot from the night before.

"Do I have my days mixed up?" he said.

"That's a strange way to say hello.'"

"Hello. Do I have my days mixed up?"

"Maybe that's common for football players."

"Are you making a concussion joke or a dumb jock joke?"

"A concussion joke would be in poor taste."

"But I was an Academic All-American. You saw that when you Googled me."

"Maybe it really is a low bar. Isn't that how you tried to play it off? Something about the one-eyed man in the land of the blind?"

"Fine. I'll assume I got my days mixed up, and it's Friday night. And you want to get together."

"Aren't we being presumptuous?"

"You called me. Unless I got that mixed up, too."

"You're assuming I called to say I want to get together. Maybe I called to say I never want to see you again."

"Why would you call to say that? All you'd have to do is never call again."

"Maybe I was thinking about our conversation from last night. The part where we talked about being subtle and being direct. Maybe I decided to be direct."

He paused. "Have you?"

I inhaled. It was loud enough for him to hear. I suppose I wanted him to. I wanted him to know I was struggling. I didn't know why I wanted him to know that, but I did. I considered saying something else. I stopped. Then the tequila took over.

"Do you want to come over?"

"To your apartment?"

"I'm not at the office."

"You work tomorrow, right?"

"I pretty much work every day. I have a fairly important meeting tomorrow morning at nine."

"It's already after ten."

"I'm sorry, are we getting close to your bedtime?"

"Maybe we are."

"That didn't come out the way I meant it."

He chuckled. "I think it came out exactly the way you meant it."

"You really are being presumptuous."

"Again, you called me. And you called me after ten o'clock and invited me over. And I think we're both adults."

"Look, are you coming or not?"

"So the offer stands? I know a little about offer and acceptance. I took business law at North Texas."

"What did you get?"

"Excuse me?"

"How did you do in the class?"

"I got an A-minus."

"Only an A-minus?"

"I missed a question on the final exam."

"What was it?"

"If a lawyer invites you to her apartment after ten o'clock on a Thursday night, does she want to give you legal advice or does she want to play Scrabble?"

"What was your answer?"

"None of the above."

"I guess you're finally getting a chance to figure out the right answer."

"What's your address?"

"I'll share my location with you. You can prove you're an Academic All-American by figuring out the rest on your own."

"Do I need to bring anything?"

I paused again. Inhaled again. "Do you brush your teeth in the morning?"

"Who doesn't?"

"Then maybe you should bring a toothbrush."

58

CARSON JEFFREY

Sunlight pushed low through dark clouds ready to drop their rain. A beam invaded the rental car, landing on the seat next to me.

I looked at the glovebox. The burner was inside. I needed to let Johnny Motts know what was happening before the team put out the final injury report and it became clear to Kansas City and the rest of the world I'd be playing. I wasn't too worried about that. I had plans in place for taking care of both of my jobs on Sunday.

I was feeling almost happy, for the first time since right before Rik Trellis stopped on his way out of the meeting room and gave me the invitation that turned my life upside down. I got a very different kind of invitation ten days later. I liked that one a lot better. It went exactly how I'd hoped. Just as I was thinking she'd decided to forget all about me, another unexpected curveball came spinning straight for my head.

I handled it well. All of it. It had been a while. It hadn't been so long that I forgot what to do and how to do it.

I got out of bed before she woke up. I found a legal pad and left her a note. I wrote the first thing that came to me. I hoped she'd laugh when she read it. I was already looking forward to the next time I'd see her.

I'd brought a toothbrush. I was holding it in my left hand

when she opened the door to the apartment. I asked if I could borrow some toothpaste. She smiled and said that, after I borrow it, she doesn't want it back.

It was hard to remember what happened next. Things moved fast. I could tell she'd been drinking. I could taste it in her mouth. If that's what it took to get her to be direct, so be it.

Direct she was. It was exciting. It was new, but it felt familiar. I remembered hoping things would continue. She fell asleep right away. That made me want to see her again even more.

I drove back to the apartment. It felt different when I walked inside. It wasn't. I was. I liked how that felt. I quit worrying about my problems. I decided to face them. Solve them. And I'd keep pushing toward my new goal.

I wanted more.

A lot more of this new life I'd stumbled into. A lot less of the old one.

It wouldn't be easy. I'd still try. I'd get through the season. I'd retire. Johnny Motts would have to deal with that. His people would have plenty of time to find someone else to do what I'd been doing. I wouldn't let some stupid thug with one eyebrow and zero necks scare me into doing something I didn't want to do. If that wasn't good enough, I'd figure out how to deal with it later.

I'd made this mess. I'd clean it up. I felt something I hadn't felt in a long time, if ever. I'd get a teaching certificate. I'd coach high-school football. I'd be productive. More than anything else, I'd throw myself into this thing with Alice and see where it could go.

I was being impulsive. I was fine with that. I'd acted on plenty of bad impulses over the years. I had a feeling this could be a good one.

I didn't know I'd been searching for this feeling. I'd found it, or at least the path toward it. I put my bag down on the floor of the apartment. I held the burner. I stared at it. I thought about all the times I wanted to throw it away.

Not this time. It was time to get to where I needed to be. The first step was to tell Johnny Motts how things are going to go.

I decided there was no time to tell him like right now.

59

JOHNNY MOTTS

I pulled the hat down some more. It wasn't gonna get no tighter. I still wanted to try, even if I could barely make out anything from under it.

I didn't need to see much. I kept my eyes on the path to the porch, the red bag I was carrying. I could feel the piece as I walked. It was pressing against my right hip like a big kidney stone.

I had one of those once. Worst pain of my life. Any day I don't have a kidney stone is a great fucking day. This didn't feel like it was going to end up being a great fucking day.

I also didn't have much of a plan. I'd pull the piece and get her to let me in. I wanted to shoot her once and be done with it. That'd be the easiest. Shot through the heart, like that old hair band song.

Just one shot. Most people hear it and they stop what they're doing and listen for another. If that's it, they'll tell themselves they never heard nothing in the first place. I didn't wanna put too much trust in that. That's why I left the BMW running. I'd need to get the fuck out of there before somebody figured out what was going on.

I decided I should steal something. Make it look like a robbery. It would've been nice to take a piece of that art. Too bad it wouldn't fit in the car.

It helped to be in a neighborhood where not a lot of shit goes on. Maybe they'd think it's firecrackers. That's really what it sounds like. Not the big loud bang them guns make in the movies.

Whatever I did when it's done would be fine, because that'd mean it's done. I just needed it to be done.

I seen the steps to the porch. I checked the hat again to make sure it was low as it could go. For all I knew, she'd laugh when she got a look at me. It's my own fault for buying the thing without trying it on first.

Better too big than too small. That guy had cameras everywhere. They won't recognize me with the hat. They'll see the mustache. I can always shave it off until the heat dies down.

I kept thinking about stupid shit like that so I wouldn't think about what was coming next. I didn't wanna do it. I had to do it, in order to keep it from being done to me. I needed to get Jimmy King under control. He had his chance. I sent him a message without sending a message. It ain't my fault he's too fucking stupid to get the point.

When I got to the porch, I tilted my head back enough to see the doorbell. I put my head back down and pressed it.

I held my breath without realizing I was doing it. I put my right hand down toward the piece. I went over the steps in my head. There weren't many, but I needed to keep them straight.

Enough time went by for me to figure out I wasn't breathing. I blew out the air in my mouth and took in more. I felt my heartbeat going faster. I tried to bring it back down.

I waited some more. I thought about ringing the bell again. I listened as close as I could.

What the fuck am I gonna do if she pulls it open and points a shotgun right at my nuts?

I thought about dropping the bag and leaving. It was too late for that. I put this thing in motion. If I didn't see it through, I was gonna end up with even bigger problems.

One more time I thought about ringing the bell again. Maybe she didn't hear it before. Why wouldn't she? She ordered food. She'd been waiting for it to show up. She wouldn't have gotten in the shower or gone to bed or nothing like that.

I moved my right hand from the piece and reached up to press the button. I heard the knob turn. The door pulled back. There she was. I figured she'd be pretty. I didn't know she'd be a fucking knockout. It threw me off.

Then I saw something that surprised me even more. It's my own fucking fault for not being curious. For not finding out more about her. The basketball player's girlfriend looked like she swallowed a basketball or her own.

"I told them to leave it on the porch," she said. "You're not supposed to be here."

I stared at her stomach. My brain told my right hand to grab the gun. It wouldn't. "They never told me that," I said.

She looked past me. "Where's your car?"

"Down the street a little bit. I thought I had the wrong address."

"Well, this is the place."

She kept glaring at me. My eyes were on that bulge. My brain kept telling my hand to get the piece. My hand kept refusing to do it.

"I paid when I ordered," she said.

"I know."

"May I have my food?"

My left hand listened to my brain when it said to hand her the red bag. She didn't take it.

"Don't you need that?"

"For what?"

"For your next delivery?"

My right hand cooperated when it was time to unzip the red bag and give her the food. I held out the brown paper bag that was inside it. My brain kept telling my right hand to pull out the piece.

"Thank you," she said.

"You're welcome," I said.

She closed the door.

60

ALICE SMITHSON

The first alarm on my phone went off at seven twenty-nine. I'd almost forgotten to set them, again. I fell back onto the mattress after turning it off.

I looked to the left. He was gone.

I felt something. Many things at once. I put my hand where he'd been sleeping. I was glad he was gone. I wished he was still there.

I turned to the pillow he used. I pressed my face into it. I breathed his scent into my lungs. I exhaled in a long sigh.

"What the fuck did I do?"

I rubbed my hands over my face. I could smell him on my palms. Maybe it was from the pillowcase. Maybe it was something that wouldn't go away so quickly.

It came out louder this time.

"What the fuck did I do?"

I sat up. I became conscious of my body. I wondered whether he was still in the apartment. I listened for sounds that would tell me he was doing something predictable, like making breakfast or brewing coffee. I hoped he wasn't snooping around. Was there anything he might notice that would let him know what I knew?

I waited, not moving and still listening. I saw a slipper I was wearing the night before. I bent down from the bed and grabbed it. I threw it at the door. I listened for any reaction to the sound.

I covered myself with the sheet, ripping it from the bed as I pulled it along the floor. I opened the door to the outer room. I called his name. It sounded strange coming from my mouth, almost like someone else was saying it. I decided he really was gone.

I was glad he was gone. I wished he was still there.

I dragged the sheet to the bathroom. I turned the water to the highest possible heat and waited for the steam to fill the space around me. I dropped the sheet. I stepped into the shower. I tried to scrub every remnant of him away.

It was a one-time thing. Never again.

I repeated those same two messages as I worked shampoo through my hair and cleansed my entire body with a soapy rag.

It was a one-time thing. Never again.

I hoped it would stick. I didn't want it to.

I became aware of the passing time. Nine o'clock would be here before I knew it. Another meeting with the man in charge. Another opportunity to inadvertently mention the situation I'd stumbled into. The situation I'd just complicated in dramatic and perhaps irreversible fashion by drinking just enough tequila to melt my restraint.

It was a one-time thing.

Never again.

I exited the shower. I wrapped myself in a robe that was past the point of needing to be washed. I opened the door to the bedroom. I called his name again.

I went straight to the kitchen. I grabbed the tequila. I considered how much it cost. I poured what was left in the bottle down the drain.

On my way back to the bathroom, I saw a folded piece of paper on the table, next to my computer. I picked it up and opened it.

Dear Alice. You have raised the standards of the Baltimore Welcoming Committee to new heights. Carson.

I ripped it in half, balled up the two pieces, and threw them onto the floor.

I surprised myself by making it to the office just after eight thirty. I'd shifted into overdrive after finding that note. I blew the wetness from my hair, applied makeup, picked one of my best courtroom-ready ensembles, made a cup of coffee, ate a banana and a bowl of strawberries, all of it with crisp, emotionless efficiency. I forced my mind to go blank and stay that way.

I had surrendered to Sally Slammer. I vowed to keep it that way, for as long as I possibly could. Hopefully longer.

I stood outside Roger McClelland's office at fifteen minutes to nine. I expected Mrs. Maxwell to tell me to wait on the couch across from her desk. Instead, she took me inside and ordered me to sit in the same chair where I'd learned about the potential case against Perry Charles. Her words carried a small hint of deference. It made me wonder whether she's hedging her bets against the possibility she'll be working for me, one of these days.

I sat there, staring at Roger McClelland's empty chair. My silenced phone was tucked into the pocket of my jacket. I didn't want to see whether Carson had called or texted. I wanted to see whether he had called or texted. I managed to ignore my curiosity as to whether he had.

Just before the clock on the shelf behind his desk reached nine, I heard Roger McClelland talking to Mrs. Maxwell. I turned in the chair and stood, waiting to welcome him into his own office.

An office that I realized might eventually be mine.

61

CARSON JEFFREY

I knew the time difference. I didn't care. I'd call and call and call until Johnny Motts answered. Just like Johnny Motts had done to me, after I got cut and he wouldn't quit hounding me about getting a job.

The line clicked halfway through the third ring of the second try. "I thought I told you how early it is here."

"Did I wake you up?"

"I ain't been to sleep yet. Consider yourself lucky, for a change."

"You told me to call whenever I have something important to tell you."

"I figured you ain't looking to chit-chat about the dump you just took. What's the news that would've woke me up if you called an hour from now?"

I had an impulse to abandon ship. I remembered my new plan. "I'm playing on Sunday," I said.

"You're what?"

"I'm playing on Sunday."

"Which Sunday?"

"This Sunday."

"How the fuck did that happen?"

"The other guy messed up his knee in practice on Wednesday."

"Why didn't I hear nothing about that?"

"They stretched the truth on the injury report. Today, they'll say he's not playing. They wanted to wait until tomorrow, but they knew that would look too fishy."

"It looks fishy all right. As fishy as a plate of fucking fish sticks."

"You've really got a way with words."

"What did you say?"

"Are you going deaf?"

"Now what the fuck does that mean?"

"Twice now I've said something, and you wanted me to say it again," I said. "So I'm wondering if you're hard of hearing."

"This ain't the time to get fresh, my friend."

"I'm not your friend."

"You think just because I'm three thousand miles away, I can't make sure you need to stick a pen in your mouth to write your name for the rest of your life?"

"I'd learn how to use my feet."

"Listen—"

"No, you listen. If you're threatening to break my thumbs, I'm telling you I'll figure out how to hold the pen with my feet and write my name that way."

"You can use your dick for all I care," Johnny Motts said.

"That would probably take a little more practice."

"Maybe you should hang up and call me back in two hours and tell me I dreamed all of this. That might be the only way out of the jackpot you pulled yourself into."

"I'm just doing my job. You're the one who's getting hot and bothered."

"Hot and bothered? I only get that way with the ladies. You're just pissing me off."

I was making myself a little nervous, but I managed to laugh. "Look, man, you've been treating me like shit ever since I got cut last week. Not that it was all that great before. I decided this morning I've had enough of it. I've held up my end of this."

"You better hold up your end of it on Sunday."

"I might have to change the signals. We might need to mix it up during the game."

"Mix it up?" Johnny Motts said.

I wanted to make another sarcastic remark, but I didn't. "I might need to change the signals. Maybe at halftime. Maybe for each quarter. I need to think it through some more."

"You better think fast."

"You'll know what they are."

"How different will they be?"

"There's only so much I can do. I'll figure it out."

"What we've been doing is simple. You need to keep it simple."

"How about if it's a run I give you a middle finger, and if it's a pass I give you two?"

"How's about you go fuck yourself? And you better hope I don't tell the people I work for that you became a smartass all of a sudden."

"You won't."

"How do you know that?"

"Because if they think you can't control me, you're the one they'll be pissed at."

Johnny Motts chuckled. I heard something in it that made me think it bothered him a little. "Don't pretend you know how this works," he said.

"I don't give a shit how it works. I give a shit about doing my job until this season is over. Then I'm out."

"We had this conversation before."

"I'm done playing football. You'll have plenty of time to find somebody else. You've even got some extra time, because I'm telling you now."

"This is a discussion we'll have after the season ends."

"There's nothing to discuss. I didn't sign a contract with you. Besides, no one ever said I had to do this the rest of my life. You can try to scare me however you want. We both know if I retire and walk away, the people you work for will let me. And they'll expect you to find someone else, the same way you found me. That's really all it comes down to, the way I see it. You're too lazy to find someone else."

"Lazy is something I ain't," Motts said, almost whispering. For the first time during the call, I wondered whether I'd gone too far. I still didn't care. I was getting out. I'd handle whatever it took to make it happen.

"I'll call you with the signals tomorrow," I said.

"You'd better, or else."

"Or else what?"

"If I was you, I wouldn't wanna find out."

The line went dead. I pulled the burner away from my ear. I looked at it and smiled.

62

JOHNNY MOTTS

The call from Baltimore made me forget about what I didn't do in Denver, for a little bit. The thing I didn't do in Denver made me more determined not to fuck around with the asshole in Baltimore.

He was getting more and more of an attitude. And now he's gonna be playing? Carmine won't be happy about that. Even if it ain't my fault, he will not be happy.

I wonder if Carmine already knows. I wonder if he wants to see whether I'll tell him. Telling him the kid didn't tell me until today won't make it better. Carmine will say he should've told me when it happened. Carmine will say it shows I can't keep my guys in line.

And he'd be right about that. I had a chance to get Jimmy King under control. It's my own fault for not knowing she was pregnant. If I did, would I have taken care of her? I think I would have. But then why didn't I do it once I found out?

Maybe I just needed time to think about it. To process it. Ain't that what smart people say? People smart enough to know somebody they're about to kill is carrying around somebody else inside their stomach before the time comes to do it.

I really am stupid. How the fuck did I make it this far being this dumb? It's time to get smart. I keep telling myself that. One of these times, maybe I'll mean it.

I need to go see Carmine. That'll be smart. I need to be straight with him. That'll be smart, too. And I need to have a plan for getting Jeffrey under control. One that I need to be smart enough not to tell Carmine about.

That's when I remembered the woman. The one Jeffrey had dinner with. I ain't heard nothing from Lego Billy about her. He should have called by now. Or maybe I should've called him. I was too caught up in the shit with Jimmy King. It's my own fault. Just more proof I need to get smart.

So I called Lego Billy. I could tell he was sleeping.

"Who died?" he said.

"Nobody yet. Unfortunately."

"What the fuck?"

"I ain't heard from you."

"I was gonna call you later."

"I don't pay you to call me later."

"I was busy."

"I don't pay you to be too busy to call."

"Christ, Johnny. You know, the world don't revolve around you."

"When you take a job from me, it does."

"You think you're the only person I work for?"

"When you're working for me, you are."

"Give me a fucking break, man."

"What the fuck is 'man'? You a pothead now?"

"Pothead? I ain't heard that word in years."

"And it feels like I ain't heard from you in years. So we're square."

"I wanted to find out a little more before I called."

"Now you're just making excuses."

"I didn't call because I needed to know a little more. I found out what I needed to know right before I fell asleep."

"You better start making sense about what you know, quick."

"I know who the guy in Baltimore had dinner with the other night."

"I'm waiting."

"Her name is Alice Smithson."

"We're finally getting somewhere. I like that."

"You won't like what's next."

"What's that?"

"She's a fed."

"What do you mean, a fed?"

"I mean she's a fed."

"FBI?"

"Worse. Prosecutor."

"Billy, you better be right about this."

"The woman I hired in Baltimore knows all about her. She's apparently a badass, Johnny."

"Are you telling me my guy flipped?"

"I don't know. That's why I needed more information."

"He either flipped or he didn't. What other information would there be?"

"He spent the night at her place."

"When?"

"Last night. Got there after ten."

"So did he flip, or is he screwing her?"

"I don't know if he flipped. And I don't know what they did last night. All I know is he spent the night there."

I didn't say nothing. I was trying to think. I didn't know what none of it meant.

"Hello?" Lego Billy said.

"You're sure about all of this?"

"I'm telling you what the woman in Baltimore told me."

"I need you to be sure."

"You wanna talk to the woman in Baltimore?"

"I'm starting to think I need to go to Baltimore."

"You're gonna take out a fed?"

"Don't worry about none of that. But if you hear anything more about this, you better fucking call me right away. Or you're the one I'll be taking out."

"You don't pay me enough to make threats."

"You just better call if you hear anything else."

I hung up the phone and threw it. That fucker flipped. Did he flip? If he hasn't yet, he will. He can't be screwing a fed and keeping a secret like this.

And I can't keep something like this a secret from Carmine.

That's when I thought for the first time in my life something I never thought I'd ever think.

Maybe I should flip, too. Maybe that's my only way out of this.

I pushed it out of my head. Well, I tried to. I need to go see Carmine. I know that much.

Even if I got no fucking idea what I'm gonna say when I get there.

63

ALICE SMITHSON

"Thank you for making the time to be here," Roger McClelland said. "I assume it wasn't easy to rearrange your schedule on short notice."

"No problemo," I said, forcing a smile through my ridiculous choice of words.

"Please, sit. We need to get past the formalities if we're going to be working together."

I smiled again, this time more naturally. His comment about working together made me feel even better about my resolve to put my indiscretion behind me.

McClelland walked behind his desk and took his chair. He wasn't carrying a briefcase. I thought it would be nice to get to the point where I won't have to lug some of my work everywhere I go. I wondered if that would ever happen.

"So," he said, "I've been doing some thinking about this new wrinkle in our Henderson Robertson case. I've got some good news. And some bad news."

"My grandfather always says to take bad news first."

"I think we have to be ready to forget about charging Henderson Robertson, if we're going to pull this off."

I wanted to ask why. I wanted to come up with reasons to argue. After all those hours, all the effort, all that stress, we were ready to get the indictment. Now we're just going to pull the plug? But I trusted there was a reason for giving Henderson Robertson a pass.

"You're taking this well," he said, eyebrows stretching. "I know how hard you've worked on nailing him. I expected some resistance."

"My grandfather also says to always take the bad news well, because there's a chance the good news will more than make up for it."

Roger McClelland chuckled a bit. "I have a feeling your grandfather was right a lot more often than he was wrong. If we're going to nail Perry Charles, I think we'll need Henderson Robertson's cooperation."

"Why?" I said it before I could stop myself.

"If we're going to go after a bigger fish, we need to be prepared to cut loose the one we have on the line."

"We have him cold."

"The man goes from being the focal point of a major investigation that was approaching its conclusion to being the key witness in an even bigger investigation. Rich people really do have all the luck."

"Some of them," I said.

"Henderson Robertson's good luck might be Perry Charles's misfortune."

As much as I hated to give Robertson a pass, the boss was right. Besides, this new case would be a lot easier to prove, if Robertson cooperates. There would be no need to figure out how to keep the jury awake through hours of testimony about digital footprints and other convoluted evidence necessary to pin an insider trading conviction on Robertson. We could get Perry Charles with testimony from Orson Fredericks and Henderson Robertson. Once Robertson understands he'd be escaping his own potential mess by turning on Perry Charles,

Robertson hopefully would sing like Pavarotti after guzzling a full bottle of Prosecco.

"Orson Fredericks wants to be interviewed in his New York office. He's concerned about you showing up at his local headquarters. He doesn't want anyone to get ideas."

"I'll go whenever he wants," I said.

"We'll set it up as soon as we can. Let's get him on the record before he gets cold feet, or before someone gets to him."

I considered my other situation. I forced it out of my mind, again.

"Is there something else you want to tell me?" he said.

Either I'm way too easy to read, or this guy is a wizard. "There's nothing else," I said.

"You're sure?"

"Absolutely."

"I know from your track record I can trust you completely. I hope you'll have that same trust in me."

"I will. I mean, I do. I agree. We're in this together. And you're right. If we can take down Perry Charles, I have no problem with forgetting all about Henderson Roberston."

"If there's anything else I need to know, I'd rather know it now."

"There's nothing else," I said, nodding with a little more gusto than I needed to. "There's nothing."

"You're sure?"

I looked down at my hands. I wondered whether they still smelled like Carson. I looked up again.

"What else could there be?"

64

CARSON JEFFREY

I pulled into the parking lot later than I wanted, but earlier than any of the players who weren't getting treatment. After putting in extra time on Wednesday and Thursday, the coaches gave most of the players a chance to get extra sleep.

The goal, as best I could tell, was to make us think we had a decent chance in Kansas City. Or maybe the coaching staff had accepted what was going to happen in two days, now that they were down to their fourth quarterback.

I still wasn't ready to give up. My chance was finally here. Throw in my brand-new decision that this year would be my last, and I was going to make the most of it. I wouldn't have one regret. And I'd have an interesting story for grandkids who'd be hearing me babble about the time I played in a pro football game and didn't piss down my own leg, at an age when I'd probably be shitting my own pants on a regular basis.

I let myself wonder whether I'd change my plans if I surprised everybody (me included) by playing well. First, I'd made up my mind. Second, it'd be nuts to think I'd do anything other than suck.

If I did anything well, it would be a fluke. Beginner's luck. Something that wouldn't be sustainable, since I was planning to play with reckless abandon.

I always loved the sound of those words. *Reckless abandon.*

That's something no quarterback can keep doing without getting himself blasted into irrelevance, or eventually throwing five or six interceptions. Cutting it loose on a regular basis works only for the most talented players in the league. I'd never be that guy, no matter what happened on Sunday.

I still wanted to do my best. I needed that experience, just once. I had to know that, when the moment finally came, I'd snatched it by the nuts and held on tight as I could. I wouldn't care about getting benched. I wouldn't care about getting taken from the stadium in an ambulance. Shit, that would probably make it easier to get away from Johnny Motts.

I wouldn't care much about that, either. My epiphany—another word I always liked but never really had any reason to use—came with a desire to do whatever I had to do to get to where I wanted to be. I didn't care about being a quarterback. My new goal was to be the husband of the woman who gave me a night I hoped to repeat as often as possible, for as long as I could.

I'd never felt that way about anyone. I knew it sounded stupid. I didn't care that I hadn't known her for very long. I knew her well enough to know. I knew she did, too. This is the happiness I'd never known I needed, because I'd never gotten a taste of it before.

I was sitting by my locker, flipping a lazy finger through the tablet with the plays the coaches picked for Sunday. I memorized everything I'd need to know. Every assignment for every player. Every part of the defense I'd need to check before I'd say the magic word that started the action. Every read I'd make once I had the ball in my hands. Three pass patterns I'd work through, and what I'd do if none of the receivers were open.

I'd trust my ability to pull the ball down and run. I never did it much at North Texas; Kansas City's defense wouldn't be ready for how fast I am, for the kind of moves I can make. They had no reason to know. Nobody had seen me do it, not for a long time.

I'd welcome whatever hits I'd take. I'd start the contact, if I had to. I didn't expect the referees to protect me the way they take care of the famous quarterbacks. As the least famous of them all, I'd be on my own. I kind of liked that.

I was used to being on my own away from the game. Now that I felt like I wasn't, I loved the idea of being a lone wolf on the football field, doing whatever I needed to do to move the chains and score some points and keep the defense wondering what the hell was going on.

Coach Gary wandered in. Yep, I'd finally figured out his name. It dawned on me to check the team's website. Gary O'Shea. A guy who, like me, had been a decent college quarterback but not nearly good enough to make it in the pros. So he started coaching more talented quarterbacks to throw the ball the right way to the right spot at the right time.

He seemed to be getting a little calmer. I'd like to believe I made him think a guy who just landed on the team can be relied upon to not fuck everything up. It was also possible he'd come to terms with the fact that, at this point, there wasn't a damn thing anybody could do.

"There he is," Coach Gary said. "The man who'll clobber Kansas City."

I focused on the tablet again. "I'm sorry you've been dealt a bad hand lately."

"You get dealt some good hands, you get dealt some bad ones. My job is to try to make bad hands into good ones."

"Does that make me your ace in the hole?"

"You could be."

I looked up. "Nobody knows that."

"We've got no chance if you don't believe it."

"I believe I'll do my absolute best to prove you right."

"That's all anyone in this business can ever ask for. You know the offense. I've never seen anyone learn it so damn fast. That counts for something. It comes down to going out there and doing it."

I stood up. I was four inches taller than Gary O'Shea. "How long of a leash do I have?"

He seemed surprised by the question. "How long of a leash does anybody have?"

"So, not very."

"Has anyone else gotten reps with the first team this week? You're playing, and you're only coming out if you get hurt or if it's a total disaster."

"What counts as a total disaster, if no one else is ready to go?"

"I don't make those decisions. They just added that kid from Kansas State to the practice squad. He doesn't know the offense, at all. I assume they'd just have him run the clock and hand the ball off and get the game over with. I haven't even worked with him. You understand that, right? I've only been working with you. We're all in with you."

"Unless it's so bad with me that handing the ball off over and over would be better."

"You know the game plan. It's already pretty heavy with runs. We'll be trying to milk the clock. We'll need to shorten the game and keep their offense off the field. Nothing fancy. Play it slow and steady. Maybe catch a break somewhere. Long kickoff return. Blocked punt. Interception. A bad call for them, which means a good call for us. It won't take much to turn things our way, if we don't go out there and make a bunch of mistakes."

"They're going to be expecting that, once they find out I'm starting. They'll think we'll be doing exactly what you're saying."

Coach Gary studied my face. I wondered whether I'd said too much.

"What was that Mike Tyson line?" he said. "Everyone has a plan until they get punched in the mouth? Between you and me, I got no problem at all if you decide to be the one who punches first."

65

JOHNNY MOTTS

I waited til noon to call Carmine. I asked if we could get together. I didn't want him to think it was nothing bad.

Even if part of it is. If Jeffrey already flipped, we got a problem. The kind of problem that could take everything down. I don't know whether he flipped. I can't even mention the chance he might flip until I know more.

I freelanced on this one. I was just trying to find out who Jeffrey might be spending time with. I stumbled into the rest of it. He's sleeping with a fed. It's just a matter of time before he spills his guts to her, if he ain't done it already.

I can't stop thinking that maybe my only way out of this mess will be to flip, too.

I need to tell Carmine about Carson Jeffrey playing on Sunday. I need to tell Carmine we'll have a plan to get the information we need before the game and during it. I don't need to tell Carmine nothing more than that.

If the kid flipped, Carmine needs to know, right? But I don't know if the kid flipped. I need to know if he might, so I can decide whether I should.

I can't flip. I took the oath. If I flip, I'm dead. It ain't if at that point but when.

Carmine told me to come by his place at three. Nothing about what he said or how he said it made me worry too much. I didn't get the idea he already knows what I need to tell him. If I only knew what I was gonna tell him.

There ain't no reason to have like a script for this. I know myself good enough to know that, whatever it is, it'll change once I'm in that chair and Carmine is giving me that look and my heart starts pumping hard and I can't control what I'm about to say and I just say whatever.

I need to be careful not to say too much. Part of me just wants to be done with it. I won't feel better about none of this until it's over.

That fucking twitch is back in my mustache again.

I left my place around two-thirty. Just as I was walking out, I saw the bag with the laptop I used in Denver. I picked it up without thinking. I guess I figured it would make me look more professional if I was carrying something other than a piece in my belt.

Yeah, I took a gun with me. I ain't gonna use it on Carmine, not in his own place. Not unless he makes a move. He won't. He don't like to do that no more. Not that he wouldn't. It's one of the things you don't have to do once you got enough money. For most people, that means not cutting your lawn. For somebody like him, it means not doing stuff that would get buried in somebody else's lawn.

I still have to be ready. I seen him mad before. If I blurt out that the kid maybe flipped, I don't know how mad he'll get. I need to protect myself, if it comes to it. Not that it would end well for me if I tried.

Sure, I'd have a chance to take out Carmine. And then one of his guys would take me out. If I was ever gonna take out Carmine, I'd need to come up with something better than pulling out my gun and shooting him while he was sitting behind his desk.

He won't get mad enough to try nothing on me there. He'll just have somebody show up the next day and say Carmine wants to see me. And they'll take me for a ride and dump my body wherever. That's how it usually goes, for the ones who know it's coming. Plenty don't even get the chance to piss or shit themselves before it goes down.

I felt like pissing and shitting myself on the drive over there. I thought about just taking him out and taking my chances with whoever else comes into the room after they hear the shots. That would be stupid. Stupider than any of the other stupid shit I ever done. It would make more sense to just flip and take my chances that way. Maybe I'd get a year or two in jail to relax before somebody finally offers the guards enough money to look the other way while they ice me.

As much as I've tried not to think about it, flipping is sounding better and better. It's not like I'd be the first guy who ever done it. I also won't be the first guy who might get whacked for doing it. The sooner I accept how this is all gonna end, the sooner I can start making better decisions.

I was still thinking it through when I parked a block from his place. I grabbed that bag and started walking. Maybe I should have just stuffed a bomb in there and blown up the whole building, me included. I'd take Carmine and a few of his guys with me. I never had much of a death wish. Maybe it's been there all along and I never noticed.

Bobo was waiting for me inside. He took me back to the same office. He told me to wait on the same couch. He looked at my bag but didn't say nothing about it.

I didn't know how long Carmine would be. I just sat there, trying not to keep thinking about all the shit I was thinking about on my way over. I looked at the bag. I took out the laptop. I remembered what I'd done outside Jimmy King's house. I figured while I was killing time to try some more of that.

If Carmine walked in, he wouldn't know what I was doing. I'd tell him I was looking at emails or checking out betting lines or looking up stuff about some of the athletes I'm working on. There's no way he'd think I'm hacking into his network to try to figure out who he reports to.

I don't know much, but I know he has somebody he answers to. I've had this feeling for a while now that he answers to somebody who ain't in this life. That he's being bankrolled by somebody in a real business.

I guess I just wanted to see whether I wasn't so dumb after all. The browser found the network and that was that. I figured they had cameras on me. I looked at the screen and didn't shift my eyes around like I was doing something I shouldn't.

I worked as fast as I could without making it look like I was working fast, if that makes sense. Typing in the stuff I need to type to get to where I wanna go as quick as I can while acting like everything is normal, like I'm just passing time until Carmine shows up.

I looked through all the websites. I never seen no computers in there before. I figured it was all from their phones. It was the shit you'd expect to see from a bunch of guys who was sitting around. In the old days, they played cards or shot pool. Now, they was watching YouTube clips and going to Facebook and playing online casino games. Somebody must have a grandkid or nephew playing basketball in some youth league in Oregon. They was watching their games. I knew Bobo good enough to know he was the one looking at the porn.

Somebody was buying and selling a bunch of stocks, too. Probably Carmine. It's like gambling. If you know what you're doing, it's a lot easier to make money than betting on sports. I need to get in that game, one of these days.

I dug into some of the moves. Somebody was picking up stock in a company called Traxxion. Never heard of it. Somebody also bought a bunch of that crypto shit. RabbitRun, what the fuck? I wish I knew more about how that works. I think somebody bought it then sold it, a while ago. I ain't too great at math, but it looks like they made a bunch of money. Yeah, I need to get into that world.

There was a bunch of emails that went in and out, too. Mainly on gmail. There was some other site I never heard of that came up a bunch. It looked like somebody was using that to send emails, too. I tried to pull up some of the messages. I felt like I was getting closer to something. But I didn't know what I was looking for.

It'll take a lot more time to figure this out. I thought maybe I should come back and sit outside in my car one night and dig deep into whatever might be there. I ain't sure I'm smart enough to do that. I've been telling myself I need to be more curious. I was getting real curious about what I was finding. I had no idea where it'd take me. That ain't keeping me from having an urge to find more. I kind of liked how I was feeling, even if I got way bigger problems to deal with before I could ever figure this out.

That's when the door opened and Carmine came in. He looked at me, sitting there with the computer open. I could tell he didn't know what to say. I waited for him to talk.

"Are you ordering a new bathrobe or something?"

"Bathrobe?"

"On that Amazon thing or wherever. Bathrobe. Slippers. Fuck, I don't know. Why else would you have a computer out?"

I closed it up, hoping I didn't shut it too fast. "I want some new rims for my car."

"What have I told you about being flashy?"

"I need to attract these athletes."

"You find them in casinos. Are you driving your car up to the blackjack table?"

I tried to laugh at that. I was already nervous again. Too nervous, too fast.

"Just be careful about attracting too much attention. You've been doing this long enough to know that."

"I was just making myself useful."

"Looking up new rims ain't making yourself useful."

"I was also looking up one of the guys I met the other night. He might be a good prospect for us."

Carmine sat in his chair. He eyeballed me. "Who is it?"

I held my breath for a second. I blew it out. I knew I needed to come up with something fast. "Billy Sullivan," I said. "First baseman with the baseball team."

"I thought you was done fucking around with that after what happened with Larry Ballentine."

"They're local. And it's the offseason. Some of them hang around the casinos until spring training."

"Just be careful where you swing this one's bat."

They're gonna bust my balls about Larry Ballentine for the rest of my life, however long that might be. That might come down to whatever happens in the rest of this conversation.

"You asked for this meeting," he said. "Let's hear what you need to tell me."

I held my breath again. I tried to come up with something good to say before I blew it out and kept on talking.

66

ALICE SMITHSON

Orson Fredericks was available to see me that same day. Which meant he wanted to see me that same day. I took the first Acela I could catch. I finalized the arrangements and charted my questions while the cars creaked through Maryland, Delaware, Pennsylvania, New Jersey.

We met at his office. He sat behind a desk on a riser, allowing him to establish dominance over whoever occupied one of his guest chairs. His hair, which seemed to be mostly real, was dyed black. Just another late-middle-aged man who didn't realize how obvious it is when they do that.

The whole thing made for a first impression that screamed out petty, insecure, and superficial. When you didn't personally earn your billions, each of those attributes is understandable.

I played into his preferred vibe. I was deferential and complimentary, without presuming familiarity. It helped the meeting go far more smoothly than I would have imagined—if I would have had time to imagine anything.

He consented to being recorded, audio only. He might have even agreed to speak under oath, if I'd arranged for a court reporter. It wouldn't have been cheap or easy to find one that fast. I also decided I'd have a better chance to get him comfortable without one.

Instead, I explained the False Statements Accountability Act. That law made it a felony to lie to a government agent. I read every word of it before we got started, in the nicest voice I could muster while reciting a federal statute. I reminded him this was the law that once upon a time sent Martha Stewart to prison.

I turned on the recorder and let him tell his story. Whatever I did must have worked, because he didn't hesitate.

"Henderson Robertson has been looking to buy a team for a while," Fredericks said. "He's clearly got the resources. They still have to want to let you in. It pays to suck up. It pays even more if the sucking up entails payment.

"I've known him for years. People like us travel in the same circles, go to some of the same parties. We've been friendly, but we haven't been friends. Out of the blue, he extends an invitation through his personal assistant for a visit to the yacht he keeps in Miami. I shouldn't call it that. It's basically an aircraft carrier without the aircrafts.

"I assume he wants to show it off. I tell my assistant to find a way to politely decline. She says she's getting the impression it's not a social thing. That there's something tangible to it. That's our unofficial word for anything that can help make an easy profit.

"I'm intrigued. I tell her to set it up, even if she has to shuffle my schedule. A couple of weeks later, there I am. Sitting in what looks like the lobby of the Paris Ritz, only bigger and nicer. He wines and dines me. We're smoking cigars and drinking bourbon from some rare bottle he must have bragged about for fifteen minutes. I keep waiting for his pitch.

"*Leave us*, he calls out. Twenty-some people scatter like cockroaches. He waits until they're gone. He turns serious, gets quiet. Intentional dramatics. He talks about an opportunity he has become aware of. An opportunity to add to my portfolio in an impactful way. He mentions that some of my partners might be interested in it as well. He asks me for the ones I trust most.

"I rattle off seven or eight names. There were more, but I didn't want him to think I'm too trusting. He asks if I have secure means to communicate with them. I tell him of course I do. He apologizes if that offended me. Which it had.

"Then he asks whether there's anyone else who should be included, if it might expedite his eventual effort to acquire an asset. Which is his way of telling me he wants to buy a team. Which I already knew. I tell him that, even though the Commissioner isn't an owner, it wouldn't hurt to add him."

That was all it took to open the door. We talked about the RabbitRun cryptocurrency, how Robertson had explained it would be added to a listing that would cause its value to increase dramatically in the short term, allowing for a quick exit and a gigantic profit.

As billionaires go, Orson Fredericks was almost likable. Even with his ridiculous hair. That's a plus. So many of them come off to the average person as assholes. Then again, most of them know how to turn on the charm when they need to. Even if they don't need to very often.

It got a little trickier at that point. I had to understand why he would be willing to betray the Commissioner. I assumed there were hard feelings. I needed to hear him explain whatever it was that made him turn on the man who runs the sport.

"Perry Charles is a millionaire who acts like a billionaire," Fredericks said. "He has systematically taken more and more control of our league. He has a small handful of owners who protect him, and who lavish him with obscene bonuses, every year. He focuses on keeping them happy. He has lost sight of the rest of us. He specifically resents me because I inherited my fortune. He has always been dismissive of me. I've had enough of it, it's that simple. I've also suspected for a long time he has found other ways like this to add extra feathers to his nest."

"Do you dislike him?" I said.

"I dislike being treated the way he has treated me. Certain teams get breaks. Jump balls go their way. We all potentially run afoul of a rule from time to time. Some get a pass. Others, he makes an example of."

"Did he ever make an example of your team?" I said.

"I haven't given him the chance. A couple of the other owners have experienced it. The double standard has become tiresome, to many. But the owners who protect him don't care, because they benefit."

I wasn't concerned about the potential for cross-examination based on some sort of personal grudge. The facts were the facts. If both Fredericks and Robertson would testify under oath in open court about Perry Charles's involvement in the scheme, it would be one of the easiest convictions I've ever gotten. The case would be so strong that he'd have to do a plea deal. The case might be so strong that we wouldn't offer one.

Henderson Robertson became the key to the case. It wouldn't be enough to pit Orson Fredericks against Perry Charles. One says up, one says down. One says white, one says black. That has reasonable doubt written all over it.

To win that specific jump ball, I needed Henderson Robertson.

The first step would be getting in touch with Joyce Fuller-Watson. From my perspective, things had changed dramatically. From her perspective, they hadn't changed at all. She would still be wired to fight, until she found out what I might be offering. Even then, I'd have to get her and her client to trust me. It wouldn't be easy. It also wouldn't be impossible.

I didn't know Joyce Fuller-Watson well enough to have her personal number. I called her office from the train back to Baltimore. An assistant told me in a mostly friendly tone that Ms. Fuller-Watson was on another call. Once I gave my name, I got the impression she'd been on the lookout for any calls from me. I expected to hear from Joyce Fuller-Watson soon.

I stared out the window of the train, watching the blur of ramshackle houses running parallel to the tracks. It was just enough of a lull to let thoughts of Carson slip back into my mind. I tried to force those memories away. I decided to sing a song in a low whisper. I went with the first thing I thought of.

I don't know why it was the national anthem. I picked it up at the part where the rockets were glaring red. The bombs were bursting in air. Fireworks. And back my mind went to the night before.

I pushed it down and went to the next line. *Gave proof through the night*. The night. Last night.

I fired off a profanity or two. I didn't care whether anyone sitting nearby would hear it over the rumbling of the wheels and the clanking of the cars. I slapped my face and told myself to snap out of it.

Sally Slammer thought she'd won. Alice was lurking, hoping for the right moment to remind Sally they were conjoined twins who shared a biological clock.

I threw my head against the top of the seat. I stared at the phone, willing the response from Joyce Fuller-Watson to come through. I thought about calling someone, anyone to distract me.

I considered making my way to the dining car for a beer. I remembered I'd sworn off alcohol earlier that day. I still needed something to get me to the conversation and, hopefully, the flurry of emails and notes and whatever else I would be doing after making my pitch to Joyce Fuller-Watson.

I bounced the back of my skull against the seat while looking at the phone. I made sure the ringer was on. I checked the bars. I kept waiting, rocking my head against the cushion in a rhythm that eventually made me think of the thing I was trying to forget.

The phone rang. The sound startled me. I fumbled, nearly dropping it on the floor. I managed to get it under control, to press the button and start the conversation.

"Thank you for getting back to me so quickly," I said.

"What can I do for you?"

Under other circumstances, I might have said something sarcastic in response to the cold greeting. But I needed to find a way to get Joyce Fuller-Watson on my side, without letting her realize she was now operating from a position of strength.

I also knew I couldn't seem too anxious. I didn't want to tip my hand until I was in the same room with Joyce Fuller-Watson and Henderson Robertson.

"We haven't spoken since our meeting," I said.

"I assume you didn't call to remind me of that."

"I have a proposal for you."

"I have one for you. Pull the plug on this pointless investigation before you end up being sued for malicious prosecution."

"You know how high the bar is to win a case like that."

"Do you think he cares about winning it?"

"I didn't call to start a fight."

"You already did."

"I know you're just doing your job. I have something that might help you do that."

"I don't need your help."

"I know you don't, Joyce. Can I call you Joyce?"

"You just did, so we both know you're capable."

I let it go, even though I didn't want to. "I'd like to schedule a meeting."

"I'm tied up all of next week."

"How about tomorrow?"

"I didn't think government employees work on Saturdays."

"We work on Sundays, too. Even though we don't have anyone we can bill by the hour for it."

"Why would I make time to meet with you tomorrow?"

"I don't want to meet with you specifically. I'd like to meet with you and your client."

I could hear her laughing. I waited for it to end. "I wouldn't waste your time," I said. "I definitely wouldn't waste his."

She didn't say anything right away. "He doesn't like you," she said. "I can't imagine what I could say to get him to agree to meet with you again."

"I promise it'll be worth his time."

"I don't even know where he is."

"I'll go wherever that might be."

"I'd wait to make that commitment until you know whether he's in the country. You don't have time to get a commercial flight if he's at one of his estates in Europe."

"I'll do whatever I can to go wherever I need to go."

"If I didn't know better, I'd think you want to trade dropping your case against Mr. Robertson in exchange for a bigger case he can help you with."

I did my best to laugh in a natural and dismissive way. "I wish," I said.

"I'll call you back."

I played my last words back again. *I wish*. It wasn't a lie. It wasn't anything. It was a statement of aspiration.

A wish. If I was going to make any wish at that moment, meeting with Henderson Robertson wouldn't have been the wish I made.

67

CARSON JEFFREY

I sat on the edge of the bed, another mattress that wasn't big enough for me. I held a tablet in my right hand and my phone in the other. The clock was creeping up on nine, and I hadn't heard from her.

I'd left her a note. The ball was in her court.

I kept telling myself that. I made the last contact. She should make the next.

Why hadn't she?

I looked at the phone again. I needed to study the tablet some more. It wouldn't hurt to keep watching some of the plays from the Kansas City defense. Sometimes, one extra look shows something that'll make a difference. Something small can become something big. The right movement at the right moment could give me the right tip I'd need to beat the defense on the right play at the best possible time.

It would have been easier to focus after talking to her. I needed to know whether she felt the way I do. That she believed what I believed. Wanted what I wanted.

It was stupid to wonder about it. If she felt the same, she'd welcome the call.

Then again, if she felt the same, she would've called by now.

That was enough to get me to pick up the damn phone and press a finger on her name.

The line rang once, twice. It rang a third time. I started to wonder whether to leave a message or let the missed call speak for itself. I wasn't sure what I'd say. I decided to hang up, if it went to voicemail.

That's when I heard her. It sounded like she was answering a call from a stranger.

"Isn't my number in your phone?" I said.

"Sorry, I was working."

"It's almost nine."

"I'm home. I was in New York today. I have to go back tomorrow."

"Sounds important for a Saturday."

"Just another day on the job."

"I wanted to check in."

"Looks like we both have busy weekends coming up," she said.

"Are you working on Sunday, too?"

"Depends on how tomorrow goes."

"Maybe you'll watch the game."

"If I have time."

"It's the first time I'll be playing in a long time. I know it sounds weird, but I don't have anyone to watch me play."

"I will, if I have time."

I thought about her words and her tone. "Is everything OK?"

"Your season lasts part of the year. Mine never ends."

I thought about telling her it's going to be my last season. I had a feeling it wouldn't be received the way I hoped. I wondered for the first time since coming up with my plan whether it was all a big, stupid mistake. That I'd misread her. Or that something changed.

I decided to be direct. "Did I do something wrong?"

"What do you mean?"

"Last night. I thought—never mind."

"Last night was last night."

"And tonight is tonight."

"Tonight I'm working. I have a big day tomorrow."

"So was last night just something that gets forgotten?"

"I never said that. It is what it was. I have no complaints."

"That's a ringing endorsement."

"I don't know how else to put it. My life happens one day at a time. Last night was what it was. Tonight is what it is. Tomorrow is whatever tomorrow will be. There's no deeper meaning to any of it."

"I thought last night was, I don't know, different. Special."

"I don't want you to think I do that all the time. Nights like last night are always special. Then comes the next day."

"So last night was a one-time thing?"

"Last night was last night."

My confusion was starting to become frustration. "We're both too old for games."

"Are you playing games?"

"I didn't call to play games. I called because after a night like last night, that's what people do."

"Thank you."

"For what?"

"For calling, I guess."

"You're welcome. What are you doing Sunday night?"

"Working, probably."

"On a Sunday night?"

"Based on what I have going on, probably."

"I know you can't tell me what you're doing. But if this thing were to continue, at some point we should—"

"Look," she said, "this is complicated."

"It didn't seem complicated last night."

"It is now."

"It'd be nice to know what I did wrong last night."

"You didn't do anything wrong last night."

"So when did I do something wrong?"

"May I be candid?"

"I want you to be."

She paused. I checked to make sure the call hadn't dropped.

"I know what you've been doing," she said.

I felt a chill shoot through the phone, into my ear and down my spine and all the way to my toes. "What does that mean?"

"It means exactly what I said. You're smart. I'm smart. Maybe smarter than you realize. I know what you've been doing. That's what complicates things for me, given what I do for a living."

I looked around the room. It felt like I was searching for a place to hide.

"I watched your last game. I saw what you were doing. I know what you've been doing. It creates a real problem for you, and for me. Do you understand that?"

"I don't know what you're talking about."

"I think you do. I think you need to do some thinking about what you're going to do about it. You have another game on Sunday. You asked me if I'm going to watch the game. Are you sure you really want that?"

"I want you to watch me play."

"Playing isn't the issue. It's what you do before the play starts."

My stomach flipped and churned. I never expected this. I should have. Just not this way. Not from her. Not after last night.

"Do you understand what I'm saying?"

"I guess I do."

"I've been trying to figure out what I should do about it. I hope you realize I have to do something."

"I have a feeling last night wasn't part of the plan."

"That's why it's so complicated."

"What should I do?"

"The better question would be what should you not do."

I closed my eyes and shook my head. "I'm sorry I put you in this situation."

"I'm sorry about that, too."

"So basically there's nothing more we can do until I figure this thing out on my end?"

"I'm not sure there's ever anything more we can do, under the circumstances."

"There has to be something."

"I doubt it. But it won't get any better if it continues on Sunday."

"Should I be concerned?"

"You tell me."

"What can I do?"

"You should come to the office on Monday. I have a colleague who can explain your options."

"I have options?"

"None of them are good. But, yes, you have options. Then you'll need to make some pretty important decisions."

My eyes kept taking in the room. This was a moment I'd love to forget but never would. It was a moment that would change my life in ways I couldn't begin to understand. I'd never played chess. But there I was, in checkmate.

"Well?" she said.

"I'll be there Monday morning at nine o'clock."

"Ask for Will Goldstein. He'll be waiting for you."

The line went dead. I squeezed the phone hard with my left hand. With the other, I threw the tablet against the wall. It smashed into pieces and left a hole.

68

JOHNNY MOTTS

"The kid is playing," I said to Carmine.

"What kid? My kid? Your kid? Bobo's kid?"

"The kid in Baltimore."

"He's playing?" Carmine said.

"He's playing."

"In a game?"

"In a game."

Carmine sat back in his chair. He was tugging at the small crop of hairs that grew out from the end of his chin. "That could be a problem."

"That's why I'm telling you."

He looked at me. His eyes got real narrow. "When did you find this out?"

"Right before I asked for the meeting."

"When did he find out?"

I wasn't gonna lie, just in case Carmine already knew the truth. If he busts my balls for not having better control of my guys, so be it.

"The other guy got hurt on Wednesday. I guess they was supposed to keep it under wraps. They're telling everybody about it today."

"Did you tell him you ain't everybody?"

"He knows not to let it happen next time."

"He shouldn't have let it happen this time. You shouldn't have let it happen, either. We need these guys to know that."

"I'm trying my best."

"We might have to send a message."

"I know."

"We don't need another Larry Ballentine situation."

"There won't be."

He wasn't acting mad. But he was making points. If he was yelling at me, maybe I would have kept my mouth shut. Now that I think about it, maybe he didn't start yelling because he knew it was the best way to get me to keep talking.

"There's something else," I said without thinking to not say it.

"About the kid?"

That was my chance to change the subject, if I could have thought of something else to tell him. I ain't smart enough to do that yet. I probably won't ever be.

"He's seeing somebody," I said.

"If I was his age and playing pro ball, I'd be seeing more than one somebody."

"It's who he's seeing."

Carmine got a confused look on his face. "The coach's daughter?"

"I don't know if the coach got a daughter."

"The owner's daughter?"

"It's nothing that could be a problem for him. It could be a problem for us."

Carmine stood up as soon as I said it. "It's only a problem for us if he's seeing my wife. Or a cop."

"He ain't seeing your wife," I said, "and he ain't exactly seeing a cop."

"That don't make it sound better."

"She's a prosecutor. A fed. A real ballbuster, too."

Carmine sprang around the desk and stood over me. He put his face down to mine. I could smell the tuna fish on his breath. "Did your kid fucking flip?"

"I don't know."

I wasn't ready for how loud he started screaming at me. "How do you not know that?"

"He had dinner with her on Sunday night. He slept at her place last night. I don't know if he flipped yet. Alls I know is he's seeing her."

Carmine stepped back from me. He calmed down, if only because he needed to think. He jerked his head around the room while he did. Then he turned his eyes back at me.

"Why were you watching him?"

I opened my mouth but nothing came out. I started stuttering. I couldn't make no words.

"Spit it out, Motts. Why were you watching him?"

"I just wanted to watch him."

"I don't remember seeing no request to spend that kind of money. Are you paying for this out of your own pocket?"

"I am."

"What are you up to?"

He was back on top of me again. That fish stink was in my nose and mouth. It was mixed with the smell of deodorant when it's right on the edge of not working no more. "I just felt like I needed to. He was acting weird. You tell me to control these guys. Sometimes, you need eyes on them to know how to."

He stepped back from me. I couldn't tell if he was for it or against it.

"So you wanted to see if there was somebody you could threaten, in order to get him to do what you wanted?"

"Basically," I said, feeling relieved he wasn't mad but worried I was walking into a trap.

"And now you've found out that the person you would have

threatened is someone you can't threaten without taking a chance he'll flip?"

I hadn't really thought of that, but he was right. So I just nodded some.

He stepped back a little more and leaned against his desk. He crossed his arms. "I'll bet all of this has made you think about flipping, too."

"I ain't flipping." I tried to act mad he'd even say it.

"I ain't saying you're flipping. I'm saying I'll bet you've thought about it. It's OK. People think about flipping. It don't matter unless they do."

"I ain't flipping, and I ain't thinking about flipping. Alls I'm thinking about is how to solve this problem before he flips."

Carmine walked back behind the desk and sat down. "You don't need me to tell you that."

"What does that mean?"

"It means you don't need me to tell you that. Or to tell you anything."

Before I could even think about it, I stood. I pulled up my shirt to show him my stomach. "I ain't wearing no wire, Carmine. You can have Bobo check me out. You don't need to talk to me like that. You can just tell me what I should do."

Carmine put his hands on the desk and smiled at me. "I'm telling you that you don't need me to tell you that."

I wanted to ask him again what that meant. He wasn't gonna tell me, and there was a chance I was gonna piss him off if I kept asking.

I've been saying I need to get smart. I figured that was my chance.

I just wish I was smart enough to know what he didn't need to tell me.

69

ALICE SMITHSON

Saturday morning, it was back to New York. I had to settle for the regional train; it was too early for the Acela. The ride was darker and grittier and louder and jerkier. It also wasn't crowded. I was able to keep a stack of documents on the empty seat next to me while collecting thoughts on my laptop.

I had no idea what to expect from Henderson Robertson, or from his lawyer. I wondered whether I'd once again be greeted by a roomful of suits.

I tried not to think about everything that had happened since the last time I'd faced him, less than two weeks earlier. I wasn't nervous then.

The stakes were higher this time. I needed to persuade the man I'd planned to prosecute to cooperate. He might think he's off the hook regardless of whether he helps deliver a conviction of the Commissioner. He might decide to stonewall or play dumb for spite, or for sport. We could still prosecute Henderson Robertson if he didn't help us. There was a decent chance he didn't care.

I welcomed this stew of possibilities and complications and unknowns, because it kept me from thinking about Carson. It was all I could do to not invite him over again on Friday night. I almost slipped during the conversation, twice, and said the same thing I'd said the night before. If I hadn't poured the rest of the tequila down the drain that morning, I probably would have.

For now, it was all business. Sally Slammer ran the show. This would be a pivotal day for my career, even if I had little control over how it would go.

The train arrived at Penn Station. I thought about walking from there. The blast of frozen wind that struck my face when I walked through the doors made me hail a taxi instead.

The cab rolled to the Manhattan offices of Traxxion Industries. I could see down Park Avenue the building where Perry Charles had his office. I wondered whether he was working that morning. I hoped he had no idea what might be coming.

While waiting for security to take my photo, I looked around the lobby. I assumed they'd all been up there for a while, making their plans for dealing with this prosecutor who had asked for another meeting out of the blue. They probably knew they had me over a barrel. They just didn't know what was inside the barrel.

I went around the corner and pressed the button at the bank of elevators for floors forty-six through seventy. I listened for the sound of the car gliding into place. The doors opened. A man stood there. He was wearing a blue suit and bright pink tie. He looked to be roughly my age.

"Ms. Smithson, I presume?" The words floated my way on a British accent.

"I am."

"They asked me to retrieve you." He used his arm to hold the door open.

"Consider me retrieved."

I stood to his left. I stared straight ahead. I could see our fuzzy reflections in the brushed stainless steel, next to each other.

He smelled good. Not too strong. But noticeable. He whistled as the elevator climbed. It was a song I sort of recognized.

"What's that tune?"

"*Sympathy for the Devil.*"

"Something from the Christmas album?"

That accent rumbled through his laugh, rich and deep.

The doors opened on the seventieth floor. "Does your job end here?" I said.

He laughed again. "Retrieve means retrieve. I've learned how to honor his orders to the letter."

"Sounds like you've had plenty of practice."

He turned back to me and smiled. I noticed his beard for the first time. It was brown and thick. "I've been doing it for nearly thirty-five years," he said.

He pushed on a large door before I could respond. It opened into a conference room with a long table that had people in full business attire at nearly every seat.

"Ms. Smithson has joined us," my escort announced. He stepped back and nodded. I moved toward one of the two empty chairs.

"Thank you, Carson," Henderson Robertson said. I stumbled a bit when I heard the name. "You can take your seats. Both of you."

The man named Carson sat five spots down from Henderson Robertson. I ended up directly across from his boss. Joyce Fuller-Watson sat to my left, at the head of the table.

"My son has become more involved in the business," Henderson Robertson said. "He grew up in England, with his mother. He's still not sure whether he wants to stay in the states."

"I may be a little too UK for the USA," Carson Robertson said.

"If you stay in the USA long enough," Joyce Fuller-Watson said, "you'll eventually have to contend with someone like Ms. Smithson scrutinizing the manner in which you acquire and manage your wealth."

"Only when laws are broken," I said, "and only when we can prove it."

"They say behind every great fortune is a crime," Carson

Robertson said. I smiled at hearing one of my grandfather's favorite quotes.

I added my own twist: "Sometimes in front, too."

"That must have been quite an elevator ride," Henderson Robertson said, looking back and forth at his son and me.

I could feel the heat on my neck. I hoped no one would notice the flesh had gone as red as it felt.

"I'm just kidding," Henderson Robertson said. "My son finds his conquests solely on Tinder."

"I shall perhaps be heading back to the UK even before this meeting ends," Carson Robertson said.

"Well," Joyce Fuller-Watson said, "that all depends on how long this meeting lasts." She then stopped and turned to me. That was my signal to get started.

"Thank you for doing this on a Saturday," I said. "I didn't expect so many of you. I recognize some from our last session. That was an important meeting, an important part of a broader investigation. As you can imagine, we have many different investigations. Sometimes, they overlap. Sometimes, that happens deliberately. Sometimes, it doesn't."

"So which investigation has mine overlapped with?" Henderson Roberston said. I shifted my eyes toward Joyce Fuller-Watson to see whether she'd show anything to suggest her client was departing from the script. Her expression told me nothing.

"Our office, like that of the office of every U.S. Attorney in every district, has considerable discretion when it comes to selecting the cases that will be pursued," I said. "There has been a development. That development potentially allows for a non-prosecution agreement, in exchange for full cooperation in another matter."

"Wait," Joyce Fuller-Watson said, "you're willing to give us an NPA on this?"

"In exchange for full cooperation in the other matter."

"Other matter?" Henderson Robertson said. "It sounds like you want me to become a rat."

"That's a strong term," Joyce Fuller-Watson said to her client.

"It's also an accurate one," he said. "She wants me to cover my own ass by serving up someone else's."

"I just want to get to the truth," I said. "We can subpoena you to testify."

"You'll have a hard time if my memory fails me. I'm seventy-three years old, young lady."

"Let's not escalate," Joyce Fuller-Watson said, still speaking directly to him. "We don't know who she's targeting. Maybe it's someone whose ass, to use your term, you'd like to serve up."

"Well, then," Henderson Robertson said, "let's hear it. Who will I be helping you put in the slammer, Sally?"

I flinched when I heard my nickname. I stammered at first, before my tongue decided to cooperate. I explained our office was investigating whether others had engaged in insider trading regarding the RabbitRun cryptocurrency. Others whose prosecutions would generate more attention and, in turn, help deter others from breaking similar laws.

"How would the prosecution of someone else generate more attention than prosecuting me?" Henderson Robertson said.

"You don't own a professional football team," I said. "And your name isn't written on every football they make."

He looked at me with that sour face. I couldn't tell whether he felt slighted or relieved.

"I would require a full and complete non-prosecution agreement," he said.

"I already said there would be one."

"Not just in this case. I want full immunity. For anything. For everything."

"What do you mean by everything?" I said.

"Is there some other meaning to the word 'everything'?"

I turned to Joyce Fuller-Watson. "Just to be clear," I said. "You want full immunity, for anything and everything he might have done?"

"I don't want it. He wants it. And if you want him to cooperate, he'll get it."

I turned to Henderson Robertson. "I'm not sure I can offer that."

"Let me guess. You need to get permission from your supervisor?"

"You're asking for something significant. Something we rarely ever give. What if you've killed someone?"

His head snapped back. "Are you accusing me of murder?"

"I'm just making a point."

"Here's my point. If you want my help, I'll get full immunity. Otherwise, you can get out of my office and crawl back to that shithole of a city you call home."

I looked back at Joyce Fuller-Watson. I could tell she was enjoying this.

"I'll get back to you," I said. I stood and made for the door.

"You have twelve hours," he said as I walked away. "And you should be glad you're getting that long."

I wanted to turn back to him and tell him to shove it. But I wouldn't need twelve hours. I wouldn't need twelve minutes.

I went to the ladies' room and called Roger. I told him the terms. He didn't hesitate. He was willing to cut Henderson Robertson loose for anything else he might have done. When you want to take someone down that badly, sometimes you'll make a deal that could turn out to be a bad one.

I still decided to wait the full twelve hours before getting back to Joyce Fuller-Watson.

70

CARSON JEFFREY

We'd have a short practice at noon before heading to Kansas City. I needed to leave by eleven thirty to get there on time. I decided to make the call at eleven, sharp. Eight o'clock, Las Vegas time. Just in time for Johnny Motts to be sound asleep from whatever he'd done on Friday night.

"Hello?" Johnny Motts said. His voice was deep and groggy. He was too disoriented to be upset.

"Good morning."

"What time is it?"

"Eleven. Well, eight for you. It's a little early, I know."

"I also know we talked about you not calling so early."

"I know we've talked about me calling you whenever it's important."

"Then this better be really fucking important."

"It is," I said. "I'm out."

"Why would they cut you? You're supposed to play tomorrow."

"They didn't cut me."

"So why are you calling?"

"To tell you I'm out."

"But you're not out. You just said so."

"But I am out. I just said so."

"You just said you're not."

"I mean I'm out. I'm done. No more information."

"It's too early in the day for you to be this fucking drunk."

"I'm as sober as I've ever been. I'm not doing this anymore."

"I've told you that's not a choice you can make." Johnny Motts was now fully awake and more than fully pissed off. "You can't make it the day before a game. Have you lost your fucking mind?"

"It's the choice I've made. I wanted you to know about it today so you wouldn't be surprised tomorrow."

"I'm surprised now. Not in the good way."

"You'll figure it out. You'll be fine."

"You won't be."

"I think I will."

"I think you don't know who you're dealing with."

"I think you aren't doing shit about it."

"I think you need to think this through a little more, pal. I think you need to think about it long and hard before you fuck everything up tomorrow."

"The way I see it, I'm fucking everything up right now. And I don't care. I quit. I resign. I'm done."

"Oh, you're done."

"What are you gonna do about it? I'll be with the team the rest of the day, tonight, and all day tomorrow. Are you gonna shoot me during the game? On the bus to the airport? On the plane home?"

"You think there's a time limit? You think we can't get to you in Baltimore?"

"I think I'll take my chances."

"I've made plenty of bets in my day. The last thing I'd do right now is bet on you getting away with this stupid fucking game you decided to play."

"I said I'll take my chances. In fact, I like my chances."

"I can't believe you're doing this. All that money you got stashed out here is gone. I'll have my guys go get it today."

"I don't give a shit about the money. Take it all. Consider us even."

"That's just for starters. This choice you're making is gonna cost you a lot more than that."

"Do you think I can't take care of myself? That I can't deal with whoever you send here to take care of me? You'd better send more than two or three."

Johnny Motts got quiet. "I'm giving you one last chance to change your mind."

"Consider it your last chance to change your mind."

"That's fucking rich. Alls you know how to do is throw a football, and you don't do that too good or you would've been playing by now. You're getting your chance tomorrow, and we both know how it's gonna go. When you get back to Baltimore, that's when the real fun starts."

"I'm ready for tomorrow. I'm ready for whatever comes after it. I haven't been able to buy very much with your money. I've been able to get enough stuff to take care of me when your goons show up. They'd better be ready for it."

"They will be, tough guy."

"You know, I hope you'll come, too. Do it personally. If you have the balls to face me."

"I've handled bigger men than you."

"Just let me know when and where. Unless you're all talk. Which I think you are."

"You're about to find out."

"Like I said, let me know when and where."

"This ain't the Old West, you stupid fuck. It don't happen at high noon in the middle of the street. It happens when it happens."

"I'll be ready whenever. I'm looking forward to it."

I hung up the phone. I held it in my hands. I thought about stomping it into smithereens, but it was now something more than it had ever been. It was evidence.

My heart thumped and pounded, from my chest to my neck to my wrists to my ankles. I hoped Johnny Motts would accept the challenge. I also hoped Johnny Motts wouldn't make it to Baltimore before I went to the prosecutor's office on Monday morning and told them the whole story about what I'd been doing.

I was willing to risk it, since that was the only way it could ever end in a way that'd give me any chance to end up with the life I was hoping for. Even if the chances of that happening had become too slim to even think about.

I knew I'd have a better chance of making it to Monday if I stopped doing what I'd been doing without telling him first. I felt like I owed it to him to let him know. I felt like it was the right thing to do.

If I'm going to start doing the right thing, I can't pick and choose when and where I'll be doing it.

That made no sense to me at all. It also made all the sense in the world.

71

JOHNNY MOTTS

The farther I got from Carmine's place, the more it sunk in. He was telling me, without telling me, to go to Baltimore and take out Jeffrey. I think Carmine was also telling me, without telling me, to take out the woman.

I can handle taking out Jeffrey. I had a feeling it was gonna end up like that anyway. I don't like the idea of taking out the woman. For starters, she's a fed. If she ends up missing, they ain't gonna stop looking for her. They'll keep coming and coming and even if they don't get me right away I'll have to keep my head on a swivel for the rest of my fucking life.

I kept thinking about Jimmy King's girlfriend. Did I not go through with it because she was pregnant, or did I stop because I knew it wasn't right to take out somebody who wasn't in this life, especially when it's a woman? I never once got rough with none of my girlfriends, even when it felt like they was pushing to see if I'd cross that line.

I started laughing. Who would have figured I got a conscience? I mean, it ain't much of one because it never stopped me from taking out guys in this world who needed to go. But it's still enough of one to make me stop short of taking out somebody not in this world, when it's somebody who ain't a man.

If I go to Baltimore to take out the kid and his girlfriend, there's a chance I'll freeze up with her. I don't wanna find out I can't do it.

I can still take him out. That won't work, either. Larry Ballentine didn't have nobody who gave enough of a shit to keep pushing for answers. She wouldn't quit. Taking out a fed's boyfriend would be pretty much the same as taking out a fed.

That's when it happened. Just like that. I decided to flip. I was lost in the middle of a maze of mirrors, and that was my only way out. If I didn't do nothing, Carmine would take me out. He was already five moves ahead of me. He was giving me a chance to make it right, if only to save my own ass. Even if I was the one who'd take the fall once the heat got turned up after Jeffery and the woman went away. I couldn't remember her name. Whatever it was, I wasn't gonna take her out. I couldn't take him out without taking her out. It was both of them, or it was me.

Unless I flip.

I needed to think it through before I made my decision for good. I changed things up and went to Mandalay Bay. I'd have a few drinks, play a little blackjack. I didn't wanna see no athletes, and none of them gamble down there. Then, I wanted to sleep on it.

Of course, before I could get much sleep at all, that fucker called me. He told me he was getting out. He basically dared me to do something about it.

That woke something up inside me. That made me forget about my conscience. I decided to go to Baltimore and take care of him. Maybe I'd take care of her, too. Once he pissed me off, it wasn't about finding a way out of that maze. It was about knocking down the mirrors and seeing what happens next.

It makes me not give a shit about what kind of problems it might cause for me. The fucker pushed just enough buttons to get me to forget all about flipping, until I get rid of him. And maybe until I get rid of her.

Am I being smart or am I being dumb? I'm being what I am. Being what I am brung me this far. The only thing that seems right at that point is to keep being what I always been.

72

ALICE SMITHSON

I stared at the same jagged landscape back to Baltimore, for the second straight day. I didn't know how I felt. I didn't know how to feel.

I wanted to think about this new Carson I'd met. He'd taken me back to the lobby after his father declared the meeting over.

New Carson offered his cell number in the event I needed anything. He said it in a way that carried implications beyond the purpose of my visit. He smiled. He used that accent. I didn't want to be interested in him for who he was or what he had, or what he'd inherit. I was interested nonetheless. I couldn't lie to myself about that, since Sally Slammer fully approved of this potential path away from Other Carson.

Until, of course, I find out whatever New Carson might have been doing that would create the same dilemma for me as Other Carson. I already knew Carson One was a criminal. I'd probably figure out Carson Two was also a criminal, in a more nuanced and complex way. If he wasn't yet, he probably would be, in time. Unless he was secretly planning to cash in his Traxxion stock for a compound on an island in the Caribbean. Maybe the Mediterranean.

I cursed my luck, if luck was even what it should be called. After years of focusing exclusively on my work, I had two interesting men showing interest in me. Two men who any woman in her right mind would want to pursue, welcoming the firewall of blissful ignorance between what the man could provide and how he went about providing it.

It kept me from feeling good or feeling bad or feeling anything about how the meeting with Henderson Robertson had gone. It made me renew the commitment to doing the right thing, to proceeding with my plan to ensure Carson One accepted the consequences. I had no interest in getting myself into a situation that might make me force Carson Two to someday do the same.

I texted Roger McClelland from the train. I suggested a meeting at the office on Sunday afternoon. Avoiding any specifics, I conveyed the importance of getting together. I told him it would be useful to have Will Goldstein there as well, and that the reasons for his involvement would become apparent. The boss readily agreed to come in. It made me feel respected and trusted.

I let Will know, also by text. He responded with various emojis and gifs. He had no complaints about having a seat at the table with the man in charge. He even promised to cancel his plans for another night of barreling through various Baltimore bars so that he'd be clear-eyed and level-headed for the session due to begin at one o'clock sharp.

The football game started at the same time. Roger McClelland probably would have it playing on his phone. I wondered whether Carson One would be doing the things I'd warned him to stop doing.

I got to work early on Sunday, setting up my laptop and files and notes in the conference room near my office. Will showed up not long after I arrived. He wore a goofy smile. The more I tried to tell him to get serious, the more he giggled and chuckled and promised through it all to get his act together the moment he smelled Roger McClelland coming.

McClelland breezed in at ten minutes after one. He was holding his phone roughly six inches from his face and laughing. "Can you believe this? That kid they picked up off the street took them right down the field. I've never seen anything like it. No one's ever heard of him. He's fast and he can throw and you should see the hit he delivered to some poor bastard who made the mistake of trying to tackle him."

McClelland looked at us. "I'm guessing neither one of you is a football fan."

"We're not," I said. "But that's not the reason for the reaction."

"What do you mean?"

"Before we talk about my meeting with Henderson Robertson, I need to talk to you about Carson Jeffrey."

Roger McClelland pressed an index finger against his screen. "How did you know his name?"

"I wish I didn't," I said.

He sat down. He turned off his phone. He twisted his head and a soft crackling sound emerged from the back of his neck. "I've got the feeling you're going to be telling me something that could be pretty interesting."

I told him the whole story. Starting at the Friday night with Will. The player with the tight shirt and loose brain who tried to hit on me. The quiet friend who played the role of surrogate joke-teller. The dinner date the evening after I noticed something strange while watching the game. My efforts to confirm I was seeing him communicate inside information, to someone. My warning that he shouldn't do it again. My invitation to come to the office the next morning and meet with Will. The options Will would be presenting.

I mentioned everything except what happened on Thursday night. I told myself that didn't count as a lie. I wondered how I would have answered if McClelland had asked a direct question about the extent of the relationship. He didn't. I couldn't tell whether he wanted to.

After I finished, Roger McClelland sat there. Thinking it through. I waited for questions that never came. He nodded, softly at first and then with more determination.

"I admire you for handling this the right way. I assume it wasn't easy. And I know it would have been much easier to do nothing. You did the right thing, Alice."

I felt a tear starting to spill over the corner of my right eye. I didn't want to make it obvious by brushing it away. I focused on keeping my mouth from trembling.

Will must have seen the droplet making its way toward my cheek. He sprang to his feet and slapped his hands against the glass-covered wood in front of him. "Let's say we turn that game on and see whether this knucklehead took our girl's advice and stopped doing whatever it was he was doing before the play starts?" Will said. "That'll give us a pretty good idea as to whether we can expect him to show up tomorrow."

Will pressed a few buttons on a small box in the middle of the table. A screen came down behind me. He hit the buttons another time, and there was the game. As I spun my chair around and pushed it out of the way, I was able to swipe the tear with the heel of my palm.

73

CARSON JEFFREY

I stood along the sideline, staring at the large flag hanging limp and lifeless from the pole at the top of the south end of the stadium. Somebody I'd never heard of sang the anthem. I had my helmet tucked under my left arm. My right hand was pressed over the eight on my jersey. I pushed down as hard as I could to keep it from shaking.

I was thinking of everything that happened before that moment. I tried not to think of everything that would come after it, including the things that might happen after we got back to Baltimore.

The flag. Representing the United States of America. Just like Alice and her coworker in the case that probably would be called *United States of America versus Jeffrey.* My reward for making it to their office to hear whatever choices I'd be facing after I admit to the things I'd been doing.

Something in my head asked, *Will you make it there?*

If I got there, I'd admit it all. No matter what. Probation or prison, at best. Something a lot worse than that, at worst. I tried to bluff Johnny Motts about having a bunch of guns ready to face whoever comes to do whatever they planned to do. I only wanted to give Johnny Motts something to think about. I wanted to dare him to personally make the trip. I didn't know why in the hell I'd done that.

Hopefully it'd be something quick and mostly painless. I didn't care if they shot me in the head or the face. It wasn't as if anyone needed to see me. A closed casket would still be better than getting thrown in the harbor or set on fire or tortured and chopped up before it all came to an end. The end didn't bother me nearly as much as the getting there.

Maybe it wouldn't come to that. They didn't know I'd be turning myself in on Monday. They'd surely wait a couple of days to come after me.

I heard that thing in my head again. *Will they wait a couple of days?*

I had work to do before any of it mattered. I was getting my chance. After all the time I'd spent standing around and watching, I was about to play.

Afterward, I'd be getting exactly what I deserved. Maybe my story would show the next target of the next Johnny Motts to think twice about saying yes to easy money.

There's no such thing as easy money. I wished I'd known that. There was nothing I could do about the choices I'd made. I was ready to own up to all of it. I was grateful for the fact that, before I got whatever I deserved, I'd have a chance to do the one thing I grew up dreaming about.

If there was any silver lining to the mess I'd made, it's that I was getting a shot to temporarily live my dream, before taking up residence in a more permanent nightmare.

I didn't realize the anthem ended until I noticed others moving. I wondered if anyone saw me standing at attention a lot longer than I should have been.

I pulled my helmet over my head and pushed it into place. I turned to find the football I'd picked to start the game with. I squeezed both ends of it. I ran my hands over its sides. I tried to remember the first time I felt that leather with the pebbles under the tips of my fingers. I wondered if I'd ever feel it again.

Our captains walked out for the coin toss. We called tails. It landed on heads. Kansas City deferred their option to the second half. Of course they did. They wanted to get a shot at the Baltimore offense led by the kid from Kentucky by way of North Texas who had no professional experience.

The time had come to do it. I embraced the chance to forget about everything and go out and play the game I love, even if the game has never really loved me back all that much. A wise man once said it can't love you back; it's just a ball. I learned over the years that, at this level, it's anything but just a ball or just a game.

I planned to treat it like the game it once was for me. Like the first time I ever played, blowing away the other kids who were playing and the grownups who were watching. From the first time I ever touched the ball, I showed everybody I was the best one on the field.

Today would be the bookend to that Saturday afternoon from all those years ago, good, bad, otherwise. I wondered if my parents would be able to see me, like they had that day. I chose to think they could. I chose to think I'd be seeing them again. Maybe sooner than later. I became determined to make them as proud as I had the first time I ever played.

And I did.

It ended almost as fast as it started. It was a blur, all of it. On the first drive, I did my thing and we scored a touchdown. Early on, Garrett McGarrett chewed me out for not sticking to the script. By the time I threw that third touchdown pass and ran the ball through and around the defense for damn near a hundred yards, nobody was saying anything.

My own runaway train approach to playing quarterback couldn't work for more than a game or two. They knew it. They still weren't complaining. They'd found something that could make a difference. They were willing to ride it as long as they could. They just didn't know the ride would end for me the second the final gun sounded in Kansas City.

The final gun. I don't know when they stopped using a pistol loaded with blanks to mark the end of a football game. As time ran out and we had thirty-eight points and Kansas City had but thirteen, the only gun I was worried about would be loaded with real bullets.

I tried to enjoy what came after the win. They gave me a hero's welcome in the locker room. They gave me a game ball. There was dancing and whooping and hollering from teammates and coaches and trainers and equipment managers and executives and a team owner who all were stunned that a guy they were still getting to know had become the savior, if only for a day.

They seemed to be surprised by my reaction to all of it. They thought I was playing it cool.

They had no idea.

74

JOHNNY MOTTS

I called Nicky No-Nose. I already owed him from helping out with Larry Ballentine. I can afford to owe him some more. It won't matter once I flip. If I still can after taking out Jeffrey. At that point, my only choice might be to run.

Nicky started asking a bunch of questions about how we're getting to Baltimore. He wanted to fly Delta for the miles. I told him I'm surprised he didn't want a seat in first class. And then he said, "Now that you mention it."

I didn't know if he was fucking with me because he could sense how bad I needed his help. Whatever. Delta flight? Fine. First class? Fine. I was surprised he didn't have a hotel in mind. It's only because he's never been to Baltimore.

I've never been to Baltimore, either. But towns are towns. Streets and buildings and stores and houses and people. I had the number of Lego Billy's contact. I didn't plan to get her involved unless it was necessary. I didn't wanna have to take her out if she ended up knowing more than she should. I didn't know if I was wired to take out a woman.

Is it sexist to think that way? Not that I'm worried about being canceled or whatever the fuck they call it now. It's just weird to think I'm treating women different from men, but in a good way. It gives them a ticket out of getting whacked. I mean, it ain't no different from holding a door for a woman, right? I'll hold a door for a woman and not a man. I'll hold my trigger finger for a woman, too.

I don't wanna find out whether that's how I am the hard way. If I end up squaring off with Lego Billy's former cop and if I hesitate for even a second, she might put a bullet through my ballsack before I realize what's going on.

I didn't tell Carmine what I was gonna do. He already gave me the nod to take out both of them. Telling me without telling me. I need to show him I'm smart. If I call to tell him I'm doing what he already told me to do without telling me to do it, I won't look too smart.

All this thinking was giving me another headache. I found them Percocets. I decided to take a couple when the plane took off.

I got my shit together before I left for the airport. Nicky No-Nose wanted me to pick him up on the way. He's lucky I need his help like I do.

I packed a bag with only the stuff I'd need. Two pairs of briefs. Another pair of pants. Another shirt. I was going all black on this one. Black jacket and black shoes. Black fedora that was a little too big on me. I told Nicky so he wouldn't dress the same. We didn't need to look like the fucking Blues Brothers.

I wanted to take my laptop but I couldn't find it. I think I left it at Carmine's. I don't need him or Bobo figuring out I hacked into the network. The good news is I had it locked with a password. The bad news is the password is 1234. Maybe they won't start guessing what it might be.

I got the kid's address from Lego Billy. I had the woman's, too. They was both saved in my phone. I packed a couple of guns in the bag I checked. If the airline loses it, I figure I can find a gun somewhere in Baltimore.

I'm still pissed at the kid. That ain't gonna change. Not by Sunday night. That's when we'll do it. I wanna get him right after he gets back from Kansas City. I don't buy his bullshit that he bought himself some guns. That's the kind of tough talk I've heard plenty of times, from guys a lot tougher than him.

Besides, it's one thing to have a gun. It's another thing to use it. As I found out with Jimmy King's pregnant girlfriend in Denver.

Still, something told me I needed the help on this one, just in case. I didn't tell Nicky No-Nose the kid might be packing. I'll tell him before we get started. He's smart enough to know something like that might be going on. If Nicky ain't smart enough to figure that out on his own, that ain't my problem.

I got enough problems. I'm gonna start solving them. My way. We'll handle Jeffrey. Maybe we'll handle the woman. Maybe Nicky No-Nose will be the one to do it. Maybe he ain't got a conscience when it comes to taking out a woman.

We'll camp outside the kid's place and wait for him to get home. Then we'll move. We don't need to take the body with us. Just fire away and go. Then maybe take care of the woman before getting on a plane and getting the fuck out of Baltimore.

I feel like the plan is too easy. It's better than it being too complicated. This is simple. We got one target, maybe two. We're professionals at this shit. We handle them and get out. In and out. It'll be better if he has no idea it's coming. He probably don't think it's coming so fast, even though he pretty much dared me to come get him.

Ready or not, mutherfucker, here I come.

The trip went pretty smooth. The flight was about twenty minutes late taking off. Weather in Baltimore. It was Saturday afternoon, just after two. We had plenty of time to get there, rent a car, find a couple rooms, and then get in position outside the kid's apartment the next day and wait.

I ain't thrilled about being stuck in a car with Nicky No-Nose for however long it'll be. He's got that weird smell. I figure I'll get used to it after a while. Plus, I've been on stakeouts with guys who stunk a lot worse than Nicky No-Nose.

I took them Percocets right as the wheels went up. Swallowed them without no water. I slept most of the way. When I woke up, I wasn't sure where I was. When I remembered, I wondered if I was still pissed enough to do it. I told myself I was. By then, it was too late to go back.

Maybe that's the real reason I brung Nicky No-Nose. If it was just me, maybe I would've changed my mind. With Nicky, I'll look like a pussy if I say once we get there that we're gonna forget the whole thing and fly home.

Besides, once I thought about the way the kid talked to me, I got pissed again. I don't care if I'm making a mistake. I don't care if I should just flip before it might be too late. The kid asked for it. The kid disrespected me. I can't accept that. No matter where things might end up.

Carson Jeffrey was checking out. His woman might be, too. And then I'll go back to Vegas and figure out what to do next.

I liked that plan. I also hated that plan.

75

ALICE SMITHSON

I nuzzled my back into the corner of the couch. I wore flannel pajamas and wrapped myself in a down-stuffed comforter. I hated turning the heat on before Thanksgiving, because my grandfather hated doing it.

I'd taken a break from the preparations for Monday. I tried to relax a little bit, to catch up on a show I'd been watching. I couldn't focus on the TV. I couldn't stop thinking about what had happened that weekend. About what would happen the next day.

It was all coming together. I could feel it. I didn't know whether the feeling was a good one.

Two very different investigations impacting the biggest sports league in the country. Two very different types of crimes. Two very different segments of society. The similarities were unmistakable. Fundamentally, people were doing things they shouldn't have been doing. Trying to make easy money, regardless of what the law allows.

Whoever had corrupted Carson One didn't pretend to be something they weren't. What you see is what you get. It was honest and authentic. Despite being immoral and illegal.

Perry Charles and those like him paraded around in civilized society, pretending not to be exactly what they were. Both were bad. Perry's type was worse, because they lied to everyone about who and what they were. They lied about that maybe even to themselves.

I stared at the screen, ignoring the life and times of one woman and umpteen men who had been thrust together into the same habitat, as Jane sorted through her various Tarzans. I decided to go to bed. Or maybe to sleep right there, since parts of the mattress still smelled like him and I hadn't washed the sheets because sometimes I wanted to cram my face into the pillow and inhale him.

I thought about that smell. I closed my eyes. I allowed myself to remember what had happened three nights earlier.

I was glad I'd poured out the tequila. I doubted even a full bottle of it would have gotten me to call him. He was showing up at the office the next day to hold his nose and take his medicine.

As I sat there trying not to think about him, I heard a knock. It wasn't loud. A gentle rapping, just enough to be heard by someone who was awake but not enough to wake up someone who wasn't. I wore the blanket like a cape as I walked to the door and pressed my left eye against the small circle.

My heart skipped a beat. Or it stopped. Or both. He was out there. Carson One. I stayed still, hoping he hadn't heard me. Praying he hadn't noticed the faint shadow that had darkened the inside of the peephole.

"Alice, is that you?"

I tried to stay still. He'd leave if I kept still. He'd give up and go away.

"I really need your help."

I tried to ignore him. I didn't want to open the door. I didn't want to talk to him through it. If I started doing that, I'd give in to the fact that it was stupid for two adults to communicate that way.

"I wouldn't have come here if I didn't need your help."

I fought hard to stay still. I tried to ignore him. I should have plugged my ears.

I could hear it in his voice. It wasn't a ruse to get inside, a first step in some plan of systematic seduction. I could tell something was wrong. He had nowhere else to turn.

He needed me. I believed it. Even Sally Slammer would approve of throwing him a lifeline.

I opened the door, still covered in the comforter.

"I was starting to think you weren't home," he said.

"I shouldn't be doing this."

"Can we talk? Five minutes, max."

"We're talking now."

"It's safer inside."

Something about the way he said it sent a wave of tingling dread through my bones. I looked at him for any clues as to what was going on. "Five minutes."

He walked past me. I pushed the door shut, twisting the deadbolt. "It looks like you did well today," I said.

"I got lucky. My luck is running out."

"Are you going to the office tomorrow?"

"If I make it."

"You're confusing me."

He looked at the couch. I could tell he wanted an invitation to sit. I offered it, making sure I sat in the chair across from him.

"My contact is a guy named Johnny Motts. I told him yesterday that I quit. He didn't take it very well. I sort of dared him a little bit."

"Dared him?"

"To come here and take care of me by himself."

"Why would you do something like that?"

"I thought he wouldn't make it here until after I made it to your office."

"I'm guessing you're here because you thought wrong?"

"I had a weird feeling as I was going back to my apartment. I thought it was dumb, but I paid attention to it. I parked a few blocks away and started walking. I saw this guy getting into the passenger side of a car with a pizza box. He had that look, you know? I got low along the line of cars on the other side of the street and worked my way down until I could see who else was in the car. Johnny Motts was sitting behind the wheel."

"What did you do?"

"I went back to my car. I drove around a little bit, and then I came here. I don't really have anywhere else to go."

"Did they follow you?"

"Probably not. If they saw me, they could have just chased me down."

"Or they didn't want to have a scene out in the open so they decided to follow you and then make their move."

"I don't think anyone followed me up here."

"It's all the more reason for this to be a quick visit."

Carson paused for a few seconds. I could tell he was thinking hard about how to say what he was going to say next.

"Is there a way you can, you know, take me into custody tonight? Arrest me, or something? Hold me in a cell until morning?"

"There's no warrant for your arrest. Tomorrow was set up to be voluntary. There aren't any charges yet. There would be no reason for anyone to put you in jail."

"Maybe I should go rob a convenience store."

"Well, that would do the trick. But then it would be a little harder to work everything out tomorrow."

"I'm not asking to hide here. I don't want to put you in any danger. I need some advice."

"I guess you could stay here."

"I said I don't want to. What if they followed me? You said it yourself. Maybe they did. Maybe they're out there now. If they're gonna try something, I don't want you to be caught in the middle of it."

I wanted to ask him why in the hell he came to my apartment. I didn't want to make him feel any worse than he was feeling.

"You should just go find a hotel and stay there tonight. Then you can go to the office tomorrow morning. Once you explain what happened, you'll be safe."

"If they won't take me in right now, why will they tomorrow?"

"Once you tell them your story, they will."

"Then what? When will I ever be safe?"

"You've heard of witness protection, right?"

He frowned. "I thought that was something in the movies."

"It's real. It's not used as much as people think. For something like this, you'd probably be eligible."

"I'm hoping for something a little stronger than probably."

"I don't make the final decisions. But they'll listen to me."

"What would it mean?"

"It would mean what it means in the movies. You go away to a new place. New name. New life."

"In case you haven't noticed, I'm kind of hard to miss. Especially after today."

"They'll work it out. They always do. You'll be safe. You might not be thrilled about where you're living, but you'll be safe."

"I thought at one point about moving to New York City and just trying to blend in."

"It wouldn't be New York. They'd want you in a place where it would be easier to keep an eye on you."

"I don't like the sound of that."

"To protect you. So if someone tried something it would be easier for them to intervene."

"I guess beggars can't be choosers. If the goal is to stay alive, I'll have to go wherever they think it'll be easiest to do that."

"You'll probably have to testify, too. In court. In front of all of them."

"I'm fine with that, unless they know how to smuggle guns into the courtroom."

I laughed at that. I don't know why I thought it was funny. "You know," I said, "you still never told me that joke."

He shook his head. He smiled, too, despite the circumstance. "Maybe another time."

I knew there wouldn't be another time. I didn't want to tell him that. He had enough to worry about. I knew I'd never see him again. Not in a private setting. If nothing else, it would be a foolproof way to end any temptation I might ever have to call him up for another spontaneous romp in the proverbial hay. Or two. Or more.

"So you'll find a hotel and then come to the office in the morning?"

He stood up. "I guess I don't have any other choice."

"I'm willing to let you stay here. I'm willing to take that risk."

"Do you have a gun?"

"I should, but I don't. After tonight, I think I'll finally get one."

"I need to be completely sure you'll have a chance to do that. I appreciate your willingness to roll the dice for me. I'm not willing to make that gamble, for your sake."

He walked to the door. I wanted to get up and go to him. I wanted to beg him to stay. I told myself the risk was low. If he was going away for good, what would be the harm in one more night together? What would be wrong with the mattress in my bedroom absorbing another full dose of his scent?

I didn't. I sat there. I watched him leave.

"Next time," he said, "I'll tell you that joke. I promise."

"I can't wait."

I stared at him as he walked out of my apartment for the last time.

76

CARSON JEFFREY

I pulled the door to Alice's apartment shut behind me. I looked to the left, then to the right. I started walking to the stairs down to the street where I'd parked the rental car.

I wondered again if they knew what I was driving. I wished I'd learned how to hot wire a car. I didn't even know whether that was still a thing.

I'd hoped to stay with her. Even with everything I was worried about, I wanted to see if what had happened on Thursday night would happen again. But I couldn't put her in any danger.

I checked out all directions before I got in the car. It crossed my mind that they had enough time to put a bomb under it. That's something they only do in the movies. Then again, I thought witness protection was only a Hollywood thing, too.

I closed my eyes and started the car. When I opened them, I searched my phone's browser for the closest hotels. I needed to go somewhere simple. Somewhere out of the way. Somewhere they'd never expect me to go.

Motel 6 in Cantonsville. Fitting, I guess. On the same day I played like someone who, if it continued for ten years or so, could have gotten all the way to the Hall of Fame in Canton, Ohio, I'd sleep in Cantonsville, Maryland. I took Route 40 out of town, heading west. The map on my phone showed it was close to I-695, just south of Interstate 70.

I was feeling a little better. Having a plan helped. The voice on my phone would guide me to the motel. Traffic was lighter than usual, and why wouldn't it be on a Sunday night that's creeping toward a Monday morning?

I followed the turns and the intersections leading away from her apartment. I kept checking the phone to make sure I was on the right path. I knew the roads well enough to sense it was taking me back toward my apartment. I had no choice at that point but to follow the instructions.

Every light was red. Every single one. It started to be funny. I also started to wonder whether it was some sort of message. I didn't have time to think much about it. The goal at that point was to get settled into a room, sleep or try to, and then backtrack in the morning to the place where I'd confess my crimes and hope for the best. Even if, at this point, the best meant getting shipped off to some new town in some new state with some new name and everything but a new body and new face that, after Sunday's game, would be recognized more than it ever had been before.

It was one hell of a way to celebrate my first pro game.

The phone kept taking me back toward my apartment. I was paying closer attention to where I was, as the car rolled from one red light to the next.

I came to an intersection where the light was still green. Right away, it turned yellow. I took my foot off the gas and coasted to a stop. I was in the first spot, waiting to go left.

I turned to the right. I didn't know why. I saw at the red light the car that was near my apartment. And Johnny Motts was driving.

I thought about flooring it through the light, but that would have given me away. Instead, I stopped the rental short of the thick white line. I waited, trying not to look over at the other car, hoping not to do anything that would make the people inside notice me.

It was too late. From the corner of my right eye I saw the passenger door to the other car swing open. My windshield exploded.

I jammed my foot as far down as it would go, fishtailing into the intersection. The rear window blew to smithereens. I drove away, waiting for what I expected to be the moment everything went black.

It didn't. The rental roared away. I was weaving in and around the other cars on the road. At one point, I realized I was in the wrong lane. The headlights of a truck coming right at me told me to swerve. I did, and I kept going.

I checked the rearview mirror. It was shattered, with a dark spot in the middle. I was too worked up to realize a bullet had gone through it.

A car was behind me, moving faster than the others. I thought about my choices. The only one that made any sense was to keep going, as fast as that thing would go. Maybe I'd attract the attention of a police cruiser. I doubted it would stop Johnny Motts from doing what he was trying to do.

I'd underestimated Johnny Motts. I'd underestimated everything. I hoped I wasn't overestimating my own ability to drive to a safe place.

I missed a turn on the way to the Motel 6. The voice on my phone started reminding me of that. I turned around and saw the lights still back there, still following. I couldn't tell if they were getting closer. The faster I drove, the more the steering wheel wobbled in my hands.

I thought about crashing the car. Would that hurt more or less than getting shot? I decided not to find out.

I figured they had a crappy rental, too. I hoped my head start would give me a chance to find a place where I could disappear into a neighborhood and work my way to a spot where I could shut the car down and make a run for it.

The burner started ringing from inside the glove compartment. Having long arms comes in handy sometimes. I reached over, opened it up, pulled out the phone, and threw it out the window. If I make it to tomorrow, they'll have to take my word for the fact that we used burner phones.

Time rocketed forward but also stood still. I whizzed past other cars. Horns were blaring at me. The voice on my phone kept telling me how to get back on the path to the Motel 6.

A car in front of me jerked hard to the left as I approached it from behind. It slammed into a pickup truck going the other way. Both spun around in the road. The car started to tumble and roll. As it was happening, I spotted a road to the left that looked like it led to a street with rows of houses on each side. I spun the rental that way and headed toward a mostly dark avenue.

I kept going, slower than before but faster than cars usually move up and down a street like that. The intersections had stop signs. I blew through them all. I took a left at the third one I came to. I got a little farther and took a right at the next intersection. It felt like I was getting deeper into lanes and drives and ways and whatever names they used for the lines of pavement where I might have a decent chance of not being found.

I slowed down. I hoped I was getting closer to a spot where I could park. Then what? Sit and wait and hope Johnny Motts wouldn't find a car with the glass blown out of its front and back ends?

It was quiet outside the car. I pulled over in an empty space in front of a house that was dark on the outside. I saw a dim light behind a curtain in a second-floor window.

I shifted into park. I cut the engine. I thought about checking out the damage to the car before realizing it didn't matter. I wouldn't be returning it to the counter and explaining how and why and when and where it ended up like this.

The phone was still trying to tell me what I needed to do to get back to the motel. I turned off the app. I looked around. I listened. I got out of the car. I took the phone and left the keys.

77

JOHNNY MOTTS

I rented another brown Ford at the airport. Nicky No-Nose made a face. I shot him a look. The best kind of car for a stakeout is a car nobody's gonna remember.

We found a cheap hotel not far from Jeffrey's building. If it was just me, maybe I would have splurged. I didn't wanna get stuck paying for two nice rooms. Besides, it ain't like I was gonna enjoy the place. My head was hurting again. I was glad I had them Percocets.

I decided to take a couple more before bed. I wondered how much I'd sleep, after getting so much shuteye on the plane.

I told Nicky No-Nose to be ready to go at noon. We'll get some food. We'll find a spot to sit and wait. We'll watch football games on our phones.

How much did I really sleep? I can't tell. It felt like not much. I rolled around on that shitty mattress all night. It made me wish I'd sprung for a nicer place.

I felt groggy and tired when I got out of bed around eleven. I took a shower. The water pressure wasn't much stronger than an old man trying to piss in the middle of the night. I tried to wash my hair real good. It didn't matter much, because when it was time to move I'd pull that black hat down on my head again.

We ate at a place that served breakfast late. I told Nicky

No-Nose not to order nothing that might make him fart later. He said everything he eats makes him fart later. I wish I'd just come alone.

I still needed the help. I got a feeling it wouldn't be so easy with this one, even if he don't have a gun. He won't be stupid when it's time for things to go down. He won't lean his head into a baseball bat, like Larry Ballentine did. Jeffrey will put up a fight. I can feel it. I hope two guys will be enough to take him out. Two guys, three guns. That should be good enough. I hope it'll be.

His building wasn't hard to find. I don't know what he's driving, but I know what he looks like. That'll have to be good enough. I made sure the place didn't have an inside garage. It was all outdoor parking. The kid will come back here, he'll leave his car somewhere, and then we'll do it.

We got settled as the early games was starting. I wanted to see whether the kid played worth a shit. I figured he wouldn't. I was surprised when he did. It made me feel even better about bringing Nicky No-Nose. No, this kid won't go out easy.

I can't believe he pulled it off. He won the fucking game. He looked like a real player. I wondered if that'll make him getting shot down in front of his house a bigger deal. I told myself it was gonna be a big deal regardless, since he's sleeping with a federal prosecutor and might have already flipped.

That's when it hit me. What if he already flipped? Will he have somebody with him? A marshal or whatever? Somebody to make sure somebody like me don't try to take him out? Maybe he wouldn't even come back here at all once the plane from Kansas City lands.

I kept worrying about that. I was getting obsessed with it. You know that feeling? You can't quit thinking about it, even if there ain't nothing you can do about it? I kept worrying Jeffrey was gonna pull up with protection, or maybe not pull up at all.

Nicky No-Nose watched the Dallas game that started at four

thirty. I tried to sleep. I figured they'd get back around nine or so. I had that thing on my phone that shows all the planes coming and going. We'll know when the jet from Kansas City lands in Baltimore. I don't know how it works after that. They'll probably take a bus to wherever they left their cars, and then they'll get in and go home.

I didn't expect them to win. What if he goes out to celebrate or something? If he shows up half in the bag, that'll make it easier to take him out. Either way, we'll wait until he comes back. Unless he don't come back at all. Which will be a problem.

I don't think I slept much while we waited. Nicky was rooting for Dallas. He's a fan of that team, and he put five grand on them to cover. I wanted to tell him to shut the fuck up a little but I was saving my energy for later.

I still can't get used to Nicky's smell. It don't help that he bought beef jerky at the convenience store next to the place where we ate breakfast. Every time he opens that bag, it smells like a cow took a shit right on the dashboard. It makes me almost miss Nicky No-Nose's natural stink.

After Dallas won and made the number, Nicky got more worked up than if he done five lines of coke. He started talking real fast. He thought about betting it all on the night game. I told him I don't give a fuck what he does, as long as he's ready to do the job.

Then started talking about being hungry. I told him to eat more of the dried beef he loves so much. He said it was gone, that he needed something more than that. He didn't wanna work on an empty stomach. I managed to get him to hold off. It helped that he kept going on and on about wanting to let it ride on Denver plus eight and a half against Las Vegas.

After the game started, he went back to complaining about being hungry. He said there was a pizza place down the street. Once he said the word pizza, I realized I was getting a little hungry, too. Besides, no matter how bad the pie stunk up the car, it wouldn't be any worse than smelling him.

I told him to go get one, if that's what he wants. When he left, I forgot I hadn't checked on any planes from Kansas City that would be coming to Baltimore. I looked at the phone and saw one had landed forty minutes earlier.

I wished I'd checked before Nicky left to get the pizza. I would have told him it was too late. So there I was, waiting for Nicky to get back with the pizza while waiting to see when Jeffrey might get home.

Nicky got back before I seen any sign of the kid. I ate a piece while I kept looking. He left that piece of shit Jeep in Vegas. I was pissed at myself for not trying to figure out what he's driving in Baltimore. I should have had Lego Billy get that information. So much for me getting smarter.

I decided to get a little smarter right then. I got on social media and started poking around some of the accounts other players set up. Maybe I could figure out where they decided to have a party after winning a game everybody thought they'd lose. I did it while I kept my eyes open for any sign of him showing up at his place.

One of them was streaming video from a place that looked like a bar. I kept searching the names of other players on the team. I saw one of them post something about drinks with the fellas at Bernie's. I searched for any bar in Baltimore named Bernie's. I found one.

I put the address in my phone and got directions. It was a couple miles away. I put the car in drive and pulled out.

"I thought we was waiting for the guy to come home," Nicky No-Nose said.

"Change of plans," I said. "I think I know where the fucker is."

Nicky went back to eating the pizza. I didn't mind that it smelled better than he did.

Everything after that is a little blurry. We got to an intersection and I looked over to the cars that would be turning when the light changed. It was him. I couldn't believe my luck.

It was good luck, until it went bad. Once I said it was him, Nicky took that to mean it was time to let loose. What the fuck was he thinking? By then, it was too late to do nothing other than deal with it. The goal was to get him, and that's what we was trying to do.

That ain't usually how it goes. Shooting at a guy in a car in the middle of the road and having him hit the gas and take off. I stopped thinking and just went. I wish I hadn't. If we'd gotten him, I would've been glad we did.

Nicky kept shooting. I wanted to tell him to stop, but I also wanted to be done with it. Take him out and move on to the next step, if the next step means going to his girlfriend's place and hoping Nicky won't freeze up when it's time to do it.

I guess my instincts took over. Shit was happening too fast. There was a crash and it fucked me up and the next thing I know we lost sight of him. I don't know whether we hit him. For all I know, he drove that car until he bled out.

I kept going, even after it was clear we didn't know where he was. Nicky didn't say nothing. I didn't, either. By then, I just wanted to be sure no cops was chasing us.

I stopped at a gas station. I pulled up the map on my phone. We went more than ten miles out of Baltimore. There was no sign of the kid. I had no idea whether he was dead or alive.

"That was something," Nicky said.

"Why did you start shooting?"

"I thought that's what we was doing. We had him. I put a bunch of bullets into that car. I think we got him."

"If we got him, he kept driving."

"Where'd he go?"

I looked at Nicky. He had sauce on his chin from the pizza. "If I fucking knew that, we'd be there right now."

"So what now?"

"I don't know. All I know is I got a fucking headache."

"Didn't you say we might take out somebody else, too?"

"That was if we got him first."

"How are gonna know if we did?"

"I don't know how to find out if we did."

"Let's just assume we got him. Let's go get the other one."

I looked at Nicky again. I had her address. I saw that sauce on his face again. Could I count on him to not fuck that one up, too? I keep telling myself I need to be smart. I tried to think of the smart thing to do. Would it be smart to take out a federal prosecutor, when we don't know whether we took out Jeffrey? I decided the smartest thing would be to do nothing, for now.

I pulled the car back onto the street.

"Where we going?" he said.

"Back to the hotel. And why don't you wipe your fucking face?"

78

ALICE SMITHSON

I sat in my office, staring at the wall. Staring at nothing. Waiting. For something. For anything.

The jury had been out nearly two days in the case against Carmine J. Positano, the mastermind of the scam that had Carson providing information and tipping plays. His contact was a soldier named John P. Monitore.

Once Carson told his story to Will, they closed in on the man Carson knew as Johnny Motts. They arrested him at the airport on Tuesday morning. He was flying back to Las Vegas with an associate, Nicholas Nocera.

Monitore flipped quickly; so much for the Omertà. (Nocera refused to talk.) Monitore took a deal in exchange for cooperation. With his testimony, Carson wouldn't have to take the stand at the trial. He was still wherever he was, wherever he'd been sent nine months earlier by the witness protection program.

Yes, Carson showed up at the office the next morning. Roger McClelland suggested I work from home that day. I had plenty to do, since I'd managed to get everything I needed to cement the insider trading case against Perry Charles. I got a grand jury together, brought in Orson Fredericks and Henderson Robertson to testify, and by Wednesday morning at ten o'clock I had the indictment.

We moved without delay. We served the warrant to search the league's offices at the same time we took the Commissioner into custody. It was unconventional and aggressive, but that's what was needed. Roger McClelland worked the political angles to make it happen the right way. Once folks higher on the Department of Justice food chain heard the basic evidence—simple and clean and clear—he got little resistance. The folks in Manhattan cooperated completely. Roger's willingness to share the credit helped. It also helped that the Attorney General herself signed off on the plan to take down Perry Charles.

Roger believed it was important to strike while both Fredericks and Robertson were ready to proceed. Before they could change their minds. Before their minds could be changed by promises they might have gotten, if Perry Charles had realized what was coming.

It was tempting to let him wander into a witness-tampering charge. It was more important to close the deal with a pair of billionaires who easily could have figured out how to complicate things just enough to kill the whole case.

The prosecution of Perry Charles had kept me occupied. It stopped me from having much curiosity about Carson, beyond what had happened after he'd left my apartment that night. I'd heard about the shootout and the car chase. It made national news, since someone had died in the crash caused by Carson speeding away from Monitore. They used the threat of a felony murder charge to put even more pressure on Monitore to give them what they needed.

I carry the guilt of swapping my own safety that night for a stranger's life. I always will. Even though I'd come clean earlier that day about my situation with Carson, I could never bring myself to tell anyone, not even Will, about Carson's visit to my apartment before it all happened. I had decided, Sally Slammer be damned, to see whether Will found out about it from Carson. He either didn't tell Will, or Will didn't tell me he knew.

Will told me Carson had used the chaos of the crash to get away from Monitore. Carson ditched his car, windows blown out and bullet holes in the metal, on a side street. He found a backyard trampoline a couple of blocks away. He hid inside the netting and waited until morning. He took an Uber to the office, showing up unshaven and disheveled for the reckoning he freely accepted.

I wanted to know where they sent him. I refused to snoop around. I'd moved on. Carson Two called and texted a few times. I never showed enough interest for it to progress. I didn't know whether I didn't want it, or whether I was avoiding it as personal punishment for my transgressions with Carson One.

I handled the Perry Charles trial with Roger McClelland. Will took care of the case against Carmine Positano. I was shocked, to say the least, when Will told me Positano was being bankrolled by, of all people, Henderson Robertson. I never asked Roger whether he would have been willing to cut the deal to get Perry Charles if we'd known that a man with so much money and power had been so closely involved with the mob. Even though there was no indication that Orson Fredericks or Perry Charles or anyone else knew about or was involved with Robertson's role as a silent partner in an operation based on betting with inside information, Robertson had clear ties to them. If we would have gone to the bottom of the Henderson Robertson RabbitRun rabbit hole, how many more rabbits would we have found?

The longer the jury was out in Carmine Positano's case, the more nervous I got. I worried he'd walk. I worried, if he went free, he'd figure out a way to get to Carson. I also worried he'd do that even if he was convicted. I hoped the guy called Johnny Motts would be the main focus of any vendetta. He was serving his sixty-five months in protective custody. It's a fancy term for solitary confinement. It's better than getting killed, but not by much.

I kept thinking about Carson. That was part of my penance, too. I'd been given a glimpse of the kind of life I could have had. Something far different than the plans I'd made for myself. I wondered if I could ever find that with someone else.

The conviction of Perry Charles was a big deal. The day the jury returned the verdict, Roger came to my office, grabbed the football he'd given me, and crossed out the Commissioner's name with a large black marker before putting a giant X through that big shield. The outcome pushed me farther down the path that would let me pivot to politics, at the right time. As the person who brought down the person in charge of the biggest sports league in America, I'd have a much better chance of winning a seat in the House of Representatives. I'd also be able to move faster from the back bench to the kind of real work that might eventually put me in line to run for the Senate. And so on.

It was what I always wanted. It was all starting to fall into place. I could feel it. And it would have been so much easier to enjoy it if I'd been able to forget about Carson Jeffrey, the quarterback who had come out of nowhere before disappearing without a trace.

The official word was that he'd been injured in the game at Kansas City. He woke up the next morning with knee pain. He was placed on injured reserve. After the season ended, Baltimore announced he was retiring due to the injury. Not many knew the truth.

I was one of the few who did. I found myself wondering far too often about where he was. About what he was doing. About whether he was safe. About who he might have met in his new life.

Whether he, like me, will continue to be haunted every single hour of every single day by what could have been.

79

CARSON JEFFREY

I rolled out of bed. It was the same damn mattress in the same damn apartment in the same damn building in the same damn city in the same damn state where I've lived from the moment they whisked me out of Baltimore and dropped me here.

I stretched my arms high over my head. I'm glad to have a job that helps keep me in shape, even if I'm not getting all that much cardio.

I work for a moving company. I fill up the trucks that roll out of town. I empty the trucks that roll in. I've learned how to carry furniture so it won't get banged up, and so it won't take big chunks out of any walls. Lately, I've been lifting at the local gym and sucking down four-thousand-calorie protein shakes. I've put on thirty pounds. Most of it's muscle. The bigger frame and the jet-black hair dye covering my mullet and goatee make me as unrecognizable as I'm ever going to be, unless I find a doctor to give me a new face.

Football's behind me. Shit, everything is behind me. I'm living day to day. I'm trying to enjoy this new life. Trying to forget the old one. I'm free but I'm not, because I'm stuck in a place I never would have picked for myself.

Anchorage, Alaska. It's supposed to be far enough away to protect me. It's supposed to be big enough to make it easy for the feds to keep tabs on me. I'd heard of the place; who hasn't? I'd never met anybody who lives here. I don't ever remember knowing anyone who even visited the place.

Now, it's home. It's been home. It'll be home. It's the price I'll keep on paying for the easy money I thought I was making. Easy money I never had a chance to spend.

I don't know what happened to the cash I left in Vegas. Johnny Motts probably made good on the threat to grab it. In Baltimore, the building manager might have had one hell of a surprise when I never came back. If he ever found the one bag I left there. Maybe it's still where I hid it.

I wonder sometimes what the team thought about everything. They lied to the world about me having an injury, as pro football teams often do. But not like this. I read a story on my phone about the knee injury, the one I never had. The one that would keep me from ever playing football again.

How many people know the truth? Does anyone from the team realize I'm hiding out for good in a place where no one will know who I am? Where the folks who used to employ me on the side hopefully won't ever find me?

I followed the news from the trial as best I could. I read about Johnny Motts pleading guilty. I read about the conviction of Carmine Positano. The jury told the judge two different times they couldn't reach a verdict. The judge told them to keep trying. They finally found him guilty. His case is being appealed. Which I guess means he still has a chance of going free. I try not to think about what that might mean.

I'd never known the name of the man who ran the operation. I only knew it went higher than Johnny Motts, because he said it did and because he was way too stupid to be in charge of anything.

How safe will I be if Carmine Positano stays locked up? He's in his sixties, and he'll do twenty-five years. I have no idea whether he has any real reach from behind bars. I don't know if his associates can find me. I don't know how many associates he might have.

Maybe I'll be able to leave this place at some point. Maybe after Carmine Positano checks out. Maybe after things die down. I'm always checking to see if anyone recognizes me in Anchorage. There's a look people get when they think they know you but don't know how or why. I guess I used to see it once in a while in Vegas. I'll probably keep looking for that look until the day I take my last breath, naturally or otherwise.

I'm not saying I don't like Anchorage. I just don't have anybody here. I don't really have a way to meet someone. If I ever do, how could I trust her? I've never been one to hang out in bars. I'm even less interested in that now, since somebody might recognize me and pass that along for whatever reward folks like Carmine offer when they're chasing a snitch.

I want a normal life. I'd gotten a taste of it in Baltimore. It gave me a dose of a feeling I never thought I'd have. I still wonder if it did the same thing for her.

I wonder if I'll ever quit wondering about it.

80

JOHNNY MOTTS

I get one hour each day away from the tiny box they keep me in. I spend all of it thinking about the next twenty-three hours I'll stay there until the next time I get out.

I never thought much about what it would be like in here. They say they're protecting me. It feels like they're punishing me. I never see nobody other than the guards. Sometimes, when they're taking me back and forth to the spot in the yard when I can breathe and smell real air, I'll see someone else coming in and going back to their own box. They don't look at me. I don't look at them.

I'll go into witness protection once I serve my time. I got no idea where. I don't really care. They tell me it'll be a new life. It's a new life I never would have picked. I figure they'll set me up with a job. I guess I can do some of that computer shit. It'll probably be almost as boring as being stuck in this box for twenty-three hours a day.

I tried to read some books. I can't focus on the words. I can read good enough, but when it's time to try to sit in that hole and do it, it don't work.

I asked for a TV. They told me that wasn't part of my deal. I wish somebody would have told me I needed to ask for that when I flipped. I guess I could have asked for a bunch of shit, like steak twice a week and pasta every Sunday. I was too willing to get it all over with. I was stupid.

That's the problem. I was stupid. I am stupid. I need to get smarter. Will I ever? Even after I get out of here, I'll keep fucking up. And I'll probably try to find a way back into that life. If I try hard enough, I'll figure out how to get back into that life without the feds knowing about it. I guess I am smart, just not the way I should be.

I don't even know if it's sunny or cloudy or raining or snowing until I get outside. The guards don't tell me. Even though I helped bring down Carmine, they treat me like every other convict. They act like I killed the pope or something. It's a shitty way to live. If I had any idea this is how it was gonna be, I never would have flipped.

At first, I was keeping track of how long I've been here. Counting the days I served and the ones I got left. It wasn't helping. I decided after a few weeks to give in to it, to wait until the day they come to get me and I think they're taking me outside for an hour but they take me to wherever I'll be living next. I won't be in this box no more, even if it'll still feel that way.

I'm always gonna be in a box. Even if I find a way out, the box is always gonna be there. And if I go too far out of the box, that's when they'll get me.

Maybe they'll get me while I'm still in here. Maybe, one of these days, that guy I see walking back in while I'm walking out will come at me with a shiv and just end it.

If that ever happens, I can fight back or let it happen. Maybe my arms will ignore my brain, like they did when I was standing on Jimmy King's porch and I seen that his girlfriend was pregnant.

Maybe that's the best way out of this for me. To welcome it when it comes.

Really, what's the point of living if you ain't got no life, and if you don't expect to ever have one again?

81

ALICE SMITHSON

The conviction of Perry Charles put me on the fast track. The conviction of Carmine Positano, even though I had no involvement in the trial, cemented things. My plans are moving toward reality. I should be happy.

I'm not. I'm sick of feeling this way. I managed in the aftermath of Will's win in the Positano trial to get him drunk enough to let it slip. I'm not sure he even remembers telling me. I've spent the past month researching everything I could about the place where Carson has gone.

I know where he's working. I know where he's living. I know the name he's using. I don't know how many federal statutes and regulations I've violated by knowing what I know. I don't plan on sharing it with anyone. Still, I'm not supposed to know any of it. I keep acting like I don't.

I've moved on to the next prosecution. I'm working with Roger McClelland again. He has gotten a bounce in his own prospects from the cases against Perry Charles and Carmine Positano.

I've typed the letter once. I've typed it again. I've revised it, reworked it, reworded it. I've accepted the fact that there won't be any easy way to do this. I just have to do it, if I'm going to.

Even now, I'm not sure I can. Sally Slammer is putting up a

good fight. Years of work and calculation and planning are at risk of being flushed down the drain for good.

I want to do it. I don't want to do it.

I don't know what I want. I want to be happy. I tell myself I'm allowed to be happy. That I'm allowed to try. I know there's only one way that will ever happen.

Sally Slammer will have to deal with it. She'll have to accept it, or she'll end up falling by the wayside as well. Another discarded item as I go after the thing I've decided I want, before it's too late to get it.

I'll keep the apartment. I'll keep paying the rent. It will be here if I need to come back. I have no idea what I'll do, if that happens. I'll worry about it then.

There are two suitcases on the floor of my bedroom. They contain only the things I'll need. I've thought about every item that has made its way inside, every item that hasn't. The cases are closed and zipped and sealed with tiny locks. The keys to the locks are in the pocket on the side of my purse. The handles of the suitcases sit there, taunting me.

I look at them. Maybe for minutes. Maybe for hours.

I pick them up, one in each hand. They aren't light, but they aren't too heavy to carry to the car and then to the counter at the airport. Was it that simple to pack the remnants of one life into two boxes while going after a new one?

What would my grandfather think about this?

I put the suitcases back down on the carpet. I look around the bedroom. I think about making one final pass through the rest of the apartment. My laptop is open on the mattress. The letter is typed and finalized and ready to go to Roger McClelland. What will I tell Will? I'll call him later, maybe from the terminal. From one of them.

I read the letter again. I moved the cursor to the spot. I held my finger over the button. I also held my breath. I looked around the room. I waited for something, for anything.

What would my grandfather think about this?

I thought about the man who reminds me of my grandfather. I smiled. I pressed the button.

I folded the laptop shut. I slid it into the bag that will hang over my shoulder while moving the suitcases. I picked them up again. I headed for the door.

I turned back to the apartment I was about to leave, for now. Possibly for good.

I had one last thing to say before I went.

"That fucking joke had better be funny."

ACKNOWLEDGMENTS

This one was a wild ride.

Ever since the Supreme Court opened the floodgates for the normalization of sports betting, I've been concerned that pro football will suffer for it. I've worried about a scandal that will impair public confidence in the game. I had an idea a few years ago for a story that would show how the combination of gambling, the mob, and pro football could go off the rails.

My former agent, Chris Bucci, had a huge role in shaping the story. In the original version, the third leg of the narrative rhythm focused on Perry Charles, the Commissioner of my fictional pro football league. After getting some feedback and preliminary interest from a potential publisher, I removed the Perry Charles chapters and turned Johnny Motts into an equal partner with Carson Jeffrey and Alice Smithson.

It made the story much better, because Motts is such a good villain. Dangerous. Menacing. Stupid. And, ultimately, a man with limits to his sociopathic tendencies that he didn't know he had, until it was too late.

While it wasn't enough to get the publisher to bite ("it's good, but sports novels don't sell" became a common refrain), it made the story better. During the umpteen times I reviewed and re-re-viewed and re-re-reviewed the manuscript, the Johnny Motts chapters were my favorites to read.

Zack Veltri, who I've known since he was a little kid playing baseball with my nephew, helped me figure out the computer hacking specifics that Motts used to monitor the activity on Jimmy King's network. I told him he'd get mentioned in the acknowledgements. I got more out of the exchange.

Thanks also to you, for getting this far. I enjoy writing things that people will read, and that people will enjoy. If you enjoyed it enough to get all the way to the very last word, I hopefully did what I set out to do.

Made in the USA
Columbia, SC
19 August 2025

61515729R00215